MW00413371

THE KING'S TOMB

(Joe Hawke #10)

Rob Jones

Copyright © 2018 by Rob Jones

All rights reserved. No part of this publication may be used, reproduced, distributed or transmitted in any form or by any means, electronic, mechanical, photocopying, recording or otherwise, without the prior written permission of the author or publisher, except in the case of brief quotations embodied in critical reviews and certain other non-commercial uses permitted by copyright law.

THE KING'S TOMB is a work of fiction. All names, characters, places and occurrences are entirely fictional products of the author's imagination or are used fictitiously. Any resemblance to current events or locales, or to persons living or dead, is entirely coincidental.

This book is sold subject to the condition that it shall not, by way of trade or otherwise, be lent, re-sold, hired out or otherwise circulated in any form of binding or cover other than that in which it is published and without a similar condition including this condition being imposed on the subsequent purchaser.

ISBN-13:978-1727678840
ISBN-10:1727678842

Other Books by Rob Jones

The Joe Hawke Series

The Vault of Poseidon (Joe Hawke #1)
Thunder God (Joe Hawke #2)
The Tomb of Eternity (Joe Hawke #3)
The Curse of Medusa (Joe Hawke #4)
Valhalla Gold (Joe Hawke #5)
The Aztec Prophecy (Joe Hawke #6)
The Secret of Atlantis (Joe Hawke #7)
The Lost City (Joe Hawke #8)
The Sword of Fire (Joe Hawke #9)
The King's Tomb (Joe Hawke #10)

The Cairo Sloane Series

Plagues of the Seven Angels (Cairo Sloane #1)

The Raiders Series

The Raiders (The Raiders #1)

The Avalon Adventure Series

The Hunt for Shambhala (An Avalon Adventure #1)
Treasure of Babylon (An Avalon Adventure #2)

The Harry Bane Thriller Series

The Armageddon Protocol (A Harry Bane Thriller #1)

Website: www.robjonesnovels.com
Facebook: https://www.facebook.com/RobJonesNovels/
Twitter: @AuthorRobJones
Email: robjonesnovels@gmail.com

DEDICATION

For My Family

CHAPTER ONE

The street lights of Lugano fell away below the Jet Ranger's windshield as the pilot raised the collective and flew toward the fir tree-lined slopes of Monte Brè. In the darkness of the chopper's rear cabin, the man known as the Oracle was staring pensively through his window, weighed down with the baggage of his life's mission.

No, *pilgrimage*. He tapped his chin with a withered forefinger while he gave the matter some thought. As the helicopter flew over the crest of the mountain and headed toward his compound on the eastern slopes, he concluded it was definitely more of a pilgrimage than a mission.

Thousands of years spent protecting the sources of eternal life had taken a heavy toll on him, but not as heavy as the search for the Citadel. In the black, hollow void he called a heart, he knew this hallowed place was more than a legend and yet no one had set eyes on its sparkling walls for millennia.

His eyes crawled over the dark waters of the Lago di Lugano and a jagged mountain ridgeline beyond it where Switzerland met the Italian province of Lombardy. He knew this landscape well. He knew every landscape well. There was only one place that still eluded him and that was the Citadel. It was out there somewhere, just where *they* had left it so long ago.

And he had to have it.

He was closer than ever before. Of the eight idols he needed to open the gateway, he had three of them – Tanit, Tinia and Viracocha – and his research had uncovered that another four were in the King's Tomb. The rogue idol, Burí, was still in the possession of the ECHO team after their raid on Valhalla. He heaved in a long breath and sighed heavily in the gloom. He had to have these other idols and he would stop at nothing and spare no one to get his hands on them.

No one.

He turned his eyes away from the night and faced the small team of Athanatoi acolytes sitting with him in the chopper. Their faces were obscured, lit a ghostly blue by the subdued night-lighting in the rear cabin, but there was no mistaking the fear etched onto every one of them. They waited obediently for their leader to break the silence.

And then he did. "Have we heard from the arms dealer yet?" he asked in Italian.

A woman sitting opposite him looked briefly at the anxious faces of the others before responding. "He followed your instructions and returned to South Africa with the sword."

"Has Julius made contact with him yet?"

Professor Julius Cronje was an Athanatoi cultist based in Johannesburg and one of their leading scholars.

"No. I think Julius is losing his nerve, and Kruger too. I think they want out."

"That is unfortunate," the Oracle purred. "Julius has been playing with treachery for many centuries. If he makes one wrong move then he will have to be terminated. As for Kruger, he has served me well, but he has more to give before he gets his reward. Much more. I cannot tolerate betrayal."

"Betrayal?"

"He knows things about us, about me. He might be trying to cut a deal with ECHO or the authorities to save his own skin." He turned to the man sitting beside him. He was tall and solid-built with a hard, square face and sad, black eyes. "You are my most loyal soldier, Blankov. I want you to go to South Africa and pull this scorpion out from under his rock. Persuade him that his fortune is best served by remaining as loyal to me as you are, or kill him."

"Yes, sir," the man said. A Slav from the northern Greek region of Macedonia, Ivan Blankov was a senior Athanatoi and one of the Oracle's most loyal lieutenants and a keen scholar of the ancient world. The fierce warrior and skilled hand to hand combat specialist thought for a moment and then said, "And Julius?"

"Let Julius do his job and decipher the sword. If he is loyal he will live, if not…" his words trailed into the darkness before he spoke up again. "We will soon have the Sword of Fire deciphered and then we will know the location of the King's Tomb. After that, there is nothing between me and the gateway."

A plasma screen on the rear wall of the chopper flickered to life to reveal the face of Davis Faulkner, the Vice President of the United States. He looked pale and anxious.

The Oracle grinned. "Something on your mind, Mr Vice President?"

"Not at all, sir."

"Good, and how are things Stateside?"

"Coming along well, sir. We're just waiting for your orders."

"Soon, Davis, soon. We have almost everything in place ready to make our move against President Brooke."

"Yes, sir," Faulkner said.

"Then I will control the United States as well."

Faulkner wiped his brow. "I think the fall-out from this one's going to take a long time to settle."

The Oracle nodded at some silent thought he was enjoying. Things were going well, it was true. Not only would he have the remaining idols within the next few hours, but with Faulkner in the Oval Office he would control the executive branch of the world's most powerful country.

Then the war could begin.

CHAPTER TWO

Diamond Falls Country Estate nestled peacefully in the eastern suburbs of Pretoria. It was a gated community, secure from the crime of the city and sprawling over one hundred acres of luscious South African landscape. Ten-room mansions hid away behind palm trees and electric fences, its inhabitants kept safe by closed-circuit cameras and biometric security systems.

Lea Donovan steadied the monocular by placing her elbows on the car's roof and carefully studied one of the properties running along the northern perimeter. "So that's where Dirk Kruger's hiding out."

"According to our intel, at least," Camacho said.

"You think he's got the sword in there, or somewhere else?"

Camacho shrugged. "Only one way to find out."

Ryan Bale raised his own monocular and swept it over the surrounding area. It was a vista of BMW X5s and Mercedes coupés parked on sweeping granite drives, sparkling swimming pools and plush tennis courts. "Eden didn't say anything about laser sensors."

Kim Taylor was leaning on the hood of their hired SUV and shaking her head. "A big bad guy like you can't be scared of a few laser sensors, right?"

Ryan looked sheepish for a moment, then regained his cool. "I'll get in there before *you* do, Agent Taylor."

"That's Special Agent Taylor, Ryan. *Special* Agent."

"Is that because they had to make special rules to get you in?"

"No," Kim said. "It's like the way you're a *special* person."

"Hearty ha ha."

Lea glanced at her watch. "Night soon."

"Don't tell me you're afraid of the dark," Ryan said.

The Irishwoman raised an eyebrow as she looked him up and down. "Afraid of the *dork* maybe, but not the dark."

Ryan laughed. He could take a joke now. The fragile boy he had once been was dead and a stronger man stood in his place. He lifted the hem of his torn, sleeveless Megadeth t-shirt and wiped the sweat from his brow. Nestled in a valley enclosed by the Magaliesberg hills, the city was a giant heat trap in the summer when the winds blew into the Bushveld from the Kalahari desert. Tonight the heat was a bastard and it felt like it was crushing his head with a vice.

"Touché," he said, letting the damp hem drop back down. "You win, you both win. I'm a *special dork*, I get it."

Kim smiled but made no reply. She was thinking about the tattoo of the snarling dragon she had just seen clawing its way around the young man's torso. Only half-finished, the black and red ink creature had stared her down with a menacing eye that made her look away.

It was a damning indictment of the misery he had been through but it represented a reborn, tougher Ryan. As he pulled a cigarette from a crumpled pack in his jeans' back pocket and fired it up, Kim declined his offer of a smoke. Like the others in the team, she quietly wondered where the young man's transformation might end.

"Wait, I see something," Lea said. She was tracking a Jeep Cherokee as it entered the community and drove in the direction of Kruger's mansion. It pulled up at his property and the doors opened. "Looks like someone's paying Dirk a visit."

Four men climbed out of the Jeep and walked to the house. One of them was casually resting a pump-action shotgun on his shoulder. They all had gun holsters. A moment passed and then the door opened and they made their way inside, one of them stopping to spit in a potted palm at the side of the porch.

"Why the extra muscle?" Camacho said. "You think Kruger got word about our arrival in South Africa?"

"Maybe," Lea said. "Remember, he's a black-market arms trader. He spends his life with mercs and gunrunners. They could be anyone like that." She changed the subject. "Everyone familiar with the schematics?"

They were. Alex Reeve over in Washington DC had easily located them online and everyone had studied the house's blueprints inside out. The only question that remained was if their intel was good and whether or not Kruger really was storing the Sword of Fire in there.

"Things could get out of hand tonight," Kim said, casting a big sister's eye at Ryan. "We need to stay focused."

"Why are you looking at me?"

"Because you're the only one without any formal military training."

He scoffed. "I've been through more than most soldiers." He dragged on the end of the cigarette and casually flicked it to the ground. "These days I'm built for fighting."

Lea laughed out loud.

Ryan looked momentarily hurt but pulled out of it before saying something he would regret. He had presumed his dramatic turnaround would buy him some more credit with his ex-wife, but all she could see was the geek she had first met all those years ago. He didn't know what it would take for her to take him seriously and these days he didn't much care. The smartass reply he thought of was already forgotten and the simple smile he gave her turned out to be much more devastating.

"I'm sorry, Ry. That was a stupid thing to say."

"Forget it. We have work to do."

Lea gave him a smile, and was pleased to be working with him again. Since reading the shocking truth about her family in the letter left to her in her grandmother's box, she had been pensive and introspective and it felt good to get back out on a mission. The fact the letter had told her that her grandmother was in fact her sister, and her father had discovered a source of the elixir of life had rocked her world, and getting stuck into another op like this was what she needed more than anything to get her head straight again.

"Right." Camacho checked his watch. "And on that, Hawke's team should almost be in China by now."

Lea huffed and rolled her eyes.

"*What*, Jack?"

Ryan leaned over to the former CIA man and lowered his voice to a conspiratorial hush, making sure to keep it just loud enough for everyone to hear. "They're still not talking, old boy."

"You're like a couple of stupid teenagers," Camacho said.

Lea opened her mouth to launch some kind of defense, but before she could utter a word, he spoke again.

"Okay, kids – let's hit the road." He took in the subtropical twilight, now rapidly fading into night. "It'll be dark enough by the time we're on site."

"And I'm on point," Lea said.

After putting on tactical raid vests and lightweight plate armor, they loaded up with HK MP5s, M4 carbines, spare magazines and stun grenades. Camacho slipped a chest rig over the top, fully laden with even more spare ammo and some CS gas canisters. Finally, he grabbed a Mossberg 500 pump-action shotgun. Last on were the ballistic helmets and night vision goggles.

Camacho hit the gas and steered the Chevy TrailBlazer around the bends in the road leading down from the hills they had used to survey the property. Cruising into the luxury estate, he gained speed and aimed directly for Kruger's perimeter fence.

The chunky grille of the two-ton vehicle smashed through the electric fence with ease and sent a shower of sparks into the hot, night air. The twisted, bent fence panels clattered to the ground behind them as he swerved the TrailBlazer around the pool and skidded to a halt a few meters from Kruger's back door.

They all jumped out of the Chevy – the tactical assault on Kruger's place was well-rehearsed and they were keen to get on with it. Their arrival had already been noticed by the men inside the house. A merc in an upstairs window leaned out and fired on them. He was using a Browning bolt-action shotgun with saboted slugs. They slammed against the wall as the sabots sprayed down on them and the rounds punctured the Chevy's steel roof.

So far, the mission had taken forty seconds.

Camacho took the Mossberg 500 to the door, swiftly dispatching three rounds on the top, middle and lower hinges. He blasted the door to matchwood and then kicked it down inside the room with a heavy riot boot. "Go, go, go!"

Fifty seconds.

Lea, Ryan and Kim instantly entered the house under Camacho's cover and fanned out into their attack positions. Two mercs charged into the kitchen with handguns raised. Camacho spun around the doorway and fired on them with the shotgun, blasting them to hell. One slumped down on a marble countertop with his head hanging in the sink and the other flew back over the island and crashed on top of a wheeled kitchen cart.

One minute.

The fighting intensified. Another merc took up a position behind an enormous Polar double-door refrigerator and starting playing games with a Beretta twelve-gauge Magnum shotgun, knocking chunks out of the ceiling and tearing the cabinetwork to shreds.

In a vicious hail of splinters and flying lead, Kim and Ryan looked at the cart and exchanged a smile. She swung around onto her back and kicked the cart with both boots as hard as she could. It raced off down the center of the expansive kitchen and Ryan rolled down into its cover, firing off a few rounds in the direction of the man with the twelve-bore.

Two minutes.

The young hacker from London took heavy fire and the shotgun made short work of the little pine cart, but Ryan already saw his destination: the basement stairs. The cart was almost gone now, with only one side and the framework left in place. He raised his MP5 and obliterated the basement door's lock in seconds. Incoming gunfire from the shotgun flew either side of him and traced over his head as he leaped to the door and shoulder-barged his way through it.

Ryan lowered the night vision goggles into place and leaped over the banister, his riot boots slamming down hard on the polished concrete floor. Scanning the basement, he saw the fuse box exactly where Alex had told him he would. He sprinted across the concrete until he was in range and then raised the MP5. Much better suited to short-range work, the young man squeezed the trigger and let the lead fly.

Three minutes.

The shaft of light shining down from the kitchen above the stairs instantly died and plunged the basement into darkness. It didn't last long and soon the subterranean space was lit up with the sudden, violent strobing of a muzzle flash from the far side of the basement. Someone was at the top of a second flight of stairs on the far side of the basement.

It happened as fast as lightning. The bullets chewed into the polished concrete floor and spat and pinged across to Ryan faster than he could take cover. The muzzle flashed. Chaos reigned. Empty shells clattered to the floor like metal sleet. The bullets traced past his head with a stomach-churning *crack crack crack* and buried themselves in the plasterboard wall ahead of him.

Ryan dived for the cover of the furnace, thinking he had made it to safety, but then he felt the scratch and burn of a bullet rip across a small exposed section of his back at the edge of the tactical vest, just below his left shoulder. He screamed as a cloud of his own blood and muscle sprayed out over his head.

He was hit.

CHAPTER THREE

Ryan crashed down behind the furnace and slammed his back against the blower chamber as he hurriedly reached around and felt his shoulder for the wound. Rounds fired over him, drilling into the steel plate of the furnace. Ricochets showered him with sparks. Metal jackets clunked to the floor.

His heart beat like a double-bass drum on a thrash metal track and he clamped his teeth together to stifle an animal howl of pain. He felt a thick pulpy wound on the edge of his back where it curved around to his left-hand side. The hacker cursed under his breath. Half an inch to the right and the tactical vest would have stopped it. A wave of nausea washed over him as his mind flooded with the fear of a bullet wound.

Hawke had told him all about the dangers of lead intoxication from projectiles lodged inside the human body. The old cowboy joke about dying of lead poisoning wasn't so funny and then there was the internal bleeding or vital organ damage to consider. Maybe Kim had been right to doubt his ability.

Sweating and desperately trying to control his breathing, Ryan searched with a trembling hand to see if the bullet had wedged itself in a bone… *God, please no…* but he felt nothing except a groove. Best guess was a round had torn through the skin and continued on its way to the far wall behind the furnace.

More firing.

He gathered his mind, reloaded his MP5 and took a breath. The wound was painful and bleeding but not fatal.

He tried to remember what Hawke and the others had taught him about close-quarter combat and spun around and fired on the enemy before they had a chance to take up a new position.

Ryan's rounds raked up the wooden staircase and buried themselves in the plaster of the supporting wall behind it. Through the goggles he saw the man who had now hit the deck at the top of the stairs and was crawling forward on his stomach with the shotgun in his right hand.

Ryan saw the moment and seized it, rolling forward until he was under the stairs. On his back, he lifted the compact machine pistol and let rip, firing on the man blindly through the top of the stairs.

He heard a scream and then the man tumbled forward, smashing through the spindles and collapsing with a hard smack right beside him.

In the ghostly green light of the night vision, Ryan saw the man take his dying breath through a bloody mouth. How did Hawke and the others do this for a living? He had a hard time imagining it until he realized with a gasp that this was his life now. Saving lives and taking lives was now part of his life and he still wasn't sure he could live with it.

The young man raised his palm mic to his mouth. "Power out and basement secured." He had already made the decision not to tell anyone about the wound. Ryan doubted it would cloud anyone's judgement. This crew was too professional to be distracted by a man down, but he didn't want to look like he was stupid enough to get hit.

He heard Lea's voice in his ear as she spoke over the comms. "Great job, Ry. We're going after Kruger so if you don't want to miss the fun you'd better get up here."

Ryan Bale didn't need an embossed invitation. He rolled out from under the stairs and ran across the basement. Sprinting up the staircase to the kitchen, he raised his gun and emerged into a room that looked like it had been bombed. "Where is everyone?"

Camacho's voice buzzed in his ear. "Going up the main stairs to Kruger's study."

"Me and Kim are heading to the bedroom suites," Lea said.

"Care to join us?" Kim said. "Maybe his wife has some panties you could try on, you big girl."

Ryan was crossing the hall now and hitting the bottom of the stairs. His back was pulsing with pain and he could feel the blood soaking into the t-shirt under his tactical vest. Up ahead he could see the rest of his team as they turned the corner on the next floor. "Oh, that's funny, but I'll think I'll stick with Jack in the study."

"Sure thing," Kim said. "If I see any your size I'll grab you a pair."

Her voice cut out and the comms went dead as everyone concentrated on the next phase of the mission. They all knew Kruger was in the house; they had seen him enter the place just that afternoon and the intel that he was stashing the Sword of Fire here until summoned by the Oracle was also good. Now was their chance to take out the arms trafficker once and for all and retrieve the ancient sword.

Gunshots rang out from another section of the house and he prayed Lea and Kim were all right. This was not his natural milieu. For one thing, people who used the word *milieu* did not generally know how to strip a rifle in thirty seconds, but he did. He had changed now and he had to accept it.

He wasn't the gawky nerd Lea and Hawke had recruited in London for the Poseidon mission. He'd been through the mill and learned the ropes from the best in the business. He'd seen things no one else dreamed of seeing. He'd fallen love. He'd watched his lover die. He knew the difference between all the bullet calibers and their uses and when to deploy a tear gas grenade or a real one.

And when to deploy the word *milieu* to devasting effect in any sentence.

With the schematics memorized, he swung a sharp right at the top of the sweeping staircase and found himself in the study. Camacho was hurriedly packing C4 on a large diamond safe in the far wall. "Jesus, you don't hang around, Jack!"

"Down!" Camacho yelled and dived behind a desk.

Ryan slammed down next to him as the C4 exploded. It ripped the front of the safe from the rest of the casing and flung it across the room like a lethal trashcan lid. The safe's door buried itself three inches deep in the opposite wall as smoke and the stench of burned almonds from the detonated explosives filled the room.

"Let's see what we got," Camacho said. "You cover the door!"

Ryan did as he was told as the American checked the safe. He heard a sigh and looked up to see Camacho punching the wall. "Nothing. Let's hope the girls had better luck in the bedroom."

Even with the pain in his back, Ryan considered the obvious joke but kept it to himself. What was worse than being sloppy enough to get hit? Making jokes afterwards, that's what. He kept his mouth shut and followed Camacho out of the door and along the corridor to the bedroom.

They found Lea and Kim rifling through Kruger's private wardrobe and drawers, but still found nothing. Lea cursed. "Nothing relating to the Oracle and no goddam sword."

"Hey!" Kim ran to the window. "They're getting away!"

An explosion rocked the house and blasted a hail of broken banister wood through the door. It blew over them like a hailstorm of razor-sharp splinters as they hit the deck to find some cover.

"Dammit all!" Kim yelled.

Lea smashed a fist into the floor. "I'm so frigging pissed off right now."

"What do we do?" Ryan asked.

Camacho looked at the smoke billowing into the room from the staircase. "We go after them! It's not too late and we never give up – right?"

The American CIA man moved forward, adjusting his goggles and raising the M4 carbine. Reaching the top of the stairs he felt some resistance as he tried to bring his right foot forward. Then he heard the tell-tale sound of a tripwire snapping beneath him.

Lea was right behind him and she heard it too. "IED!"

The explosion was savage, blasting each of them backwards through the smoky air like so many rag dolls. Lea and Ryan collided mid-air and crashed to the floor outside Kruger's room. Camacho was blown straight through the study door and Kim flew over the mezzanine rail, tumbling through the air toward the parquet floor.

"Kim!" Camacho yelled. He crawled out of the study and scrambled down the stairs with his gun raised.

Ryan and Lea were right behind him, each taking the steps two at a time.

"Is she okay?"

"I'm fine…"

She had been saved from a broken neck by a table. It had snapped under her weight but arrested her fall enough to ensure she survived with nothing more than some bruises. She snatched up her gun and dragged herself to her feet. "Let's get going!"

They ran over to the door, coughing the smoke from their lungs. Ryan was first, emerging from the chaos and jogging out onto the expansive bull-grass lawn.

The others ran over to him.

"We have to get after them!" Kim said.

"It's too late." Ryan swore and kicked a wad of turf into the air. "They're long gone and they were generous enough to destroy our SUV before they went. If anyone wants a challenge it's in a thousand pieces all over the yard."

Each member of the team felt the same crushing sense of defeat as Kruger's Maserati Levante made the corner at high-speed and vanished from sight.

Lea stared at the fleeing vehicle and knew she had failed. "Fuck it sideways!" She turned in a circle and screamed out loud. "Shit, you're wounded, Ry!"

"It's nothing, really." He was playing it cool, but he was already feeling a little dizzy from the blood loss.

"Get your vest off."

He removed the tactical vest and dropped it to the floor.

Lea gasped when she saw the thick matted blood caked over his t-shirt. "Jesus, Ry!"

"It's nothing…"

And then he went down onto his knees, his head spinning.

Camacho and Kim grabbed hold of him while Lea lifted the t-shirt and checked the wound. "You need medical attention."

And next on their radar were the flashing blue lights of the South African Police Service hurriedly swerving around the bend with sirens wailing. They skidded to a halt outside the burning house and police leaped from their vehicles with guns raised.

"Drop your weapons now!" the lead officer yelled. "You're under arrest."

CHAPTER FOUR

The ECHO Gulfstream cruised thousands of feet over the rice paddies of Guangdong Province. The moon broke the horizon over the South China Sea and the fading dusk of another tiring day gave way to the night.

Hawke had just woken after the long flight from London. Scarlet Sloane was sitting at a table with Vincent Reno and Danny Devlin playing Texas Hold'em. By the looks on the two men's faces she was winning big style and as he walked across the cabin and joined them it was just in time to see her slide another pile of fifty-dollar bills onto her side of the table.

"There's no escaping fate, boys," she said with a wink. "I'll enjoy spending this."

Hawke pulled up a chair and looked at Reaper and Devlin with sympathy. "I'd fold before it turns into strip poker."

"Fold?" Devlin furrowed his brow with fake confusion. "That's what I'm waiting for!"

Hawke said nothing. Tension had been high in the ECHO team since his bust-up with Lea and for a time he'd blamed the Irishman, but a few texts from Scarlet had set him straight on who was really to blame and it turned out wasn't Devlin but him. Sure, the former Irish Ranger had pushed his luck on their last mission to locate the Sword of Fire, but he knew in his heart his old friend was right.

He ran his hands over the box in his jacket pocket. The engagement ring was still there, next to his heart but now cold and redundant. It needed the heat from Lea's hand to come alive, but he was starting to think asking her would be a mistake and that marriage for him was some kind of a curse.

His first wife was brutally murdered on their honeymoon and he'd delayed asking Lea for a long time. When he had finally decided to take the step, they'd argued and broken up within hours. Maybe the smartest thing he could do was toss the ring in the garbage and forget all about it. That had to be the best thing for both of them.

"I'm out." Reaper folded his hand over onto the table and yawned.

"Smart but boring," Scarlet said. "I'd have the shirt off your back in the next round."

"Now you're talking!" Devlin said.

Scarlet raised an eyebrow. "I won't stop there, Danny. You'll be down to your underwear in three rounds and I'm not sure how that benefits any of us, darling."

Reaper clapped a heavy hand on her shoulder. "C'est vrai. The only way you win when playing strip poker with a man with Danny's body is to lose and go naked yourself. It saves the eyes."

"You guys shoot straight from the hip," Devlin said, and turned his cards down to the table beside the Frenchman's. "I'll quit while I'm behind."

Hawke watched Scarlet smirk as Devlin and Reaper moped down to the end of the plane with empty pockets. She cleared the cash off the table and swept it into her jacket pocket with the single fluid motion of a seasoned Vegas pro swiping her winnings into a chip rack before taking them to the cage.

He opened his mouth to speak but she won that fight too and spoke before he got a word to his lips.

"Someone needs to make the first move, Joe."

Hawke looked down the cabin at Devlin and frowned. "Maybe I over-reacted when I saw him hugging her."

"You think?"

"I presume you're being sarcastic."

"Clever you. I gave Lea a hug once," Scarlet said. "Does that mean I'm in love with her?"

Hawke took a deep breath, puffed his cheeks and blew it out again. "I was going to ask her to marry me, Cairo."

"So get on with it and stop being such a bell-end."

Hawke contemplated the friendly advice, delivered as ever with Scarlet's usual panache.

Dammit all, he had known he was wrong the second Lea had walked away with Devlin back in London, but now wasn't the time for regrets. Lea had gone to Pretoria to bring Kruger down, secure the sword and get a lead on the Oracle and he was leading a team to Hong Kong to rescue Lexi. He had to focus, not stress about the rocky road of his private life.

"Bell-end, eh?"

"You said it."

Hawke narrowed his eyes. "No, you said it."

"What are you, a lawyer?"

"You think we could make it work?"

"What makes you ask the question?"

He shrugged. "Just wondered."

"I don't think so, darling. I'm not one for settling down. You know that – I'd eat you for breakfast."

"I'm being serious."

They watched the progress of their flight on the little screen. Still over Guangdong Province, and with their journey almost at an end, they now turned into their final vector. She let out a heavy sigh. "Look, I know you're only a man so I'll explain it in simple terms. You were a bell-end. We established that, right?"

"Right."

"Exactly right, but you're a bell-end that wants to make things right."

"I'm not sure I like bell-end being used in anything but the past tense. A one-off sort of thing rather than a permanent condition."

"Bear with me."

"Fine."

"So the way you make things right is to grovel profusely and then go ahead and do your wedding ring thing."

His eyes narrowed. "Grovel profusely for how long?"

"There are no rules. It's an indeterminate time decided only by Lea, darling."

"Got it."

Scarlet's phone rang. She checked the screen and said "Eden" before taking the call. "Hey, Rich. You have something new?"

"Yes, I have something new." His voice was weak thanks to his recent recovery from an induced coma, but the tiny speaker on the phone made him sound even more fragile.

"What's up?"

"A reliable source has managed to refine the target's whereabouts in Hong Kong today."

The team shared an excited look.

"Turns out our man Rat is hopelessly addicted to gambling, but it's mostly illegal on mainland China so when he wants to lose some money, he likes to travel to the casinos in Macau, or the…"

"Or the racecourses in Hong Kong?" Hawke said.

"You read my mind."

"Any idea which one?"

"Better than an idea. Rat will be at the Happy Valley Racecourse on Hong Kong Island this evening. They're running a big race there tonight and Mr Rat wants in on the action."

"Tonight?" Devlin asked.

"Happy Valley Racecourse runs races on Wednesday nights," Eden said. "An old friend of mine, Monty Devane, happens to be on the board of the Hong Kong Jockey Club and he's already working with their security to try and track him down. He'll brief you when you arrive. In the meantime, I've arranged with the British Embassy for you to be fast-tracked through the airport by an officer with MI6 named Chris Raynes. He will introduce you to another man in the Special Duties Unit."

"Who are they?" Devlin asked.

"The SDU is a tactical unit within the Hong Kong Police Force whose main work is in counter-terrorism."

"And they're happy working with us to track down one of the Zodiacs?" Scarlet said. "They're Chinese agents after all."

"It's complicated," Eden said. "There are factions within the top of the PLA and not everyone is supportive of the way the Zodiacs work."

"I get it," she said. "Sounds like we're all set up and ready to go."

"I've done all I can," Eden said. "Now it's over to you."

When he disconnected the call, a silence filled the cabin. No one had talked to Eden about the coma he had suffered, but they were all pleased to see he was having such a strong recovery. If he had died, the leadership of the operation would have passed to Hawke and Lea, and that wouldn't exactly be easy with the way things were right now.

Hawke broke the silence. "All right – get some sleep everyone. It's not long till we land in Hong Kong and we're back on the clock. It could get rough. Lexi needs us in a big way right now and this could easily be our last chance. The Zodiacs aren't the easiest people to track down and I don't like Rich's chances of being able to get us this close a second time."

"I agree." Reaper cracked his knuckles.

Scarlet sniffed. "Another game of poker anyone? You know what they say – sleep's for pussies."

"Count me out," Reaper said. "I need to rest. I'm not as young as you."

"And you can forget me as well," Hawke said with a wry smile. "I've seen you play too many games to go up against you."

"What a couple of jessies," Devlin said, sitting down opposite Scarlet. "I'll play you Cairo, and I'll kick your ass too."

Scarlet gave the deck a professional riffle shuffle and started to deal. "This I have to see."

Hawke smiled and walked over to the couch where he collapsed down onto it and stretched out ready for what Ryan had started referring to as a nanonap. He wasn't exactly sure what one of those was – in his day back in the regiment, it was "forty winks", but he was prepared to give it a go.

He'd need the rest if the Zodiacs were as ruthless as the briefing notes described them to be.

CHAPTER FIVE

When they landed at Hong Kong International Airport out on the Zhujiang River Estuary, they stepped out of the crushing humidity and into the air-conditioned cool of the airport arrivals terminal. Hawke glanced around at the impressive building and remembered all the times he had been through here on his travels.

The memory that stuck in his mind most was the week he spent here with Liz not long after they met. They had flown in on a Friday night and met with some of his Royal Marines friends. They'd visited the Ladies' Market and Temple Street. Joked all the way around Disneyland and ridden the funicular railway to The Peak. As the past always seemed to be, it was a more innocent time with easier laughs and less stress and when he thought about it he started to feel like someone had hollowed him out with a combat knife.

After some confusion about where to go, they met with the MI6 agent who used his diplomatic status to expedite them through the customs process. He gave them the names of the SDU men and told them they would meet them at the Jockey Club. Then he casually slid his Panama hat back on and vanished into the crowd.

They stepped outside back into the humidity. Eden's recent fight with a coma hadn't dulled his senses or affected his planning skills, and an Escalade was waiting for them outside the airport exactly as he had described.

They climbed inside and before they had even buckled their belts the driver was whisking them along the north coast of Lantau Island. Endless high-rises flashed past them, the view of the apartments obscured by laundry drying on poles hanging out of the windows. Neon signs blinked in the haze, their Chinese symbols making unknown promises to the Westerners as they moved through the bustling metropolis.

As they crossed the Tsing Ma Bridge on their way east into the New Territories, Hawke took in the breathtaking view of the ships out on the water. He lowered the window and felt a rush of hot, humid air on his face. Yachts and container ships fought for space out in Victoria Harbor as they swept south along Route 3. He saw the luxury high-rises of Tai Kok Tsui tower over them and then they slipped into the Western Harbor Crossing tunnel.

They emerged on Hong Kong Island and the driver weaved them east again through the dense traffic until turning south on Route 1. Glimpses of the city's underworld flashed by, offering a tantalizing view of the metropolis's exotic underbelly teeming with life in the hot night.

Hawke saw the escorts hanging off the arms of overweight businessmen and the triad gangsters busy with their extortion rackets and their trafficking. He'd seen it all before, but it never failed to turn his stomach. He was woken from his thoughts by the sensation of the car slowing down. He looked up to see the driver pulling up in the taxi rank of the racecourse. He killed the engine and turned to face them, propping his elbow on the top of the leather seat for support.

"This is your stop."

They checked their weapons, climbed out of the Escalade and scanned the building's exterior for any sign of trouble. None of Hawke's many trips to this part of the city had ever brought him to the Jockey Club, but everything he'd ever been told about it made the place almost recognizable.

Happy Valley was one of the greatest racecourses in the world. Planted in swampland at the north of the island back in 1845, it rapidly grew into one of the most famous horse-racing tracks in Asia and later anywhere on earth. Today the course is surrounded by towering apartment blocks and the lush, steamy slopes of Mount Cameron to the south.

Safely inside the grounds, Hawke realized for the first time just what a task lay ahead of him and the rest of the team. The place was an enormous, sprawling venue stretching out ahead of him in all directions.

Hemmed in by dozens of towering skyscrapers, it felt like they were ants in a bowl, and the added pressure of the intense humidity only made things harder. With sweat pouring down his back, they met up with Officer Eddie Cheung and his SDU men, made brief introductions and then Hawke ordered his team to break into sub-units and make their way to the agreed positions.

Spectators holding cocktails or pitchers of cold lager bumped into each other as they jostled for the best views of the track. The horses and their riders were coming into view now, and preparing to start another race around the course. Excitement rippled through the growing crowd of people, many of them anxiously gripping betting stubs in their hands as they stared up at the screens and made their wishes.

From the position he had taken up, Hawke surveyed the seven-storey stands running along the western edge of the track. Capable of taking well over fifty-thousand people, these stands gave the perfect view of not only the course, but also an inner field containing several hockey and football pitches as well a rugby field. Running along the tops of the stands were numerous arc lights blazing down on the course.

"Anyone see him yet?" Hawke asked.

Scarlet was the first to speak. "Not from where I am."

"Nor me," Devlin said. "But I've been watching a very beautiful woman over in the bar on the Pavilion Stand so he might have slipped by me."

"Stop being a tit, Danny."

"Sorry, Cairo. You know me."

"Unfortunately that's true."

"What about you, Reap?" Hawke said.

"Not yet."

Hawke called Eddie Cheung over the comms. "Eddie?"

"We think we have something, Hawke – a potential sighting in the Grandstand. I'm just getting verification now via facial recognition software."

Hawke kept his eyes peeled. "Stand by everyone."

Eddie's voice crackled over the comms. "It's him, Hawke! I repeat, we have conformation via the facial rec system. Rat is at the rear of the Grandstand, wearing a black denim jacket and a white t-shirt."

"I have him!" Reaper said.

Scarlet said, "Me too."

"Okay everyone," Hawke said. "Close in on him, and keep it subtle."

With the crowd hysteria reaching a peak, Hawke moved down through the stands with the men from the SDU close behind him. He reached the bottom of the stands and made his way toward the exit. The roar of the crowds boomed all around them as people cheered their racehorses on and willed them to finish ahead of the rest of the string.

He weaved through the crowd of spectators, keeping his weapon out of sight in the holster. The last thing he wanted now was a mass rush for the exits as people fled what they believed to be a terror attack.

He turned into the bottom access aisle of the Grandstand and started to walk up the steps to the top. He and Scarlet looped arms and tried to look like a couple as they meandered closer to the Zodiac agent. Only the closest inspection would reveal the earpieces they wore, and the guns beneath their jackets were imperceptible to all but the most skilled observer from the world of law enforcement and espionage.

Hawke let go of Scarlet's hand and wrapped his arm around her shoulder.

"I love it when you take charge," she said with a wink. "Who says we couldn't have made it?"

"Pack it in, Cairo."

"We're almost there," Reaper said over the comms. He and Devlin were on the other end of the Grandstand now. The SDU agents attached to them were a few paces behind.

"He's on to us!" Reaper said. "I repeat, he knows we're here."

"Dammit!" said Hawke. "He must have recognized one of the SDU men in the crowd."

"He's on the move!"

"Everyone get after him!"

CHAPTER SIX

Hawke burst into action, using his formidable upper-body strength to slam spectators aside as he pushed through them in pursuit of Rat. Some objected, but they settled back down again when his jacket flapped back to reveal the flash of the Glock's grip in his shoulder holster.

The young Chinese assassin spun around and fired on him, the bullets cracking above the sound of the cheering crowd.

"Get down!" Hawke yelled.

Only the gaggle of people around him heard the command. They hit the deck with their drinks and betting stubs still in their hands, no time even to scream. Hawke dived down and hurled himself in a forward roll. When he exited the roll he was gripping the gun and squinting as he aimed at Rat. He moved to fire on the man and stopped himself, cursing. *Too risky, you idiot.*

He pounded along the top row of the Grandstand after the assassin, grimly aware he was chasing a man several years younger but up for the challenge nonetheless. Either side of him the SDU men were drawing their weapons and barking commands into their palm mics as they closed in on their mark.

Rat fired again. The bullet traced over Reaper's head as he slammed into the ground. The bullet missed, but far behind him he heard a horse grunt in pain and turned to see one of the animals in the race collapse into the turf. The jockey was crushed under its weight and a sense of confusion in the crowd started to morph into fear as they realized the horse had been shot.

Hawke knew things were about to get badly out of control. Of all the situations he tried to avoid, pursuing someone in a crowded public space offered the most opportunities for innocent bloodshed and carnage. Now the racecourse authorities were using the tannoys to calmly instruct everyone in the venue to move slowly to the exits.

Great, it just got much harder to take Rat down, he thought. "We need to move quicker," he said into the comms. "He's heading across to the pavilion stand, Danny. You're closest."

"Ah, for *fuck's* sake, Hawke. I just got myself a beer!"

"Stop pissing about, Danny," Scarlet said.

"I'm on him already," Devlin said, his voice suddenly businesslike. "Bastard's slowed down to a walk to blend in, but I know a rat when I see one."

Up ahead, Hawke saw some officers in the regular Hong Kong Police Force swarming around one of the entrances. "Looks like we have some back-up."

Devlin's voice crackled over the comms. "He's walking past the Pavilion Stand and continuing north. He's either heading toward the Racing Museum or the Jockey Club HQ, or maybe… no wait. He's turning left. All units, the mark's heading toward the exit at the northwest section of the course, just past the Happy Valley Stand."

"I have him," Scarlet said.

"Moi aussi," Reaper said. "I see him now. He's very calm."

"He just walked through the line of punters at one of the betting windows."

They made it to the betting hall and pushed through the long lines of gamblers who were still trying to make a wager.

"Over there!" Scarlet said. "I see him."

Hawke saw him too. He was heading for a fire escape in the far wall of the betting hall, and looking pretty shifty as he did it. Glancing over his shoulder, he saw the ECHO team and decided to make a break for it. Bursting into a run, he kicked open the fire door with his boot and vanished into the darkness beyond it.

"He's doing another runner!" Hawke yelled. "Get after him!"

They sprinted through the shifting crowd, pushing their way through until they reached the fire escape. With Devlin right behind him, Hawke kicked open the door. Finding himself in a corridor lit by emergency lighting, he lifted his gun into the aim and made his way toward the only other place Rat could have run – a set of concrete steps leading down to what he presumed was an underground car park.

They reached the top of the steps and Eddie Cheung and the SDU men filed down first. Seconds later, they came under heavy fire. Rat had ambushed them and was blasting them with his handgun. He was deadly accurate, instantly killing the SDU attachment who had been in the lead.

Hawke and the others slammed into the cover of the stairwell doorway and prepared to fire back. He and Scarlet were one side and Reaper and Devlin on the other, each of them holding their guns up to their chests ready to attack.

Hawke indicated with two fingers that he and Scarlet would go in and the others were to provide cover fire. When he gave a curt, shallow nod to everyone, they all knew it was the sign to go. He and Scarlet spun around and opened fire in the doorway. It was a relentless and ruthless attack, and by the time Reaper and Devlin moved in to provide the support fire, Rat was hit, struck in the shoulder and spun around like a top.

The Zodiac agent stumbled over at the top of the steps and crashed all the way down to the bottom. The concrete steps were unforgiving, and on the way down he broke his left wrist and sustained a concussion. Lying in a heap at the base of the stairs, he tried to lift himself up but quickly gave in, howling in pain as he applied pressure to his wrist to lever himself up. He collapse back down onto the floor and clamped his eyes shut as he gave a silent prayer.

Scarlet was first to reach him. When she saw the state he was in, she stuffed the gun inside her holster and pushed the toe of her boot down on his throat.

"Well look at that," she said. "Looks like we caught a rat."

Hawke walked over to her and also holstered his weapon. Upstairs at the ground level the crowd was growing restless as the race drew to a premature conclusion and the authorities continues to order them out of the grounds. Excited voices garbled over the tannoy system and another confused roar filled the grounds, but down here a very different atmosphere was unfolding.

The Englishman leaned over, twisted a fistful of the man's collar in his fist and dragged him up to his feet. "You're coming with us, sunshine."

"Where are you taking me?"

"I have a good friend I think you should meet."

Hawke pulled his fist back and then piled it into the man's face, instantly knocking him unconscious.

CHAPTER SEVEN

A lithe, tall woman in her late twenties was waiting for them in the basement of the safehouse. "Sam, meet the team," said Hawke. As he spoke, Reaper and Devlin bundled Rat over into a chair in the corner of the room and started tying the struggling, hooded man to it. "This one's Vincent, but we call him Reaper, and that's Danny Devlin. The scowling woman with the cigarette hanging off her lip is…"

"Cairo Sloane," the young woman said.

Scarlet raised an eyebrow. "My reputation precedes me."

"Something like that."

Scarlet looked her up and down, ignoring Rat's squeals and grunts as he struggled to free himself from Reaper's vice-like grip. Devlin calmly continued to tape him into the chair. "And who might you be?"

Hawke answered. "This is Samantha Dearlove."

Scarlet lit the cigarette and shook her hand. "Delighted, I'm sure."

Devlin finished taping Rat's legs to the chair, checked he was secure and stood up to his full height. Reaper tore the bag from the man's head and tossed it on the floor.

"We get anything for returning this scrote back to its rightful owners?" Scarlet said.

Dearlove shook her head. "He's part of the Zodiacs. Officially they don't even exist and if any of them get caught the Chinese Government just cut them loose. So he's worthless as far as any sort of trade goes, if that's what you had in mind?"

Scarlet shrugged. "He's worth something to *us*, darling. He snatched one of our team and he's our only lead. Without him we have no chance of getting her back."

Dearlove was strictly by-the-book and already she was starting to regard the ECHO team with increasing anxiety. "Let me speak with him first."

Scarlet sighed and looked at her watch. "If you must, but remember we're up against the clock here."

Dearlove stared them down. "On my own, please."

The others gave Hawke a glance. He shrugged and turned to the MI6 agent. "You have five minutes."

They waited outside as Dearlove used all her training on the captive, but when she appeared at the door it was obvious she had failed to extract anything from the assassin. "It's as we thought," she said dolefully. "He's clammed up."

"My turn," Hawke said.

Dearlove gave a nervous sigh. "We don't want an international incident on our hands."

"Leave it to me," Hawke said with a cocky wobble of his head.

"Not too rough, Hawke. I mean it," Dearlove said anxiously. "Don't forget he's the property of the Chinese Ministry of State Security and sooner or later they're going to get wind of this."

"C'mon, you know me," Hawke said. "I'm the poster child of restraint."

Scarlet laughed and nearly spat out her cigarette.

"All the same, this isn't the movies, Hawke," said Dearlove haughtily. "Do try and control yourself."

Hawke walked back across the basement. Rat wasn't even breaking a sweat as he turned a confident smile on him. The prisoner even managed a smug nod of the head.

"How you doing, Ratty?" He picked up a lug wrench and held it casually in his hands, testing its weight and balance.

"If you think you can beat the information out of me, you are sadly deluded. There is nothing you can do to me that is worse than what the Ministry will do to me if I speak."

"We'll see about that." With the forehand swing of a Wimbledon champion, he brought the head of the lug wrench crashing down on his leg and smashed his right kneecap to pieces.

Rat screamed and struggled to escape his bonds, but Devlin had stuck him down too tight. His screams turned hoarse but the Zodiac man clamped his jaw down, gritting his teeth hard to restrain himself.

"That's going to take a good surgeon to fix up, mate," Hawke said.

"Screw you!"

"Careful, lad. You've only got one other kneecap."

The man grunted and writhed, fighting the urge to lose his temper and insult Hawke. He was a prisoner now and there were protocols to follow, but it didn't look like these guys were too bothered about protocols.

"My turn," Scarlet said, sliding another lug wrench off the top of a toolbox on the floor beside the bound prisoner. "I'm not going to lie to you, Rat. This is going to hurt you more than it's going to hurt me."

She took the lug wrench and aimed between the man's legs. He fought to bring them together and protect himself but each leg was taped securely to its own chair leg. It was impossible to close the gap, and it was clear that he sensed his terrible vulnerability.

Scarlet swung the wrench and brought the end of it crashing down on the tiny patch of seat that was visible between Rat's legs. The weight of the steel combined with the accuracy and power of Scarlet's swing to smash a fist-sized chunk of the wooden seat to pieces.

Rat squeezed his eyes shut and screamed.

"Next stop is your nuts, Rat Man," she said coolly, and brought the wrench back over her head for the next attack.

"All right, all right! Stop!"

"You're going to give me something?"

Rat was breathing heavily, fighting hard not to show weakness in front of his enemy, but the agony of a smashed kneecap was too much to bear. In his struggle to hide his pain from Hawke, he started to hyperventilate and his face turned red. He opened his eyes and looked up at Scarlet with a terrifying mix of fear and real, burning hatred in his eyes. "Yes, just please get her away from me."

"No," Hawke said bluntly. "Not until I hear the quality of your information."

"What do you want to know?"

"We'll start with the location of my friend, Lexi Zhang."

Rat visibly deflated and closed his eyes. His breathing had calmed now, and he'd had time to assess the situation. He might be a ruthless, trained assassin but today his greed and stupidity at the racecourse had gotten him into a lot of trouble. Now his life was reduced to a fight for his survival, and everyone in the room knew it.

"They'll kill me," he said at last.

"So will we," Scarlet said.

Dearlove moved forward from the corner. "This has to stop now."

Reaper put his hand out and stopped her from going any further. "Let them work. They won't kill him, but we need the information."

She gave the Frenchman a doubtful look and then nodded her assent. "But I'm keeping a close eye on this. If it goes much further it has to stop or I'm calling into my superior. What's going on in here is torture."

"Where is Lexi Zhang?" Hawke interrupted bluntly. He knew Samantha Dearlove better than to accept she cared about the torture of a man like Rat. Her concerns were entirely for her career advancement and that ranked considerably lower on his scale of concerns than the kidnap and potential execution of a member of his team. "I want to know right now or things are going to get ugly."

Rat was working hard to stay in control. Recalling his training. Thinking carefully about how his boss back at the Ministry, the much-feared Zhou Yang, would deal with him when he found out he'd given up the location of the traitor Dragonfly to save his own worthless skin.

"Is it Beijing?" Hawke asked.

"Yes, but they're not keeping her in the Ministry itself," he said, glumly accepting his fate. "She's in a government facility used by the Zodiacs. There is no way you can get to her. That is why she is there. It is one of the most secure sites in China."

Reaper, Devlin and Dearlove shared a look of hope. Hawke was getting somewhere after all.

"Tell me more about this facility. I want to know exactly where they're holding her and how I get there."

Rat managed a laugh. "You're crazy! I already told you it's one of the most secure government sites in the entire country. You'd have more luck trying to break into Fort Knox."

Scarlet swung the wrench again, and Rat spilled all the information they wanted in a hurry. "She's in the basement of a building called the Torture House."

"Of course she is."

"It's on East Chang'an Avenue near Tiananmen Square."

"Turns out you can be a very helpful rat when you have to be," Scarlet said with a smirk.

"Now you trade me for her?"

"Never mind trading you for a hostage, buddy," Hawke said, staring at him without so much as blinking an eye. "You're going back to the UK on an RAF transport plane. You'll fly into Brize Norton and then disappear."

Rat was deflated. "You will regret this."

"I think not, pal," Hawke said. "But you're going to regret hurting my friend."

He swung a powerful uppercut into the man's face and knocked him out for the second time in the hour.

Dearlove gasped. "Was that strictly necessary, Hawke?"

"Not at all," the Englishman said with a grin. "But it sure was fun. Now, we need to get to this building he's just described and work out a way to get into the basement levels."

"And how hard can that be?" Devlin said.

"Exactement," said Reaper. "We will be in and out with Lexi like this." He snapped his fingers to indicate the lightning nature of their raid.

"Either that or breaking into one of the most heavily guarded government sites on earth is a suicide mission," Scarlet said, lighting a cigarette. "And we'll all be dead within twenty-four hours."

Hawke laughed. "Always the optimist, Cairo."

"You know me. And we're one Zodiac down now, as well. Only three more to go."

"Let's go get our friend."

*

Two thousand kilometres north, Lexi Zhang awoke to the sound of a door slamming. She was certain it was day, but the world was black. Her breath was warm on her face and when the confusion cleared she realized she had a bag over her head.

Footsteps clipped on the stone. A man sighed. She heard a lighter fire up and then smelled smoke.

"I'm very disappointed in you, Xiaoli." The words were delivered in quiet, calm Mandarin.

Zhou.

Shit.

She kept her voice level. "I'll never talk."

"I think we both know you will."

She said nothing.

"Not only will you tell me everything I want to know about your treachery, and any other details I desire to know, but you will also beg me to make your death a quick and painless one."

"Screw you, Zhou."

"When did you first cross to the other side?"

"Who killed my parents?"

Another deep exhalation and the smell of smoke. "The Zodiacs."

"Which one?"

"Why does it matter?"

"Because whoever did it is going to die very painfully."

He sighed. "I understand you're angry, but you don't seem to grasp the situation. You are a prisoner now. Chained up in a location quite unknown to you. Soon you will be tortured until I am satisfied you have been squeezed dry of all information, and then you will be slowly killed. There is no possibility of you exacting revenge against my men."

"Which one!"

"When did you first defect?"

"I will never talk."

She heard him tap on the door. The hinges creaked and then she heard Zhou speaking with some men.

"Good news, Xiaoli. Pig is here."

She said nothing.

"He thinks you are very beautiful. He particularly admires your hands. He says he finds your nails very tantalizing. So much so, he wants to pull them out and keep them for himself."

She felt her skin crawl. "You bastard, Zhou."

"Tell me what I want to know or I will let him go and get his toolbox and take a pair of pliers to you."

"Son of a bitch!"

"We'll leave you now. Give you some time to think. When we return, you will talk or I will give him carte blanche to do as he pleases with you." She heard them walk to the door. "And then you will talk, believe me."

CHAPTER EIGHT

After watching the police load Camacho and Kim into a cruiser and drive into the night, Lea and Ryan climbed into the back of an ambulance and gave the paramedics a weary smile.

One was an older man with red cheeks and thinning hair. He climbed into the back alongside her and immediately made Ryan comfortable and started up a morphine drip. The other was a young man, with a neatly clipped beard and tanned skin like polished bronze. He turned the key in the ignition and the engine growled to life under the hood.

Lea expected him to pull away and make his way to the closest hospital in Pretoria, but instead the rear doors opened and a tall man with a moustache got in. He was wearing a dark suit and the seat groaned when he sat down on it. He slammed the rear doors and buckled his seatbelt. "I'm Officer Paton," he said blandly. "I'm here to escort you back to the hospital until we can ascertain why you've been blowing up houses in my city."

"There's really no need," she said. "We're the good guys, and Ryan's not going anywhere with a gunshot wound like this."

The paramedic smiled at her, but from Paton there was nothing but another empty smile. "Orders from above. Sorry."

The ambulance pulled out of Kruger's property, weaving in and out of the various fire trucks that had arrived to extinguish the blaze. Looking at Ryan, she saw he was in less pain now. Morphine was dripping into his system via a canula in his right forearm, and a silly smile was slowly spreading on his unshaven face.

"You doing okay, now?" she asked, passing a hand over his shaved head.

"I'm fine, but I think they wrecked my favorite Megadeth t-shirt."

"Tosspot."

"I'm serious. These are collectors' items now!"

She smiled and checked her phone. "My phone says it's a left."

The driver disagreed. "This way is faster."

"No, it's not," Paton said, leaning toward the front. "We should be in Equestria now."

"We're meeting Fluttershy?" Ryan said with a chuckle.

"How much morphine are you giving him?" Lea asked.

The paramedic was too busy checking Ryan to reply.

Paton kept his eyes fixed on the driver. "Turn around."

"Relax. This way is faster."

Paton reached for his phone. "I said turnaround."

"And I said relax." The driver half-turned and pulled a silenced gun from the side pocket. Lea gasped as Paton tried to knock the weapon from the man's hands but he was too slow. The driver fired and killed the paramedic, then he turned the weapon on Paton. He buried three rounds in the detective, bursting his chest open and spraying blood all over the back of the ambulance.

Holy crap! We're being kidnapped!

Lea tried the door. No dice – it was an emergency vehicle and the door locks were activated as a matter of protocol. Worse, the driver now slammed shut the plastic partition between the front and rear of the ambulance, turned back around in his seat and stamped his foot on the throttle. The heavy vehicle surged forward and pushed her back in her seat. She screamed as Paton's corpse slumped over on her and she pushed it down into the footwell in the center of the ambulance beside the dead paramedic.

She looked at them both with pity and said a quick prayer. When they had gotten inside the ambulance she had doubted Paton was a policeman. She had thought maybe he was one of Kruger's men. Now she knew the answer – he was a detective all right and the young guy behind the wheel with the nice Ladies Man smile was the one in Kruger's pocket.

"Just relax," the driver said.

Ryan looked at Lea and she stared back at him wide eyed. The doors were locked and there were no windows. They were trapped. She leaned back into the seat and raised her legs, slamming her boots into the plastic partition as hard as she could. It didn't budge, but the driver did.

He turned again and raised the silenced gun. "I said relax," he said with a snarl and pulled the hammer back. "Or die."

"Who the hell are you?" she said.

"Definitely not Fluttershy," said Ryan with a sideways glance. "I don't think he even *knows* any of the My Little Ponies."

Lea said, "And neither should you, you freak."

The driver had laid his gun down and was steering the ambulance south through Garsfontein. He signalled and joined a highway. Under the more powerful LED luminaires she now saw the right side of the man's face in the mirror for the first time. A line of thick scar tissue ran in a semi-circle from the right jaw line, through his right cheek across both his lips and around to his nose. It was one of the most disfigured faces she had ever seen, and despite what had happened she felt strangely sorry for him, as she might for anyone who had undergone whatever had happened to him.

"I asked who you were, please."

"I'm no one, Miss Donovan."

"Then where are you taking us, No One?"

"All will become clear soon enough, in the meantime just try and enjoy the ride."

He turned again and she saw a sign indicating they were on Moonlight Road. The city was fading away and bushland was opening up on both sides of the car. Long lines of confetti bushes flashed past in the arc lights.

Further out, where the lights ended and the South African night took over she saw the occasional marula tree dotted here and there in the scrub. An hour passed. The landscape grew monotonous but then she felt the revs drop away and she and Ryan exchanged a silent glance. Scarface was slowing down.

He indicated to the left and pulled off onto a smaller road, and ultimately onto an unsealed track. Red dust billowed out behind the ambulance as they drove over the rough surface. The man slowed again and rounded a bend to reveal a large clearing and just beyond it an airstrip. Idling at the end of the runway Lea recognized a Raytheon 400XP private jet. "Jesus *Christ*, Ryan. Take a look."

He saw the jet just as the driver was steering them over toward a parked pick-up truck. "Rainbow Dash doesn't need a stupid jet. She has wings."

"You're starting to worry me now."

"Only just *starting* to?" he said with a smile. "Thanks for the compliment."

Lea looked at the Raytheon again and sighed. "Hope you brought your toothbrush, Ry."

"We're here." The driver braked and brought the ambulance to a stop beside a Toyota pickup. Killed the engine and turned the gun on them again. "We're going to get out now, and you're going to be good, or I will shoot you. I have the authority to do it."

"From Dirk Kruger?"

He climbed out and opened the rear doors. "Out."

They obeyed and he was smart enough to keep a sensible distance between either of them and his gun. He gestured to the right. "Over there, to the plane."

Scarface force-marched them over to the jet. Somewhere in the east, the horizon was starting to pale and a weak pink light was starting to grow in strength behind a line of paperbark thorns and sagewoods. As they approached the airstair a man appeared from the control tower and walked over to them.

"My name is Venter," he said warmly. "Please, let me welcome you aboard." He gestured at the airstair. "Mr Blankov is looking forward to meeting you."

"And who, might I ask, is Mr Blankov?" Lea asked.

"You'll find out. Now get in the plane."

The muzzle of Venter's gun glinted in the dull glow of the jet's portside navigation light. Lea helped a dizzy and confused Ryan up the airstair and into the tiny cabin of the private plane. When Venter was inside, he closed the door and stepped into the cockpit leaving the two of them alone with Scarface. He shut the cockpit door and the aircraft started its take off roll.

"How are you feeling, Ry?"

They both felt the aircraft surge forward as the pilot activated the throttles.

"Like a troop of gorillas crapped in my head. You?"

Lea winced at the imagery. "Not like that, but not great. You think Jack and Kim are okay?"

He shrugged.

The jet's nose pitched up as the powerful engines propelled them up out of the veld and into the dark African sky. Their stomachs floated up inside their bodies and their ears started to pop.

Lea sighed. "I just feel like we really let the team down."

"Don't be ridiculous," Ryan said, swallowing to relieve the pressure. "How were we to know Kruger's private residence was rigged to blow? Holy shit, who the hell has his own house wired to explode in case it comes under armed assault?"

Lea weighed it up and smiled. Sometimes he knew just how to bring her back to the surface. "I guess so. I think you're going to have a helluva scar on your back."

He shrugged. "Meat and potatoes to a hero like me."

"Get outta here, ya fool."

"Talking of scars…"

She narrowed her eyes. "What are you talking about?"

He gestured at Scarface at the front of the cabin. He was casually fitting a gas mask to his head. He pulled the straps to tighten the seal around his face and then leaned back in his seat.

Lea looked from Scarface to Ryan. "What the hell?"

Ryan visibly slumped in his seat. "Oh *crap.*"

A thick orange gas started to seep from the air-conditioning ventilation system above their seats. Lea leaped from her seat and darted over to Scarface, but he'd known the moves to this game before it had even started.

Drawing a Vektor Z88 semi-automatic pistol from a leather holster he lifted it in the air and pointed it at her face. "Get back to your seat, ECHO, and enjoy the ride."

Lea knew the game was over. If she charged him he would fire the gun and at this range there was no chance of missing. She would get plugged with a nine-mil lead slug and bleed out on the floor of this plane, and they would still take Ryan wherever they were going.

Defeated, she blew the man a kiss and walked back to Ryan, who was already knocked out colder than a snow cone and slumped down double in his seat. Her head started to feel woozy now, and she thought she might be sick. She grabbed hold of the top of the seat and looked over at Scarface. Her double vision meant there were now two of them. They were still holding their guns and pointing them at her.

The plane started to spin all around her, and then she fell down into her seat.

CHAPTER NINE

Ryan awoke to the sound of elephants trumpeting. He was lying on a soft leather couch with his face squashed into an expensive silk cushion, and when he lifted his head he felt drowsy and sick.

He felt his back. The wound had been dressed by someone when he was unconscious. That was something, he reassured himself, and pressed the heels of his hands gently into his aching eye sockets. He rubbed his face and tried to get his bearings. Shot in the raid on Kruger's place. Morphine. Kidnapped. Gassed.

Why the fuck am I not just hacking for living?

He blew out a breath and opened his eyes. During the gassing on the plane he had presumed he would awaken in Kruger's basement but instead he was on a plush leather sofa surrounded by scatter cushions. He crawled up to his elbows and saw Lea sleeping on another sofa, then he swung his legs around onto a thick red rug and took in his new surroundings.

They were inside a luxury safari lodge. Leather chairs, heavy oak tables decorated with hardback books and bowls of nuts and fruits. A set of gazelle horns was mounted on one of the support pillars. He blinked and tried to shake off his headache. Looked around some more. There were no walls, just open-air punctuated by thick wooden pillars here and there, and above his head was a thatched grass roof. Several ceiling fans circulated air around the lodge and lowered the temperature by a few degrees, but the heat was still stifling.

He walked out to the balcony which overlooked a large waterhole and saw the elephants that had woken him a moment ago. Three of them were standing on the shore drinking and washing. Another loud trumpet sounded in the hot air and sent a blue crane bursting into the sky.

He heard running water from some kind of feature and followed the sound to a small fountain at the end of the balcony where a set of steps led both up and down. He walked up to the higher level. The elevation of the top storey offered a generous view across the plains of what he presumed was the Transvaal and he realized how isolated they were. There were no people anywhere either, so he made another assumption that this place was private and not a commercial site inside one of the national parks.

He went back down and found Lea sitting up in her chair. She looked like she'd been slapped to sleep and dragged backwards through the night. "Hey."

"Howdy," he said. "Glad you could join me."

"What is this place?" She looked through bleary eyes at the bowl of walnuts and peaches on the table in front of her. "Jesus, I'm thirsty. I'd kill you for a drink."

"Thanks. I think it's some kind of safari park. There's a pitcher of water behind you."

She turned and poured herself some, drinking deeply from a tall glass. "Iced, too. Seems our host is very thoughtful."

"Apart from the fact he gassed us into unconsciousness, yes."

"Yes. You said this was a safari park?"

Before he could reply, an elephant called out again.

"Well, we're not in Dublin, that's for sure," she said.

"No, not Dublin. Looks like the Transvaal to me, but I'm no expert."

"Impressive."

They turned to see the owner of the cool, well-educated voice. He was a tall, lean man in a white shirt with the sleeves rolled up neatly to his elbows. He wore stone-colored chinos and polished brown leather boots. Crocodile belt. As he approached them he removed a wide-rimmed bush hat and placed it on one of the tables. "My name is Blankov. Welcome back to reality."

"Who the hell do you think you are?" Lea said, dragging herself to feet. She swayed and fell back down on the sofa.

"Please, the effects of the gas can last for several hours. Just take it easy."

"Thanks for caring," Ryan said. "Remind me to beat the living daylights out of you when I'm back on my feet."

"Is that any way for one scholar to talk to another?"

"A scholar?" Ryan said. "Forgive me, but scholars don't usually kidnap people and force them to breathe oneirogenic anaesthetic against their will."

Blankov looked confused.

"Sleeping gas," Lea said. "That's how Ryan says sleeping gas."

"Of course he does – he is a man of learning. I know how to recognize a genius when I see one, Mr Bale. I have been around a very long time indeed."

Ryan felt his skin crawl when he heard the words fall from Blankov's mouth, but it was Lea who spoke first.

"Oh my God. You're one of them."

Blankov nodded his head. "If you mean Athanatoi, then yes, I am. In fact, I am a devout believer in the mission of the Athanatoi. That is why I had to have the Sword of Fire. Only this can lead the Oracle to the tomb of Alexander the Great and the final idols."

Lea almost gasped, but managed to swallow it down. She regained her composure and acted as cool as she could. "The final idols?"

"The legend is quite clear. One must have all the idols to open the gateway to the Citadel."

"What do you mean by Citadel?"

He grinned. "I see I have the advantage."

"Uruk?" Ryan said.

Blankov glanced down at him. "The capital of ancient Sumer? You impress me once again, but no, not Uruk. The Citadel is far older than Uruk. In fact, it's the oldest center of civilization on the planet, as you might expect considering it was once the capital of the world."

Lea and Ryan exchanged a look, and when she spoke her voice was almost trembling. "What the hell are you saying?"

"Yeah, what do you mean the capital of the world?" Ryan added.

Another grin, but much wider. "I see I have the advantage once again, but we will have time to discuss this and many other things later on."

They heard footsteps behind them and turned to see Scarface opening an internal door. A tall man in another broad-rimmed bush hat and black shirt sauntered into the room and gave Blankov a nervous look.

Blankov seemed to enjoy the fear he caused the man. "Ah, here is Mr Kruger."

CHAPTER TEN

"So you can see what we're up against," Hawke said, turning his face from the laptop screen back to the rest of his team. "If the information is good and I think it is, we're looking at one of the toughest jobs we've ever had. Rat's description of the interrogation rooms inside the Torture House's basement level does not make for a good bedtime story."

In the safety of their Beijing hotel room, Scarlet, Reaper and the Irish Ranger stared back at him with the cool, unfazed expressions he would expect from three people with their experience.

They had been through a lot together, but he sensed they all understood the uniquely dangerous nature of this mission. The Torture House was part of the Ministry of State Security and breaching its defenses was an almost impossible challenge. Making a successful egress with one of their prisoners would bring a whole other world of pain into their lives.

Scarlet spoke first. "She's not worth it. We should leave her there and fuck off back to Elysium. The place needs a lot of work so the sooner we start the better." She popped a roast pork egg roll into her mouth and gave Reaper a sly wink.

Hawke cocked his head and gave her a withering glance. "Stop being naughty, Cairo. Anyone have any *serious* ideas?"

"We need to forget about going in guns blazing," Devlin said, casting a curious eye over the pile of dinner they had ordered from room service moments earlier –

wonton soup, beef lo mein, crab Rangoon, chicken chop suey. "There's no way we can match them. There are too many of them and the place is too complex."

He took a bite of something from one of the cartons and instantly felt the sting of Sichuan peppercorns and chili sauce. "What the hell is this?"

Reaper peered inside the carton. "I might be wrong, but I think that might be the beef tripe and ox tongue in hot sauce."

Devlin had an overwhelming urge to spit it from his mouth as fast as possible but the optics of spicy ox tongue sprayed all over the wall weren't great, so he opted to drop it inside an empty carton and wipe his mouth with a tissue. "Yummy."

Scarlet rolled her eyes. "Can't take you anywhere."

"Danny's right, though," Reaper's hand passed over the tripe and instead he picked up a sweet and sour spare rib and started to go to work on it. "The answer is to go underground. We cannot fight them man to man."

Hawke nodded. "Exactly what I was thinking. Alex's schematics show that the Torture House is where Rat said. If you look closely there's an extensive network of sewer pipes running under the entire compound. My assessment is we can find a way into the place via the sewage pipes."

"I love my life," Scarlet said wistfully. "It's so glamorous."

Hawke smiled and winked at her. "Stop whining, Sloane. You love it."

Scarlet raised her middle finger and worked hard not to smile back as Hawke pinned up the schematics Alex had emailed to him earlier. He indicated a point on the paper. "This is where I suggest we start our ingress. If these are accurate it looks like the main pipes run from the center of the compound to a number of different areas in the surrounding area. We need to find somewhere we can work from without bringing too much attention on ourselves."

"What size are these pipes?" Devlin asked.

Hawke leaned into the blueprint and studied the scale for a few seconds. "Three feet diameter."

"One meter?" Reaper said, frowning. "That's going to be tight. I'm a very big man."

Scarlet sighed. "Must everything always come back to your pants, Reap?"

He gave a Gallic shrug. "God blessed me, what can I say?"

"We'll all get through the pipes," Hawke said. "But with our special packs it's going to mean crawling."

"Mmm," Scarlet said. "Crawling through sewer pipes! Somebody pinch me."

Hawke snorted. "It's not nice, but we didn't join the Special Forces to sit at home clutching hot water bottles and wearing pink fluffy slippers. Sometimes we have to get dirty."

Scarlet sipped her beer. "I bet you love your pink fluffy slippers, Danny."

"You been spying on me again, you weirdo?"

"Point is," Hawke said, "Without the little surprise in our packs we're never getting Lexi out of there, so we have to be able to get them inside."

"So how do we get in?" Scarlet asked.

Danny said, "We know we need to access the sewage system and the closest access point is on the street corner to the west of the Torture House."

Hawke shook his head. "To access that we'd need to go down through a manhole cover on one of the world's busiest and most heavily surveilled streets. Plus we'd need something like a maintenance truck and some fake costumes, which is hard enough. Even harder is trying to make a bunch of Westerners look like they work for the Beijing Municipal Commission of City Administration. We'd be in the back of a security bureau truck within five minutes. It's a non-starter. Any other ideas?"

Reaper pushed open the window and rolled a cigarette. Lighting it, he blew the smoke outside and shrugged. "We need somewhere much quieter. What else is there on Alex's schematics?"

Hawke took another look, tracing his finger along the paper schematics until he found something to the east. "When in doubt, go to what you know. Just opposite the Ministry is the National Museum of China."

Scarlet joined Reaper for a smoke. "I like it."

Hawke called Alex and her face appeared on his iPhone screen. "We think we have a way in thanks to your schematics."

"Oh yeah?"

"Yes – the museum. Any good?"

"Already on it, Joe." She busily tapped at her keyboard until a smile appeared on her face. "This is our way in."

"What ya got?"

"I'm looking at the internal schematics of the museum right now, courtesy of the CIA website and it looks like you can forget about having to use the sewage system."

"Thank heaven for small mercies," Devlin said.

"Oh, *bugger*," said Scarlet. "I was *so* looking forward to that."

"There is a utilidor in the museum that leads to a sewage pipe connecting into the system beneath the Torture House. Don't worry – it's disused and walled up, so you'll need to blow it to get through."

Hawke felt hopeful. "Why are they connected?"

"The museum was finished back in 1959 as one of the Ten Great Buildings of Mao's Great Leap Forward. The government building at the coordinates given to us by Rat was built at around the same time and they share an underground tunnel system that was built to facilitate maintenance. The Smithsonian has a similar set up in DC. I think it should be possible for you to use this tunnel."

"How do we get there?" Scarlet asked.

"You could walk," said Alex.

"No." Hawke shook his head. "We could walk to the place, but not away from the place. When the balloon goes up we'll need a vehicle. Could you hire us an SUV, Alex?"

"No problemo."

Scarlet and Reaper shared a high five and Devlin peered back over into the beef tripe box. "But how hungry am I?"

Hawke laughed. "Looks like we've got an ingress strategy."

*

Tiger watched Zhou Yang as Pig approached the prisoner. He was holding a pair of pliers in his right hand and humming to himself as he drew closer to the woman tied to the bed. Monkey was slouching against the wall with his eyes closed and a cocktail stick between his lips.

Zhou raised a hand. "Halt."

Pig came to a sudden stop and turned to look over his shoulder at the boss.

"Agent Dragonfly." Zhou casually crossed his arms. "It is essential that you give me quality answers to my questions, or my agent here will be forced to employ a series of persuasion techniques I am sure you are familiar with, as we have already discussed."

"Go to hell, Zhou."

Zhou never flinched. "You have spirit. You have courage. And I agree with Pig. You have very beautiful nails."

Lexi looked up at him, eyes narrowing.

"The ancient practice of denailing is classified by the United Nations as a form of torture, but I think this is an over-reaction. It is in fact a thing of beauty, a classic element in the art of persuasion used successfully for millennia. You will answer my questions truthfully or I will order the Pig here to start pulling your nails out. He will ensure to destroy the nail matrix so they never grow back."

Lexi bristled but kept her mouth shut.

"Now, when did you first become a traitor?"

"I will tell you nothing!"

He chuckled. "On the contrary, you will tell me everything, Agent Dragonfly. The only point of contention is how many fingernails you will have left to paint by the time you do the talking."

Lexi struggled on the bed but the restraints were just too tight.

Tiger took a step back as Zhou ordered Pig forward to the prisoner.

"Last chance, Xiaoli. Your family is dead, your friends have deserted you and now you are about to be mutilated. We will not stop with the denailing. The Zodiacs here are experts in bone-breaking, kneecapping, tooth extraction, pressure points and a host of other unpleasant activities."

He leaned in until their noses were almost touching. "Believe me, Xiaoli, you *will* tell me everything I need to know about your treason."

A casual flick of his hand was Pig's order to move in with the pliers and as he moved in beside her and took hold of her left hand, a broad greasy grin appeared on his sweating face. "I am going to enjoy this. You're a filthy traitor and now you're going to sing for me."

Tiger sighed and uncrossed his arms. He wondered if he should have brought ear plugs. Sometimes their screams seemed to split his head in two.

CHAPTER ELEVEN

Ryan Bale wasn't sure how to react when he saw Dirk Kruger walk into the safari lodge. Of all the ECHO team, he had more reason than anyone to despise the arms trafficker. It was Kruger who had kidnapped him in the notorious Seastead battle during the Atlantis mission. He felt the memory wash over him like icy water.

Dragan Korać, the former Serbian military commander and warlord had blown up a boat beneath the enormous sea platform and knocked Ryan unconscious into the raging ocean. Kruger had saved his life, but only to use his brilliant mind to help locate the Lost City.

This man had kidnapped him, beaten him and tortured him for information and been part of the force who had murdered his girlfriend, Maria Kurikova. Now, standing a few feet from him he felt an overwhelming desire to destroy him as painfully as possible.

Without knowing it, he had moved forward a few inches, his fists clenched so hard his knuckles had gone white. He felt Lea's hand on his stomach as she held him back. He blinked in the shaded light of the lodge as he looked over to her. He saw she felt the same hatred as he did. She lowered her voice to a whisper. "Not now, Ry."

Kruger gave Blankov a suspicious glance and then flung his sweat-stained broad-rimmed bush hat on a chair. "You have more lives that a cat, Mr Bale."

"Get fucked, Dirk."

The corner of Kruger's mouth turned up. "Woah – are you a tough guy now, or something?"

"Tough enough to wring your neck, for damned sure."

Kruger eyed up the young man for a moment, judging his physical strength. "It takes more than muscle to wring a man's neck, Bale. Doesn't matter how strong your arms are. It's about how strong this is." He tapped his temple. "You think you could choke the life out of a man? Watch him die right before your eyes, at your own hands?"

"I don't think it, I know it. Even easier to kill a rat like you. When I kill you I'll dance on your grave."

Kruger thought about speaking but instead he tapped his fingers on the desk for a moment and then glanced at Blankov for the next move.

The Athanatoi chief turned and looked out over the veld. "This is a very impressive park, Mr Kruger."

"Yes. We have everything here at the park. The elephants you already saw, but we also have rhino, buffalo, hippo, leopard, hyena, eagles… and lions."

"Of course, lions," Blankov said. "Talking of which, shall we all go outside?"

Kruger led Blankov outside to the elevated deck running around the outside of the first floor. Venter and Scarface raised their guns and frog-marched Ryan and Lea outside, a few feet behind them.

Out on the balcony, Kruger gestured to a table beside some steps which led down to the ground level. On the table were a pitcher of iced water, some glasses and an expensive laptop. The trafficker stared longingly across the veld with his hands in his pockets and sighed. "It's always good to be home, but my mission's not over yet – not by a long shot." He turned and ordered them to take a seat. Ryan looked over his shoulder at the men with guns and obeyed.

Blankov spoke next. "Ever heard of Professor Julius Cronje?"

Ryan and Lea kept silent.

The Athanatoi man wasn't to be baited. "He's a leading authority on ancient languages, specializing in pictograms and symbolism. We invited him here to the safari park to help us with the symbols on the Sword of Fire."

"You mean you kidnapped him?" Lea said.

"Yes and his son, too."

"You bastard."

Blankov waved a fly off his face. "Julius is one of us."

"Athanatoi?" Lea asked.

He nodded. "Yes."

"And you kidnapped him?"

"He's a traitor," Kruger added.

Ryan said nothing. He was past the point of rage and knew what had to be done to this man. It was just a matter of staying alive long enough to kill him. He decided to let Lea do the talking.

"How is he a traitor?" Lea asked.

"After careful consultation with the professor, he decided that he didn't want to help the Oracle after all," Kruger said.

"Shame."

"I'm not finished."

"You will be soon."

A shit-eating grin spread across the South African's cracked, tanned face and revealed a set of uneven teeth. "As I was saying, Professor Cronje took exception to the hospitality I extended him here at the park and refused to give me the information I required, but it turned out he was much more agreeable after I threatened to throw his son to my lions."

"You disgust me."

Blankov spoke next. "You see, immortal or not, Julius has the same weaknesses as anyone else. Family is one of these weaknesses. Loving people is a weakness. It makes you vulnerable. Academic principles and ethics are one thing, but faced with watching lions tear your son apart and eat his guts, they go right out of the window. We soon agreed it was better that he told me the meaning of the symbols and in return his son would be allowed to live. I call it the art of compromise."

Outside below the balcony they heard a heavy animal breathing hard and padding about in the dust. The smell of wild big cats floated up through the slits in the teak decking.

"But after translating half the symbols, the traitor tried to modify the terms of our agreement,' Blankov said.

"What do you mean?" said Lea.

Kruger chuckled. "He means that Julius Cronje didn't take my threat seriously and thought he could barter with me."

Ryan gripped the arms of his chair until they almost snapped. In his head, he repeated the same mantra over and over again. *Later... you'll kill him later.*

Lea brushed a mosquito away. "I don't understand."

"Have you ever thought about when terrorists take some people hostage and make their demands? How they say, we'll kill the hostages if you don't do this or that? Ever wondered why the authorities don't simply spin it around and say, you'll let the hostages go or we'll kill you all and your families too? It's because they're weak and the terrorists know they won't do it."

Lea yawned and looked at her watch. "Is it nearly bedtime?"

Blankov offered a cold smile. "The traitor Julius Cronje thought his knowledge and my desire to access it was a more valuable commodity than the strength of my threat. He translated the first half of the symbols, and after proving himself he decided to make a counter offer. If I let his son go, he would translate the other half."

Below, they heard a lion roaring and growling.

Kruger sipped his iced water and picked up his bush hat. "Julius tried to play fucking poker with me. With *me*! And you know why?" Before she could say anything, he said, "Because he didn't take me or my threats seriously. He thought he was the one driving our little bargain, so I made sure he found out the hard way what happens when you try and play games with me."

"What are you talking about?"

"I killed his son."

"Oh my God."

Kruger said, "Needless to say we now have a full translation. What he wouldn't do to save his own son's life, he did to save his own."

Lea felt deflated. They already knew what the symbols meant. "So you know where the King's Tomb is located?"

"Yes," Blankov said. "And now Julius must also pay for his treachery."

Kruger set the hat on his head and his eyes disappeared into the brim's shade. He pushed his chair away from the table and stood up. He turned and looked over the balcony. "How's my baby?"

A man called up and told him the lion was in good form. "But a little hungry and restless, just as you ordered, boss."

He turned to face Lea and Ryan. "Did you hear that? Just as I fucking ordered."

CHAPTER TWELVE

Jessica Clark tightened her legs hard and flexed her hamstrings and quads. The Weston Gym in Downtown LA was quiet tonight, just the way she liked it. Outside in the street a police cruiser screeched past with sirens wailing and a news chopper was hovering over a building on the next block.

She stretched her calves now, pointed her feet to the ground and let go of the bars until she was hanging upside down. She brought her hands up to her face and started to crunch up until her face was parallel with her waist. Thirty reps was the usual, but today she was heading for fifty.

Thirty-five.

It hurt. The pain in her abdominal muscles was something else, but she knew better than to let it get to her.

Forty.

Burning around her torso as the lactic acid seeped into her muscles. Up she went, *crunch* and back down. The sweat ran from her forehead, trickling into her eyes on the way down and running into her ears and mouth when she crunched up.

Forty-five.

Crunch and back down.

That pussy Garcetti used to mock her for only being able to complete fifteen reps of these upside-down crunches. If he were here now she'd make him eat his shorts.

Fifty and she stopped, suspended upside down like a vampire bat. The blood rushed to her head and she glanced over at her zip hoodie and cell phone. She left it on silent in the gym, but she could see it was buzzing. Someone was ringing.

She reached up – the fifty-first crunch – and grabbed the bars. Slipping her legs out of the top of the bar she spun the right way up and her training shoes hit the gym's carpet tiles with a gentle thud.

"Hello?"

"I didn't realize you were into heavy breathing, Agent Cougar."

"Fuck off, Garcetti."

"And I thought you loved me."

"You've got the personality of a sweat sock, why would I love you?"

"My manly physique?"

She laughed. "Garcetti, you have to unhook your top pants button before you sit down or your gut will make it fly off like a champagne cork and put someone's eye out."

She heard a wistful sigh. "So how many crunches you up to?"

"Seventy." *What was the harm?*

"That's impressive stuff, Jess."

"Why are you bothering me, Tony?"

"I have a job for you."

"Oh, yeah?"

"Mm-hm."

"Any details?"

"There's an international team of assholes running around the globe, hunting for treasure and ancient relics and generally poking their snouts in where they do not belong and the boss wants them deleted from the program, so to speak."

"When you say boss, you mean who exactly?"

"The VP."

"Got it."

"Yeah," she heard a cigarette light up. "Thing is, these assholes are causing problems and it's time they got taken out. Faulkner was very clear about offering you total *carte blanche* in order for you to get rid of them. You can do whatever you want and there'll be no questions asked." He chuckled. "Hell, you might even get the Medal of Honor."

"Only the President can award that decoration, pinhead."

"Oops, my bad. I was getting ahead of myself. Anyway, that's your head's up, so get yourself ready or whatever the hell it is you do. I'll call when I have more details, maybe even with a kill order."

When Garcetti hung up on her, Jessica gave the phone a look of disgust and slipped it into her pocket. She showered and picked up her gym bag. Walked out to her car. It was dark and she was parked in a side street to dodge the fee.

Three men stepped out of the shadows.

She scanned them for all the usual stuff – who was the boss, who was the strongest, the weakest, the fastest, the slowest.

Then the top dog pulled out a .38 Special. "Gimme your wallet."

She sighed. "You can't be serious."

"Hand it over, cupcake."

Jessica sighed inwardly and glanced at the TAG Heuer Aquaracer on her wrist. She was already late and now this. She dropped her gym bag on the sidewalk and cussed.

He laughed. "What, am I inconveniencing you? Hand your fucking shit over."

She pulled her purse from the bag and stepped into the man's shadow. Handing it over to him, he moved almost sideways to keep the gun on her but out of her reach and then stretched his hand out to take the money.

She struck like a bolt of lightning.

Flicking the purse into his face, she darted her right hand forward and grabbed his wrist. Twisting it around hard so the thumb side rotated around clockwise until his palm was facing skyward. That was as far as the joint went without breaking, which she made happen next with ruthless force.

The wrist bones shattered and split. He screamed out in pain, but she was only on the starter course. The main meal was yet to be had and now she was hungry. In the confusion, she reached out and grabbed the gun by the silencer, pushing it up into his hand until the grip slipped out of his palm.

She went with the momentum of the disarming action and swiped the gun up away from his hand and into his face where the top of the barrel collided with his nose and smashed the upper lateral cartilage into a mushy pulp.

The other two guys flicked a look at one another and ran into the fight.

Jessica was already three moves ahead. She swivelled around on her right ankle and struck one of the men in the balls with a powerful flying side kick. He went down like a dead moose and cracked the back of his skull on the side of a garbage can.

The top dog spat a wad of blood and lunged toward her, working with the other remaining guy like a tag team.

Jessica rotated back toward top dog, lifting her right leg up and driving a hefty crescent kick into the side of his head. She heard his jaw break and thought she saw it dislocate a little in the direction of the blow. He was down and out, but she finished him with a chin strike and knocked him back into the pile of garbage cans where the other guy was still out cold.

The third guy raised his palms and started to step away from her, a tire iron in his right hand. "I'm sorry, okay? I don't want any trouble."

"I guess that's too bad, huh?" She glowered at him, her eyes turning icy cold and brimming over with pure hate. "'Cause you got it."

He ran for it, but she was faster. She hunted him down before he made the end of the street. Hooking his legs out from under him she brought him crashing down into the slime of the gutter. His face slammed down in the grime as he tried to scramble away from her. He got to his feet and gripped the tire iron hard. This was it. The bitch wasn't going to let him go so he had to take her out.

He swung the steel lever at her and she stepped not away but into the arc of the swing. Opening her hand, she brought her arm up and moved it in the iron's direction of travel. She gripped the lower end of the weapon near the man's hand and rotated her arm around until the elbow landed in his face and broke his nose.

He grunted and fell away from her. She seized the moment and yanked the tire iron from his hand, disarming him of the weapon in less than five seconds from his initial attack on her. She spun around and brought the steel rod down on the top of his skull and then twisted around until she was able to smash him in the face with the back of her other hand.

It struck him like iron and blasted his head back allowing her to land a punch on his left temple. He stopped fighting now and seemed to hang in mid-air for a few seconds until he started to sway on the spot like the town drunk. It was not an impressive effort, she thought and landed the final blow.

She extended the tire iron to the full reach of her arm and spun around at her waist one-eighty to maximize the momentum of the steel bar. It landed on his jaw and shattered the teeth on the left-hand side of his mouth. He fell down and landed face-first in the gutter slime, a Whopper box cushioning the final impact.

She dusted her hands off, picked up her purse, walked over to her gym bag and blipped open the doors to her RAM 1500. Climbing inside, she tossed the gym bag on the passenger seat and fired up the engine. “Three minutes,” she said with a frown. “That’s a full minute per asshole. I have to sharpen up.”

CHAPTER THIRTEEN

Hawke took in the darkness of the National Museum of China's enormous main entrance hall. The size of the place was breathtaking. Its smooth marble floors stretched out like a football pitch and its glass and steel windows towered a hundred feet up to the ceiling. He estimated it was easily big enough to accommodate a full-size passenger jetliner.

Breaking in through a skylight had been easy enough, but they all knew it only got harder from here. In the darkness, they crossed the expansive floor and headed toward a series of shallow marble steps leading up to three colossal double door arches. Sixteen Chinese characters on a bright red sign hung above the door. Hawke nor anyone else could read them but they knew from the schematics it was the entrance to the museum's Level 1.

"That's right, yeah?"

Alex's voice crackled over the comms in everyone's ears. "Sure is, Joe. I'll make a linguist of you yet."

He smiled. "That's more Ryan's field of expertise."

"Wonder how the boy's getting on?" Scarlet said, her boots clipping on the polished marble steps.

"They haven't called in yet," Alex said.

"Are we worried?" Reaper said.

"Not yet," Hawke said. "They know what they're doing."

They moved through the doors and stepped inside the *Ancient China* section on Level 1. A special exhibition on the Silk Road had been attracting a large crowd of interested people and a series of stone sculptures from the

Song Dynasty also seemed to be a big hit, but tonight all was silent and dark. And he was interested in only one thing – finding the access point to the utility tunnel Alex Reeve had located on the museum's schematics.

As he scanned the space for the fire door, he felt good, but anxious. Earlier that morning he'd gone for a long run around the eastern shore of Kunming Lake. It was a good way to burn off some adrenaline and stay calm before an op like the one they were going to execute tonight.

It had been busier than he'd expected, with people everywhere he looked. Some were Beijingers, walking dogs or jogging or just making their way to the office. Others were tourists greedily snapping pictures of the Summer Palace which rose majestically above the northern edge of the lake.

He'd beaten his personal best and returned to the hotel feeling pretty good about himself. After a shower and something to eat during their briefing they'd stepped out onto Chang'an Avenue and made the short walk from the hotel to the museum.

They slipped through a fire door and found themselves behind the scenes of the giant museum. "It should be down here."

"I think that's it," Reaper said.

On the door was a warning in Mandarin. Scarlet looked on her phone at an image Alex had sent her. They corresponded. "This is it."

The door was locked, but not for long. Reaper's delivery of a hefty riot boot almost smashed it off its hinges and then they were in.

The utilidor was a long passage constructed deep beneath the museum whose main function was to accommodate the vast building's utility lines. These included electrical cables, steam pipes and fiber optics among others. It was an eerie world of damp walls and echoes and smaller conduits receding away into total darkness.

Reaper gave the place an unforgiving glance. "At least it's not a sewer pipe, hein?"

"That fun comes later," Scarlet said.

"Alex said it was disused," said Hawke.

They followed the corridor for several hundred meters until they reached a maintenance office. The door was locked, but Reaper's famous shoulder-barge soon had it on the deck and then they were in. Stepping inside, they found themselves in a small room full of clutter and junk.

Hawke saw it first. "I'm looking at the floor, Alex. I see the disused sewage pipe you're talking about and it's got a steel grate fixed on it just as you said."

"Which is what the C4 is for," Scarlet said.

"Right," Alex said, "but don't use all the explosives. You'll need some at the other end when you reach the Torture House."

Hawke packed a small quantity of explosives around the grate. "All right, we're go," he said at last.

Reaper detonated the C4 and blew the ironwork clean off the pipe's entrance. The explosion was small and contained and thanks to their underground location it went totally unnoticed. When the smoke cleared, they left their cover and made their way over to the hole in the floor.

"So we're really going inside that horrible little sewage pipe?" Devlin said.

"Look on the bright side," Scarlet said.

"There's a bright side?"

"Of course not," she said deadpan. "Get in the fucking pipe."

"Once again, it's disused, Danny," Hawke said.

They lowered their packs inside the pipe and jumped down after them, crouching down on all fours and crawling into the gloom.

Hawke led the way, his head-mounted torchlight shining a beam down into the pitch-black darkness. The concrete-lined pipe offered no surprises, except for the occasional dead rat and was precisely as their planning had shown them it would be. He pushed on, crawling on his hands and knees with his team behind him.

"That's not smelling so great," Devlin said.

"Please stop whining," Scarlet said.

They made their way along the pipe, lighting the total darkness with their flashlights as they drew nearer to the section beneath the notorious Zodiac Torture House.

"Can't say we lead a boring life," said Devlin.

"There," Hawke said. "Up ahead I see the wall Alex described from the schematics."

They reached the wall and the pipe opened out into a space large enough to stand in. The wall was made of breeze blocks and totally blocked them from going any further.

"This is Act Two for the C4," Hawke said.

Devlin ran his hand over the wall. "Are we sure we know what's behind it? For all we know the entire PLA could be waiting for us!"

Scarlet smiled at him. "Not scared, are you?"

"Just sayin'."

She got right up in his face. "Hey Danny, what's big, brown, seriously unpleasant and behind this wall?"

"I don't think I want to know," Devlin said.

Scarlet fixed two deadly serious eyes on the Irishman. "Humpty's Dump."

He burst out laughing. "Oh, *man*… you've got one fucking great sense of humor, Cairo Sloane."

"Just ask her boyfriends," Hawke mumbled. "The line of broken men stretches around the equator."

Scarlet regarded him with contempt. "That kind of talk's not pretty, Josiah. Especially considering you're in that line."

"Ouch," Devlin said.

Reaper laughed and handed Hawke his bag. "This has to hurt, non?"

Hawke said nothing. He pulled another quantity of C4 from the bag and placed it on the wall's weakest sections. "All right, get back down the tunnel."

*

Pig pushed the nose of the pliers deep under the fingernail on Lexi's left forefinger and squeezed down on the handles until the grip was solid and unbreakable. He had already torn out her thumbnail and she had passed out in agony. After a long wait for her to regain consciousness she had finally woken and he was keen to do more damage. He turned and nodded at Zhou. "Ready."

"This is your last chance, Agent Dragonfly. You have already lost one nail. Why suffer more than you have to?"

"I had my last chance a long time ago."

"I am impressed by your courage. I would expect nothing less from someone with your training and experience. However, you must realize there is a fine line between courage and stupidity."

"Not such a fine line in your case."

"When I give Pig the sign – a simple nod of my head – he will tear out another fingernail, the one he is now gripping with the pliers. As with your thumb, he will do it slowly. It will not break off, but he will instead extract the entire nail including the matrix. As you now know, this is more pain than most people can possibly imagine. After another extraction you will be screaming and pleading for mercy and yet there are eighteen more nails on your body. I want you to think very carefully before answering my next question."

"You sure do talk a lot, Zhou."

The man in the black suit kept his calm. He knew what she was doing and it wasn't going to work on him. "I want to know how much information has been lost to the enemy. When did you defect to the other side? When did you step over into the ECHO camp?"

"You will never know."

Zhou nodded at Pig without warning and the Zodiac assassin pulled the nail from her finger. Unlike the thumbnail, it did not come easy at first and he was forced to dig the pliers in harder, pushing the pointed ends beneath the nail.

Lexi screamed so hard she went hoarse. She had promised herself she would show no weakness, but when the pain came all over again, it came even harder than before. It felt like someone was pushing the nail *in*, not pulling it out. She'd had the same sensation when a dentist extracted a tooth in her childhood, only this was a thousand times worse. She had passed out early on with the thumbnail, but this time she was wide awake.

Eventually, whatever was causing the resistance gave way and Pig wrenched the nail from her finger. Blood spurted out behind it and sprayed up his shirt and face, but his only response was a low, sick laugh as he watched her struggle and squeal.

She felt her heart thumping and pain streaked from her pulsing, burning hand to her head.

Zhou stepped forward, hands in pockets and voice soft and calm.

"When did you cross over to the other side, Agent Dragonfly?"

The rage rose inside her like a tsunami. "Go… to…hell, Zhou!"

Zhou gave a weary sigh, glanced at his watch and indicated to Pig. "Move on to the next nail."

CHAPTER FOURTEEN

They moved out of range of the wall and Hawke detonated the explosives. In the enclosed space the explosion was much fiercer and quickly filled the tunnel with heat and smoke. For a moment, it seemed that it would never clear, but the draft blowing down the utility corridor behind them sucked the smoke away and they were good to go.

They moved forward, Devlin still laughing.

"What's so funny?" Reaper asked.

"Sorry, still thinking about a talking egg taking a shit on that wall."

To Hawke's relief, the next section was also precisely as Alex had described from the schematics and they were able to step over the destroyed wall and climb up inside the access tunnel without any problem. As expected, they soon reached the final hurdle.

"I see the manhole up ahead," Hawke said, wiping the sweat and grime from his face.

"Hopefully it should move out of place. We're directly inside the compound now and blowing it will make more noise than a Chinese New Year."

"No one's blowing my manhole," Devlin said with a chuckle.

Scarlet looked at him with sympathy. "Oh, Danny. Really?"

He shrugged. "I just throw 'em out there."

Hawke carefully raised the heavy cast-iron manhole plate an inch or so and scanned to see if the coast was clear. "We're good to go," he said. "Bang smack in the middle of the courtyard just as we thought."

Leaving their packs behind, they climbed up out of the sewage pipe in silence and after replacing the cover they crossed the courtyard in the darkness of the night and slammed their bodies up against a wall. In the safety of the shadows, Hawke spied the route they needed to take to get inside the Torture House.

Hawke heard the faint sound of men talking somewhere above. Looking into the courtyard he saw the shadows of the roof in the strong moonlight. He could clearly make out the shadows of two men up there. "Two guards on the roof," he whispered. "At least."

He scanned the courtyard and saw several guards' rifles stacked in tidy tripods in the corner. "Looks like they're ready for trouble."

"I think they're always ready for trouble in a place like this," Devlin said.

When the two men were out of sight, they silently crossed the courtyard and reached the door they were looking for. It was beneath the corner of a classic Chinese gabled roof and shaded from the bright moonlight by a veranda.

Through the door now and inside to find a man behind a desk. He looked up with confusion, eyes wide. Hitting an alarm, he reached for a pistol on his desk but it was too late.

Hawke smashed a hefty punch into the man's jaw, twisting his head around on his neck and knocking him over onto the floor. Kicking the man out of his way, he blinked in the bright light. Where was the door leading to the cells?

He saw it on the other side of the room, partially obscured by a large curtain, but another man entered the room and lunged at him. Hawke managed to land a haymaker on his temple, but the man rolled with the blow and fired one back at him, driving a tight, bony fist into the side of Hawke's face.

His head was knocked to the side and his vision started to slip out of focus. Stars swam all over the room and through those stars he saw the man completing a three-sixty twist and bringing his fist around for another attack. He watched as the man rotated at his waist and fired the second punch, but the stars had gone and he ducked just in time to miss the impact.

Behind him, Reaper and Devlin were engaged in a heavy fist fight with a number of other soldiers who had entered the room from the courtyard. Scarlet was moving ahead and opening the door that led to the cells.

The Frenchman and Irish Ranger took out their opponents just as Hawke drove a heavy fist into the man's stomach and blasted the wind out of him. As he bent double in pain Hawke brought his knee up into his face and smashed his nose into a pulp. Working fast now, he grabbed the man's hair in his fist and yanked his head back before powering a final punch into his face and knocking him clean out.

Reaper slammed the door shut and Devlin slid the bolt.

Ahead, Scarlet yelled out to them. "This is it! I see the steps."

They ran down a dark stone staircase until they reached a small space that looked like a dungeon. Three doors on either side and only one of them lit from the inside.

"That's it." Hawke charged forward and tried the door.

Locked.

He shoulder barged it. It shook in its frame but stayed put. A second one and more progress.

Now he heard screaming from inside the room.

Lexi's voice.

The third charge broke the door down to reveal the horrifying sight of Lexi Zhang tied to a bed, but no sign of anyone else.

"Lexi!"

"Joe! Am I glad to see you!"

"Are you okay?"

"Just about."

He stared down at the blood pouring from her left hand and saw at once that she was missing several fingernails. "Who did this to you?"

"Pig, under the orders of Zhou."

"Where the hell are they?"

"They left me here when they heard the alarm."

Hawke hurriedly untied her, staring in horror at the damage to her fingers. He ripped away a section of his shirt and wrapped it around the bloody mess. "You'll be okay, Lex. We'll make sure of it."

"And now let's get out of here," Scarlet said.

They raced up the steps and reached the corridor, but this time it was teeming with soldiers.

Devlin said, "Looks like we're in deep shit."

"You think?" said Scarlet.

"If you think getting out of the Torture House is hard," Lexi said, still breathing hard from the torture and gripping the cloth around her hand. "Imagine how hard it will be to get out of China."

"Thanks for that, Lex," Hawke said. "You always know how to cheer me up."

The soldiers streamed down the staircase and raced down the long corridor toward them.

Scarlet cracked her knuckles. "This is it, ladies."

"Just the five of us versus fifty PLA soldiers," said Reaper with his famous shrug.

"They don't stand a frigging chance!" Devlin said.
Hawke shook his head. "Where to start?"

CHAPTER FIFTEEN

Driven by a fierce loyalty, the wall of muscle and bone that was Vincent Reno stormed forward into the swarm. Charging into the enemy ranks, he lashed out with one hand curled into a heavy, deadly fist and the other gripping a dagger drawn from his belt. Spinning, kicking, crushing and then hurling those who dared to attack him out of his way, the man they called Reaper proved once more his indispensable position in the team.

Scarlet was next into the fray, body-slamming a soldier away from the Frenchman and taking him out with a razor-sharp scissor kick. Armed with a combat knife in each hand, she slashed at the enemy and forced them back. Vermillion arcs of blood sprayed through the air around the two ECHO team members as they fought their way through the men. Nothing could stop them from rescuing their old friend, not even here in the heart of the Chinese homeland.

Armed with handguns, Hawke and Devlin fired on the soldiers further along the corridor, taking out two of them before the third and final man freed his gun from the holster and took cover behind a stairwell wall. Supercharged with adrenaline from the unexpected assault, Lexi lifted the gun Hawke had given her into the aim and unloaded the magazine in a ferocious fusillade directed at some of the crowd closing in around Reaper and Scarlet. Men screamed as their chests bursts open and sprayed blood up the walls behind them. Others scattered for cover.

Working as one now, the Frenchman and former SAS officer took advantage of the few soldiers brave enough to continue engaging them under Lexi's fire. Reaper fought hard, with the power of a pro MMA wrestler and the speed of a ninja. Ducking and diving, dodging and blocking and then returning fire with a barrage of rib-cracking power punches and crippling elbow strikes. He grunted and he sweated, but he never flinched and he never slowed. Fighting Reaper was like fighting a mountain.

Hawke and Devlin worked their way up the corridor with a Buddy System, or bounding overwatch tactic. The Englishman went first, charging down the corridor as Devlin backed him up with suppressive fire. Hawke slammed into a shallow doorway and now provided the cover while Devlin sprinted forward, all the time closing in on the soldier defending the distant stairwell. Now Devlin took cover and fired on the man while Hawke took his turn in the offensive forward position. Reaching the stairwell, Hawke reloaded his gun and prepared to spin into the void and take out the soldier.

Behind them, Lexi tossed her empty gun aside. It clattered to the tiled floor as she leaped into the brawl with Reaper and Scarlet. Filled with hate and loathing at how she had been treated in this place she relished the chance to take some back for herself, to prove to herself that she wasn't a spent force and that they had failed to break her. The first soldier was a man who was trying to attack Scarlet from behind.

She grabbed his shoulder and spun him around, smacking the heel of her hand into the dead-center of his surprised face and crushing his nose to pulp. She finished the job by swinging her elbow around full-force and smashing it into his mouth, knocking his front teeth out and nearly making him swallow his tongue.

He staggered back, raising his hands to feel the damage she had inflicted on him and she delivered a devastating Wushu butterfly kick, instantly knocking him out.

The second man lunged at her but slipped on his comrade's blood. Flailing in the air for a few seconds, Lexi drew on her terrifying knowledge of martial arts and put him down hard with a merciless Krav Maga eye-strike. Illegal in professional competitions, ramming rigid fingers into your enemy's eyes was a certain method of taking him out of the fight.

As he doubled over and screamed in pain, Lexi ended their date by landing a couple of hard slaps around his face before driving a spinning crescent kick into his head. Out cold before he hit the floor, she kicked him in the balls for good measure and then turned back to the fight.

Reaper was gripping two wriggling men by the backs of their heads. He brought their skulls together with a toe-curling cracking sound and they slumped to the floor at his boots. Scarlet was running the blade of her knife across the chest of another. Blood burst out through his fatigues and he yelled out in terror. More soldiers now came from every angle, running down the stairs behind them and emerging from a fire exit beside it.

"Something tells me they don't want to let you go, Lexi," Scarlet said.

Lexi winked. "I have that effect on people."

Up ahead, Hawke spun around into the void and emptied his magazine into the soldier defending the stairwell. The bullets tore into his chest and blasted out the other side, ricocheting off the steel banister rail and burying themselves in the green and white painted plaster walls.

Devlin joined him at the stairs, gun raised into the aim and ready to fire. "All done?"

Hawke nodded and raised the palm mic to his mouth. “Northern stairwell cleared. We’re good to go.”

Scarlet’s voice crackled back in his ear. “Having some trouble back here, darling.”

Hawke shared a look with Devlin. “Must have sent in reinforcements. Stay here and make sure the stairs stay clear, I’ll go and sort it out.”

He sprinted down the corridor and was shocked by what he saw. The lobby was now a warzone with Scarlet, Reaper and Lexi fighting at least twenty PLA soldiers. Tasked with defending the inner sanctum of the Chinese State, the men and women in uniform were fighting as fiercely as they could, but his ECHO friends were more than a match for them. By the time he had reached them the action was over.

“Turns out you didn’t need me after all,” he said.

Scarlet shrugged. “What can I say?”

“Where now?” Lexi said. “I hate this place.”

Hawke glanced at the bloody rag wrapped around her left hand. “To the courtyard. We have a little surprise waiting there.”

They headed back to Devlin and reached the small courtyard where they had broken into the Torture House compound. To Lexi’s confusion, Hawke then leaped down through a manhole cover. Working quickly and efficiently and exactly according to plan, he picked up their backpacks one by one and passed them up to the rest of the team.

Lexi nervously scanned the courtyard for any sign of the soldiers. “What the hell’s going on? They’re sealing the perimeter! We don’t stand a chance.” As she spoke, a series of search lights switched on and lit the night as the soldiers started to scan the perimeter for any sign of the invaders.

Hawke lifted himself out of the hole. "Right, everyone open their packs and let's get out of here."

With confusion still etched deep on her face, Lexi followed the others and unzipped the chunky backpack Hawke had passed her from the sewer pipe. She opened it up and was astonished by what she saw.

"I don't believe this."

"Believe it and hurry the hell up!" Devlin said.

She pulled a strange, heavy black object from the bag and set it down on the cobblestones. "What the hell is this?"

Scarlet said, "It's a jet-powered hoverboard, a bit like the Flyboard Air but with its own proprietary software and turbojets. Its top speed is one hundred miles per hour, it has a ceiling of ten thousand feet and can fly for fifteen minutes before running out of fuel."

"Am I dreaming this?"

"No," Devlin said. "And to be fair it's more of a nightmare."

Hawke fitted a small pack onto his back. "There's enough A1 kerosene in these packs to last around ten to fifteen minutes and after that you're hitting the deck. How high you are when that happens is up to you, but I'd recommend no more than ten feet. These remotes control the throttles and after that just follow my lead."

"Are you insane?" Lexi asked. "We'll never get away on these things!"

"We'll never get away any other way," he said. "The perimeter was completely sealed the moment the alarms went off. Besides, where's your spirit of adventure?"

Lexi sighed and shook her head as she stepped onto the board and secured her boots inside the straps. "I saw someone doing this on YouTube once," she said, turning cynical eyes onto Hawke. "He had a *parachute*."

"No room for parachutes."

Soldiers tumbled out of the courtyard door and saw them. They raised their guns and started firing.

Hawke fired his board up first and the four miniature, jet-powered turboengines burst to life. Rising up into the air he turned and fired on the men with his Glock, forcing them to take cover.

Scarlet and Reaper were already powering their jetboards into the air behind him, hands on their weapons and spinning around to fire on the men. Hawke thought Lexi was having some trouble with her board, but Devlin covered her while she fired it up and got it moving. Breaking a Chinese citizen out of a government facility like this would lead to some serious questions at the highest levels, especially if anything went wrong and they were already on the wrong side of most governments.

Lexi was higher in the air now and Devlin was just a few seconds behind her, wobbling about as he fought to control the jetboard while simultaneously firing on the soldiers.

They gained speed rapidly, the 250 horsepower jet turbines easily lifting them up to the elevation of the outer perimeter wall. Another alarm declared loud and clear that they were leaving the compound. Searchlights lit them up like Christmas trees as they flew over the top of the outer wall and headed down toward the street.

Hawke was in the lead, racing down from the top of the wall and slowing up around twenty feet above the street. Below him, soldiers poured out of the main gate and sprinted after them with rifles.

He flinched as a bullet traced past him and then another struck the casing on one of the jetboard's four turboengines. The soldier who had fired on him was still giving chase, stopping every few yards to raise the rifle and take another pot shot.

The five-strong team now converged around fifty feet in the air as they continued to flee. Below them, a motorbike raced out of the main gate and headed in their direction. Tiger was driving it and Monkey was riding pillion, armed with two PLA-issue P19 semi-automatic pistols.

He teased some more speed out of the jetboard, suddenly shooting up into the air once again and leaving Tiger far below in his wake. Lexi was at his side now, deftly manoeuvring the jetboard as if she'd spent half her life flying one.

"Zàijiàn, you bastards!"

Spinning around in the air, she raised her weapon and opened fire on the soldiers sprinting across Tiananmen Square. Spraying them with rounds, she forced them to take cover behind their vehicles, but in the distance, she saw at least another half a dozen PLA trucks giving pursuit.

We'll be lucky to get of this with our lives, she thought, then saw Tiger and Monkey speeding up on their bike and continuing to pursue them.

"This is not good!" she screamed. "They're gaining on us!"

"What's the plan, Hawkster?" Scarlet asked.

With only a few minutes of kerosene left before the jetboards fell out of the sky, Hawke knew there was only one plan. "We get back to our car and get to the rendezvous point as fast as we can!"

CHAPTER SIXTEEN

Hawke steered the jetboard down to Tiananmen Square until he was no more than two or three feet off the ground. "Get down low!" he yelled. "Harder for them to see us."

The rest of the team followed him and descended until they were almost the same height as the crowd of people now scattering from them in every direction. Most were scared, some were bemused and others simply filmed all they could on their phones.

The jetboard engines roared. CCTV cameras swivelled. Somewhere in the distance they heard a helicopter. Tiger revved his bike and closed the gap as Monkey raised both guns cowboy-style and fired on the ECHO team with a vengeance.

Hawke twisted around and returned fire while still flying away from them. Reaper and Scarlet made the same manoeuvre. Devlin and Lexi raced ahead toward their Maxus D90 SUV which was still where they had parked it earlier.

Out of rounds, Hawke clicked the release and the empty mag fell away onto the square. He smacked a second one into the grip and emptied it all over the pursuing Zodiac men and their bike. Hitting either of the assassins would work for him, but if he missed and hit the fuel tank there was the possibility of it killing or injuring innocent bystanders.

He raced backward through the night, hot wind whipping at his hair as he fired again on his pursuers. Empty jackets spat from the ejector port and clattered to the ground below. The gun kicked back in his grip with each shot, but holding the throttle remote meant firing one-handed and the bullets were going everywhere except where he wanted them.

Tiger's Kawasaki growled like a hungry beast, accelerating easily with the twist of the throttle as he weaved in and out of the terrified crowd. Monkey fired again, almost hitting Reaper. Somewhere behind them they heard the sound of the helicopter engine grow louder and then police sirens and lights on the streets to the east and west of the famous square.

"Ever heard the phrase *we're in deep shit*, Hawke?" Devlin said.

"Keep going!" Hawke shouted back to him. "We have to get to the Maxus before the fuel runs out in these engines."

The chopper was even louder now but still no sign of it. Tiger was closing in and not far behind were at least half a dozen cop cars and PLA jeeps. Hawke suddenly found it easy to imagine being in a Chinese *laogai*, or gulag, for the rest of his life.

He glanced over his shoulder and saw the Maxus. He slowed the board gently and it rapidly lost altitude. The rest of the team also brought their boards to the ground and leaped off.

Hawke joined them dived into the Maxus D90. Firing it up, he wasted no time in flooring the throttle pedal and steering away from the kerb. The enormous Chinese SUV growled in response and lurched forward like a hungry tiger as the Englishman slammed his door shut and buckled his belt.

Soldiers crawled from everywhere like ants, but this time they were armed with automatic rifles. Hawke saw a handful on the right emerging from a set of concrete steps. Unable to get away from them before they fired, he frantically spun the wheel and plowed the two-thousand kilo monster right through them.

One on the side managed to dive away and fire off a few rounds before he crashed back down the steps. One smashed into the grille and disappeared beneath the SUV and the third tried to leap away but was too slow. He bounced up over the hood and smashed into the windshield leaving a chaotic array of spider-web fractures all over it and obscuring Hawke's view.

The SBS man wanted to slam the brakes and send the man flying off the hood, but by now the other soldier on the concrete steps had gotten himself back together and set up an offensive firing position. Tucked away behind the reinforced concrete he was now firing on the D90.

"Swerve!" Lexi yelled.

Hawke spun the wheel and the man flew off the car. They all heard the rounds spraying across the tailgate as they made their way toward the rear window. Seconds later all the glass on the back of the SUV blasted out in a shower of lethal shards and sprayed into the back of the car.

"Holy shit!" Lexi screamed.

"Bastard's a good shot," Scarlet said calmly. "Shame to do this, really." She smacked a fresh mag in the grip of her Glock, popped her seatbelt buckle and turned in the rear seat. Lifting the weapon into the aim she rested it on the top of the seat and squinted down the sights. "Steady as you like, Joe."

She fired on the shooter and hit him with the first round. It neatly punctured the center of his forehead just an inch below the line of his helmet. In his death throes, he released the assault rifle and fell back down the concrete steps without a scream. Scarlet turned back and winked at Lexi as she was buckling her belt back up. "If only you could fight like that we wouldn't be in this mess."

Lexi snarled. "Why, I ought to…."

"Go to shooting lessons?"

Lexi leaned forward, ready to fight, but Reaper gripped her by the wrist. "We're family," he growled, turning to Scarlet. "Reunited. Now, kiss and make up."

Hawke sent the Maxus screeching into a sharp bend and stamped on the throttle when they were back on the straight.

Scarlet laughed. "Kiss and make up… you wish, darling."

"Yeah, you wish," Lexi said.

Now Reaper laughed. "See, you're already on the same side!" He checked his gun and pushed down the window. "This is nice, n'est-ce pas?" Leaning outside with the wind flapping his bandana, he started laying down some fire on an army MengShi 4x4 on their tail.

Hawke saw the MengShi gaining on them and wrenched the steering wheel hard to the left to take the next bend. "Your friends," he said to Lexi. "They're not very nice people. They're so keen to get you back they've recruited a Fiery Thunderbolt."

"A what?" Scarlet said.

"It's a recon chopper," Lexi said. "And they're not my friends."

Running alongside the Maxus around five hundred feet in the air on their left was a Harbin Z-19 attack helicopter. Hawke craned his neck to peer up at the chopper. "Good stuff. We've got rockets, we've got gun pods and we've got Hongjian air-to-surface anti-tank missiles. Can I interest anyone in some clean underwear?"

The chopper spun around like a black angel of death, flying sideways as the pilots aimed the pod-mounted

23mm machine gun at the fleeing SUV and opened fire on the ECHO team. The rounds chewed into the asphalt behind them and chased them at high-speed as they raced south along Qianmen Street.

Ripping over the busy junction at Zhushikou West they tore past Temple of Heaven Park and continued south, but shaking the hunters off their tails was proving to be harder than they had thought.

The Harbin chopper was now directly overhead and rotating on its axis so it was now side-on to the fleeing Maxus. The door opened and a man they recognized as Zhou leaned out with a megaphone. Behind him he saw Pig. "Pull over or we will kill you!"

"Looks like we're running out of options, Joe!" Reaper said.

"What have you got us into?" Devlin said with a grin. "I could be in Flynn's right now taking the top off a pint of black, you know?"

Hawke smiled back. "Nothing I can't get us out of – and I'll share that pint with you when all this is over."

Scarlet sighed. "I wonder what it feels like to be hunted by half the Chinese Army?" She turned to Hawke, deadpan, her words dripping with sarcasm. "Oh wait, it feels like *this*."

"I'm doing my best, Cairo."

They approached a large concrete and steel bridge supporting the Beijing-Shanghai High-Speed Railway. In the distance to the west Hawke saw the unmistakable outline of a Fuxing Hao high-speed bullet train racing along the line. Its sleek steel hull glinted in the arc lights of the railroad line.

"This is going to get ugly," he said.

Scarlet flicked a glance at him. "What do you mean?"

"Behind us," he said, nodding toward the rear-view mirror. "The Z-19 is opening fire on us!"

The chopper swooped down until it was below the top of the buildings lining Singin Street and let rip with its nose-mounted GPMG. Rounds ripped along behind them like dancing devils, savaging the asphalt road service and ricocheting up into the air six ways from Sunday.

"This is too close!" Lexi said. "It's over!"

The bridge approached them at lightning speed.

"They're firing another missile!" Hawke yelled. "Hold on to your arses!"

Above them on the bridge, the train gathered speed on its journey to Shanghai.

Hawke sucked in a breath and spun the wheel hard to the right sending the Maxus lurching over onto two wheels. They squealed loudly and black rubber smoke billowed up in their wake as the Hongjian air-to-surface missile ripped underneath them and smashed into one of the bridge's concrete stanchions.

"Holy shit!" Lexi yelled, covering her face with her forearm.

Hawke spun the wheel hard to the left and brought the Maxus crashing back down onto all four wheels. The axels creaked and groaned as the heavy vehicle swerved all over the road. He fought hard to correct the skid and avoid the collapsing bridge up ahead. "Look out!"

After a supercharged explosion, the section of the bridge directly above the destroyed support column now collapsed in a massive smouldering heap of crumbling concrete and an enormous cloud of smoke and dust. They all saw the bent, broken rails twisting down from the tracks, pointing like the gnarled fingers of a gravedigger at a freshly dug grave.

"The train!" Lexi yelled.

"It's going too fast!" Devlin said.

Reaper shook his head. “That thing goes over four hundred Ks per hour!”

The train derailed and crashed down off the bridge and plowed down into the burning void created by the missile. For a few seconds the thick black smoke obscured it. When the wind cleared the smoke, they saw the train was wedged nose-first in the gap and the carriages behind it were buckling up on their couplings. Alarms blared and people screamed as Hawke spun the Maxus across two lanes and ripped under the one remaining clear section of the bridge.

The chopper saw it too late.

The pilot tried to pull up but they were going too fast. By the time the smoke cleared they were almost on top of the bridge. They struggled to pull up in time but in their zeal to destroy the fugitives they were going too fast.

When the Z-19 collided with the wrecked bridge it exploded like a grenade. Burning jets of kerosene sprayed out like a fireworks display as the crumpled airframe crashed into the asphalt just a few meters from the smashed train.

“What the fuck just happened?” Scarlet said.

Reaper shrugged. “Hawke’s at the wheel, so nothing unusual.”

“Zhou and Pig just got roasted,” Lexi said.

Devlin shook his head, his heart pounding in his chest. “Holy Mary Mother of Christ, that was *nuts!*”

Lexi closed her eyes. “Innocent people will have died on that train.”

“We didn’t do that,” Hawke said flatly. “And where the hell’s the MengShi gone?”

“You can’t see it anymore?” Scarlet asked.

Devlin turned in his seat and scoured the street behind for any sign of their pursuers. “It’s not behind us anymore!”

"Look out!" Reaper yelled.

The MengShi had peeled off and taken another route to get ahead of them and now it was pulling out of a side street.

Hawke stamped on the brakes but it was too late. The front of the Maxus smashed into the rear of the MengShi and spun it around one-eighty. Clipping the other vehicle sent them into a spin and by the time Hawke brought it under control he saw some police up ahead had thrown a stinger across the road to bring the fun to an end. As they plowed past the crumpled MengShi, their front tires ripped open on the stinger and instantly deflated.

He struggled with the wheel to keep the vehicle level but their speed was too great. The Maxus swerved violently to the left, smashed through a barrier and piled down an embankment at the side of the highway.

In the space of just a few seconds they tipped over and rolled down the rest of the slope at speed. The roof crumpled down and the airbags fired off. Reaper cradled his head in his arms while Scarlet tried to tuck her head down between her legs. Lexi screamed and covered her face and everyone held on for their lives until they came to a smoking, steaming stop, upside down at the bottom of the highway embankment.

Hawke managed to unbuckle his belt as Reaper kicked out the shattered windshield with his riot boots. Twisting in the battered, twisted SUV, he saw Scarlet struggling to unbuckle Lexi's belt. The Chinese assassin was out cold, just like Devlin.

"It's jammed!" Scarlet now frantically tried her door. "And the bloody petrol tank's on fire, Joe!"

And then it exploded and lit the night with white-hot flames.

CHAPTER SEVENTEEN

Unlike in the movies, the explosion did not instantly destroy the entire vehicle, but was instead limited to the tank and now flames spilled out of it and covered the rear of the Maxus.

Hawke quickly scanned the interior of the car to check his team. Reaper was good to go. He was still struggling with his belt as he finished smashing the shattered windshield out. Devlin was still out like a light and Scarlet was woozy and continuing her struggle with the door. Lexi was unconscious and bleeding from the mouth and nose. Her window had cracked with the force of the roll down the slope and exploded in her face. She was lucky to be alive.

Reaper immediately produced a combat knife and slashed his belt in two. He crawled out through the windshield and ran around to the back. He opened Devlin's door, crawled inside and slashed open his belt before dragging the Irishman out behind him, away from the smoke and flames.

Smoke filled the interior of the Maxus as Scarlet crawled out through Reaper's open window and joined him as he tried to resuscitate the former Ranger.

Hawke was next out, crawling out through the shattered windshield and working hard to clear his lungs of the toxic smoke. He got to his feet and turned in the night to see Lexi still trapped in the back seat, strapped in by her belt and hanging upside down in the burning vehicle.

With cold sweat running down the back of his neck and over his back, Hawke didn't hesitate to run into the fire. The sight of Lexi inside a burning car slowly filling with noxious smoke shocked him but his training banished all emotion as he worked out the best way to get her out.

The door was jammed. The gas vapor burned like a storm from hell. He shielded his face from the intense heat of the fire as he lifted his boot and smashed the remaining glass in the rear window. He kicked it three more times until it broke out of the frame completely and then he was able to lean in and hack Lexi's belt in two with his knife.

The flames roared in the night, engulfing the entire rear section of the car now, burning the seats and carpet and roofing felt. Black smoke poured from the interior of the destroyed Maxus as Hawke dragged Lexi from the back and hoisted her into a fireman's lift.

Pounding away from the vehicle, he just reached the safety of the concrete traffic barrier when Tiger swerved the Kawasaki to a halt at the top of the embankment. Monkey jumped off and slid the bolt on his gun with a howl of insane laughter. Tiger killed the engine and pulled his own weapon.

Devlin regained consciousness and got to his feet. "What the hell?"

"You got knocked out," Reaper said.

"You never said a word the entire time," said Scarlet. "I preferred you that way."

Behind them, the highway flashed with the blue lights of countless emergency vehicles. A PLA jeep skidded up behind the Zodiac's motorbike and a dozen soldiers leaped out the back and started running down the embankment.

Over Hawke's shoulder, Lexi started to come to, coughing and moaning incoherently. "Where am I?"

"What sort of food do you get in Chinese gulags, Lex?" he asked.

"What the fuck?"

"Humor me."

"Pork broth, without the pork," she said woozily. "Why?"

"No reason, just hang on tight!"

They started sprinting away from the devastation of the crash site with the soldiers at their heels. Tiger and Monkey stayed higher up the embankment and fired off a few pot shots. Their rounds pinged off the hot asphalt around Hawke's boots as he ran with Lexi over his shoulders.

Scarlet and Devlin pounded the pavement beside him while Reaper spun around and let off a few rounds from his gun. Tiger and Monkey ducked down behind the traffic barrier at the top of the embankment and the soldiers scattered and sought cover wherever they could find it before returning fire.

The rounds from the more powerful rifles chewed into the concrete and snaked their way closer to the ECHO team. "Over there!" Hawke yelled.

They jogged down a second shallower embankment and found themselves back in civilization. Neon signs hung from shabby buildings and steam poured from vents in the sides of restaurants.

They burst through the door of the closest building. A small room with yellow-painted walls and a number of greasy tables around the outside. A man with a meat cleaver looked up with confused eyes from his work of parting a chicken. He lifted the heavy blade over his head and started shouting in Mandarin.

Still over Hawke's shoulder, Lexi called back and an argument began. The man lifted what was left of the bloody chicken up with his other hand and started screaming some more. Lexi laughed and hurled back more abuse.

The Englishman considered the situation and wondered if he'd run into an episode of the Outer Limits.

Devlin scratched his head. "What the *holy* fuck is going on?"

"I take it he's not going to serve us then?" Hawke said.

Lexi laughed. "You don't want to know what he's saying."

Reaper turned from the front door. "Tell him the People's Liberation Army want to see his menu."

They ran past the screaming man through a door into the rear. In the kitchen now, steam and smoke filled the air again, but this time the flash of woks and the smell of ginger and chili replaced the smell of burning car seat stuffing.

"Which way?"

A chef snatched a knife-sharpening steel and held it up as a weapon.

"Hang on," Hawke said. "Why am I still carrying you, Lex?"

She shrugged. "I thought you were just being an English gentleman."

Hawke twisted his mouth and dropped her from his shoulders. "Your ride is over."

"If I knew it was a ride I'd have dressed for the occasion."

He looked at her. "Really? Here and now?"

The soldiers teemed in through the door and flooded into the kitchen. Still no sign of Tiger and Monkey, Hawke noted, but this was plenty enough trouble as it was. The fight kicked off when Reaper snatched up a wok and piled into three men beside one of the industrial-size stoves.

Smashing the cooking pan into one of their heads, he swung it back in the opposite direction and panned another of the soldiers a second later. Both men fell back onto the stove, plunging their hands into the gas flames and screaming in pain as Reaper headbutted the third man and finished him with a bone-crunching haymaker.

The man fell back and crashed into more soldiers like a bowling ball colliding into a dozen pins. One of them scrambled to stop himself going over and reached out to grab something to stop his fall. He hit the handle of another wok and flicked it up into the air, spraying himself and his colleagues with hot oyster sauce and Sichuan peppercorns.

Lexi and Scarlet were taking out their frustrations on some soldiers closer to the man with the sharpening steel who was now running from the kitchen with fear on his face. Devlin was pounding another soldier in the corner, holding him up with one hand while landing punches on his jaw with the other.

Hawke scanned the room for another way out when he saw a door behind some industrial refrigerators. It was at the other end of the enormous island that ran down the center of the kitchen. It seemed to lead to a downward staircase and he thought it looked good as a possible escape route, but then Tiger and Monkey burst through it with their guns and started firing on him.

He slammed himself up against the wall behind the refrigerator and called out to his teammates, alerting them to the arrival of the Zodiacs. Searching the enormous kitchen for their locations, he saw Reaper first, deep in the brawling mob. Catching sight of his skull and crossbones bandana, he called out to him.

"Zodiacs, Reap!"

The Frenchman spun around. "And just as I was getting bored, too!"

CHAPTER EIGHTEEN

Reaper didn't hesitate and quickly launched himself into the assassins, lashing out with tightened fists and razor-sharp elbows as he worked his way through the soldiers to get to the Zodiac men.

They fired on him, hitting a soldier in the heart and killing him on the spot. The soldiers reacted fast and badly, drawing their weapons and raking the two assassins with a vicious fusillade.

Tiger and Monkey were the hardest trained men in the country. They took cover behind the island in the center of the kitchen and calmly reloaded. When they fought back against the soldiers it was a bloodbath and seconds later not a single one of the PLA men was still alive. Their cooling corpses slid down to the kitchen floor beneath walls covered in blood. Tiger and Monkey reloaded and turned their guns on the ECHO team and the traitorous asset. They would kill them all.

Reaper had a different strategy planned. He pounded across the kitchen and vaulted over the island. His tactical Foreign Legion-issue boots smashed down on the tiles with a heavy thumping noise as he turned on the assassins.

Tiger swivelled around to look up at the invader, unable to believe he'd had the nerve to do what had just happened. Monkey excitedly slapped the floor with his free hand and laughed like a madman.

Reaper grabbed hold of Monkey's throat and hurled him back into the wall beside the staircase. The Zodiac assassin smashed into the plaster at an awkward angle and tumbled down into the stairwell, smashing his head on the banister rail as he went.

For a second, the Frenchman thought the job was done, but then he saw something that shocked him to the core. Monkey sprang up over the banister like he had the power of flight and raced toward him, a knife drawn in the air.

Reaper never flinched. He ducked, swung around and landed the bottom of his clenched fist in the middle of Monkey's face. The assassin swooned for a moment as his eyes rolled up into the back of his head. He was a fast and experienced martial arts warrior but the former legionnaire had caught him by surprise. He fell to the floor and rolled out of sight under the island.

Reaper scanned the room for the vanishing Monkey. "C'est quoi ce bordel!"

A few steps away, Hawke swung a powerful right-hand cross at Tiger, but his opponent was too fast for him. He ducked, easily dodging the blow and fought back with a lethal hook kick, smashing Hawke's legs out from under him and sending him tumbling over backwards.

"Need a hand, buddy?" Devlin said, wiping blood from his mouth.

Hawke gave him a look. "Not right now, thank you."

Tiger attacked again, launching himself at maximum velocity at the fallen Englishman, but Hawke rolled away to the left, leaving Tiger's punch smashing into the floor tiles beneath him.

Monkey rolled out of the island at the other end of the room and leaped to his feet behind Lexi. Cockily, he tapped her on the shoulder and when she turned he winked.

Even with her damaged hand, her reaction was ruthless and she started pummelling him in the stomach. She moved so fast he had no chance and she cursed as she beat the wind from his lungs, never letting up long enough for him to get his breath back and return fire. The murder of her parents at the hands of these men had raised a hatred inside of her she never realized she could feel and now she fought with a ferociousness never before seen by the ECHO team.

Now, her work was nearly done. She grabbed hold of the semi-conscious, dazed Monkey by his hair and walked him backwards to one of the stoves. Pinning him up against the work surface, she started gripping his throat.

The assassin squirmed as she squeezed ever tighter on his throat. His face started to turn purple and when he pleaded for mercy, his voice was weak and hoarse. He begged her in Mandarin to release him.

"I will release you only to hell!" she spat back at him, tightening her grip even further. One glance at her mutilated, bloody hand was enough to keep her resolve to kill him clear in her mind.

He kicked and flailed until a fat blue tongue popped out of his mouth and his eyes looked like they were about to explode. "Die, you piece of shit!" She slammed his head down under the surface of a pan of filthy old cooking oil and held him there. He kicked and squirmed some more. "You killed my parents, you son of a bitch!"

His head burst out from the oil and he gasped for air. "No! Tiger killed your parents!"

Lexi felt rage burn inside her and she pushed his head under again. "Die, you bastard!"

Scarlet reached out a hand and rested it on her shoulder. "He's dead, Lexi. You killed him."

She looked down and saw Monkey's limp body slide down to the floor. She had killed him.

Tiger saw it too and fled from the chaos into the night.

Lexi watched him vanish. "He killed my parents, Joe!"

Hawke watched him go. "I'm on it!"

He pursued him hard, smashing his way through the door. The stairs he had seen turned out to be a fire escape leading down to a car park at the rear of the restaurant. He pounded down the metal steps three at a time. Beijing was towering all around him. The sound of sirens was still in the air, as were the police choppers and their searchlights. One of the biggest manhunts in modern Chinese history was unfolding all over the capital city, The hounds were everywhere and he was the fox.

But right now he was more interested in a tiger.

With Rat in British custody and Zhou, Pig and Monkey all dead, Tiger was the last surviving Zodiac and letting him go was unthinkable.

And then he saw him, fleeing at full speed into the night. He was sprinting under a line of streetlights toward another side street. Hawke knew that for the Zodiac assassin, losing him in the backstreets of Beijing would the easiest thing in the world. He had to catch him now, or he would be the mother of all loose cannons, hell bent on revenge against them and with the skillset to deal it out.

He sprinted after him across the car park, pounding on the asphalt as fast as he could power his legs forward. Tiger was younger than him, faster and probably more agile, but he thought he might just have the edge when it came to upper body strength.

And luck.

Tiger darted into an alley lined with garbage cans and the Englishman followed him into the darkness. The assassin was already at the far end and wheeling around the corner. Chest pounding and lungs on fire, Hawke forced his aching legs to work harder and faster as he turned the corner and scanned the street for his enemy.

A busy street lined with shops on both sides. Towering above them were several storeys of apartments, marked by washing on poles hanging out of the windows and blowing gently in the neon breeze.

Tiger was on the other side of the road, slowing to a jog now and heading for what looked like a laundry.

Hawke was wrong. The Zodiac assassin wasn't aiming for the laundry but a Mazda parked up out the front of it. As Tiger approached it, someone inside flung open the rear door and he dived inside.

The former SBS man was running out of options. If the car took off into these side streets that was the end of the chase. But the Mazda wasn't taking off anywhere. Instead it revved and turned in a tight circle in the middle of the street before heading right for him.

Hawke narrowly avoided the impact by flinging himself into a forward roll and he got back to his feet on the other side of the road. As the Mazda rushed past him a man in the back seat beside Tiger leaned out of the rear window and twisted a submachine gun around, spraying lead all over the asphalt. The rounds chewed into the surface of the road and spat chunks of tarmac up into the air all around him.

He dived onto the hood of a passing cab and landed with a smack on the windshield. His back slammed into the glass and smashed it, leaving the driver struggling to see the road. He opted for stomping on the brakes and sent Hawke flying off the hood of the car and crashing down on the hot, hard road. He turned the fall into another roll to absorb the energy and dragged himself back up just in time to avoid another hail of bullets from the Mazda.

He ran to the side of the road and took cover behind one of the market stalls. The owner started shouting in Mandarin at him and waving a slice of durian in his face. His tirade was brought to an abrupt stop by a savage fusillade of automatic bullets raking into the front of his stall and blasting his stock to pieces. He swore loudly and hit the deck beside Hawke, then spoke in rapid Mandarin.

"Just what I was thinking, mate."

More police sirens and lights.

"They're having a busy night." Hawke cradled his head in his hands as another wave of gunfire ripped over their heads blasting lotus roots, taros and starfruits all over their heads.

The driver of the Mazda hit the gas hard, spinning the wheels and making them squeal like pigs. Two thick clouds of burned rubber smoke spewed out of the rear wheel arches and then the car took off, swerving down the street. It turned a corner and vanished into the night leaving crowds of terrified people peeping out from behind wherever they had sought cover.

Hawke thrust a hundred dollars into the stall holder's hands and looked at him with an apology on his face and a shrug on his shoulders. "Gotta go, mate. Not all that interested in explaining this to the law."

He slipped away into the crowd and called Scarlet. Reaper had done the decent thing and stolen a Haval H9 SUV he'd found around the back of a noodle bar near the restaurant. He started the long walk back to the rest of his team and found them leaning against the side of the Haval, sharing a smoke. Lexi was safe but not out of China, so the mission was only half done. They still had to get back to the other team and finish the hunt for Kruger and the Sword of Fire.

"Talking of getting out of China," he asked. "Rich sort it out yet?"

Scarlet nodded. "As planned. The ship leaves tonight – if we can get there."

"We can get there."

The rest of the night was quiet as Hawke drove the Haval out of the city and joined the highway stretching around the west coast of Bohai Bay. Leaving the industrial landscape of the capital behind, they cut through endless tracts of Chinese countryside before finally arriving in Qingdao at four in the morning.

The port city nestled on the western reaches of the Yellow Sea and they quickly located the Naja Maersk moored up behind one of the massive container cranes in the northern section of the port. At over four hundred meters in length and nearly two hundred thousand tonnes, it was one of the world's more formidable container ships and tonight it was their passage to freedom.

Sailing under a Danish flag, it was due to leave port and sail through the South China Sea before crossing the Indian Ocean. From there it would head north through the Suez canal until eventually reaching Rotterdam. Under the protection of Captain Poul Kampmann the ECHO team would sail out of Chinese waters and then get picked up by a chopper from a US carrier group under the direct orders of President Jack Brooke himself.

Hawke pulled up and killed the Haval's engine. Dumping it at the side of the road behind a cargo shed, they walked across to one of the gangways on the stern's starboard side. Waiting there was a man smoking a cigarette and wearing a black beanie. He introduced himself as Ulrik and then showed them up the enormous gangway.

At the top of the steps a man in a roll neck jumper met them and waved them on board. A thick carpet of silver stubble carpeted his jaw like an expensive rug and his pale blue eyes had a hint of mischief about them.

"I'm Captain Kampmann," he said, nervously glancing behind them down at the docks. "Were you followed?"

"They tried," Hawke said, "but they failed. Listen, thanks for taking this risk, Captain. Smuggling a fugitive out of China is a big deal. We all have a lot to thank you for."

The man finished his anxious scan of the port over their shoulders. "Let's just say your organization was very generous when it came to paying me for my troubles. We're due to leave in a few moments, so please, Ulrik here will show you to your quarters. There you can freshen up before dinner and then we will rendezvous with the US Navy helicopter as soon as we are out of Bohai Bay."

As they walked deep inside the safety of the goliath container ship, Devlin turned to Scarlet and said, "Thing I want to know is why Humpty would take a dump behind the wall anyway? Has he *no* fuckin' manners?"

Lexi looked at him in confusion, "What the fuck?"

CHAPTER NINETEEN

Davis Faulkner was in the back of Air Force Two when the call came. They were flying thirty-seven thousand feet over the Midwest on the way back from a Vice Presidential trip to Seattle. Below, storm clouds were forming above the cornfields of Minnesota, but it was the storm on the end of this phone call that unnerved him.

"Sir."

"Mr Vice President, how good of you to take my call."

Faulkner leaned forward in his seat and fiddled with the end of his tie. "That's no problem at all, sir."

"Let's get straight to business, Davis."

"Yes, sir."

"We both want you in the Oval Office, am I right?"

"Yes, sir."

"Good, good."

Faulkner heard the creature wheezing. He sounded like he was getting weaker.

"The problem I have, Davis, is that our attempt to blow your President out of the sky in England failed and so as you know, I have been working on something much more certain to do the job."

"Sounds promising, Oracle."

"I will of course need the assistance you can provide in your capacity as Vice President of the United States."

"What do you need, sir?"

"My people will need unfettered access to a certain American coastal city, land sea and air."

"I probably can swing that, sir." A smile spread on his lips. This really was going to happen. He really was going to become President.

"Probably?"

Faulkner's smile dropped. "It'll be done, sir. Whatever you want."

"Better."

"What's the plan, sir?"

The Vice President listened carefully as the Oracle briefed him on the plan to kill the President. It was brutal. It was treason. It was going to put him in the Oval Office in less than two days.

When the Oracle hung up, Faulkner realized his hands were shaking. His Chief of Staff, Joshua Muston stepped over to him with two coffees in his hands. "Captain says more turbulence is on the way, sir."

Faulkner accepted the coffee. "There certainly is, Josh. There *certainly* is."

"I don't understand."

"That was Wolff."

Muston paled and took a seat opposite his boss. "Oh, God."

Faulkner's eyebrows lifted half an inch. "Pretty much, yes."

"What did he want?"

"He wanted to tell me I'm going to be President in a few hours' time."

Muston seemed to have forgotten about his coffee. "What's going to happen?"

For a long while Faulkner was silent as he took in the storm clouds so far below, swirling, bubbling. "Let's just say this country's going to have a very bad day tomorrow."

CHAPTER TWENTY

The savage heat of the Transvaal veld beat down on them as they watched the horror unfold in front of their eyes. They had driven a short distance from the complex to an area of caged animals and now Lea studied Kruger's face for any sign that he might be bluffing. Out here in the bleak isolation of his home turf he looked bigger than usual, more powerful. More in control. Out here he was god and he knew it.

He turned away from where his men were struggling with Julius and looked over at her, staring into her eyes. Not a flicker of emotion was on his face, not the vaguest hint that he was playing games. Turned black in the shade of the bush hat's broad, battered rim, his eyes were as cold as ever, almost defying her to challenge him, to try and save the traitor's life.

"I can tell you're impressed," he said at last.

He's right beside you, dammit! Why don't you do something to stop this?

Because her hands were handcuffed behind her back and she was surrounded by men with automatic rifles. That's why and she hated it. She felt powerless because she was powerless. The frustration burned inside her, hotter than the African sun, but it wasn't enough to save this man's life and she knew it.

But did she really want to save his life? He was Athanatoi after all. But then, he had also decided to turn away from the Oracle and had refused to help him in his quest to take over the world. That was enough, she thought. Bad people could become good and when she watched Julius struggling in the arms of his captors, she knew he had genuinely turned.

The captive called out over his shoulder. "Blankov, I don't understand! I never did anything to you. I even translated the symbols!"

"Only because I had your son killed and no – you never did anything to *me*, that's true." He sounded almost sympathetic. "But you did something against our glorious leader."

"But can't you see, he's insane?"

"Hush, Julius, hush. After so many centuries, your time has come."

Julius struggled in Kruger's arms. "Please, come with me! Together we can beat the Oracle, Ivan!"

Blankov wasn't listening. Neither was Kruger. Lea knew he wouldn't. She knew him well enough to know that nothing would drive a man like him to show pity. To Dirk Kruger pity was weakness-and there was nothing worse than showing your enemy you had any weaknesses, any break in the armor. She guessed if anything, Blankov was even worse.

"Sadly, Julius, I cannot on this occasion accommodate your pleas."

"This is madness!" Julius looked like he was about to throw up.

Lea watched helplessly as Venter and his men lashed the ropes around him and dragged him to the enclosure. Kruger was standing the other side of the enormous cage. He was tapping the mesh and calling out to the lion as it paced up and down in the heat. Now, it turned and padded over to him. Approaching the arms dealer, it growled and reared up on its hind legs, bringing its powerful front paws crashing down on the steel mesh. Its claws scraped down the metal and produced a tinny, grating noise.

"They're very intelligent," Kruger said, waving a fly from his face and scanning the empty savannah beyond the cage. "The most intelligent beast out here and that's for damned sure."

"It's got fifty IQ points on you, Dirk," Lea said.

Kruger smiled, then he brushed away another fly. When he turned, she saw his back was covered in the tiny bush flies. He ambled through the baking dry heat, dust kicked up by his boots. "I'm glad you can make jokes, Donovan. I wonder if you'll find it so funny when you see what I have in store for you and Mr Bean here."

Ryan bristled at the mockery. Since Maria's death he'd worked hard to turn himself around and make himself stronger. To be tough enough to stop anything like that from ever happening again and not having to rely on people like Hawke, Scarlet and Lea to pull his arse out of the fire when things got nasty.

To hear the man he hated more than anyone laughing at him nearly pushed him over the edge. He fought it back down and held his tongue. The next time he spoke to Kruger it would be the last words the bastard would ever hear.

The South African leaned into the back of the flatbed and pulled out a bottle of ice-cold lager. He cracked it open and downed half the bottle in one. The heat had instantly created a sheen of condensation on the brown glass. "Gotta sink these babies fast before the sun warms them up, don't you agree?" He handed her another bottle.

Lea looked at him with contempt. "I don't drink with murderers."

"Suit yourself." He turned the bottle upside down and let the lager run out into the hot sand. Tossing the bottle into the back of the truck, he finished his own drink and belched loudly. "It's time, Venter."

Lea watched his men hauling Julius over to the cage. He was still kicking and screaming, but some of his energy had been sucked away by the sheer terror of his situation. She knew from Kruger's earlier bragging that this wasn't the first time these lions had eaten human flesh and she guessed in his long life that Julius had seen them feasting on victims more than once. Knowing what was about to come must have made it ten times worse for him.

"The Zulus call them *ingonyame*," Kruger said happily. "It means the 'master of all flesh' and I guess I don't have to tell a couple fucking smartarses like you two why that is."

Lea struggled against her bonds. "In the name of everything that is holy, Kruger, please."

"You mean like the *ukweshwama* ceremony when the Zulus sacrifice a bull to their gods? That kind of holy?" He watched Venter give Julius a hard, backhand slap to stop his struggling. Blankov oversaw the proceedings in silence. "Wait till you see this." He casually cracked the lid off another lager on the tailgate of the truck and sank a few more gulps. "There's nothing like it on earth."

Ryan shook his head. "My God, you're sick."

"Maybe, Mr Bale, but if I am, there's no cure." He walked around the cage until the sun was at his back and then clicked his fingers and pointed at Julius. His men opened the cage and pushed the Athanatoi man inside, making sure to keep their hunting rifles trained on the lion for the few seconds the door was open.

The lion eyed up the man in the cage. Julius was hurriedly untying the last of the ropes from his arms and legs and kicked himself free of them. He was hyperventilating as he picked up a thick piece of rope and tried to make it crack like a whip. Kruger and his men laughed as the rope thumped down into the ground and kicked up a cloud of red dust.

"Don't try and run," Ryan said calmly. "That thing can run fifty miles an hour, which is twice as fast as the fastest human. If you run you're dead."

Julius stared at the beast. "Great advice, my friend."

"And stay calm," he continued. "Right now it feels threatened."

"How the hell do you know that?" Lea asked.

"It's moving its tail. When it's trying to hunt it stays totally still so not to alert its prey of its presence. If it's moving its tail then that means it feels threatened in some way."

"Maybe by your freakish level of general knowledge," Lea said. "I know I am."

Julius called out, "What about that tree?"

"Forget that too. Any lion can climb any tree twice as fast as you can and will only enjoy dragging you out of it."

The animal roared loudly and started to charge at the man. It was ferocious. It quickly hit its maximum speed of fifty miles per hour and was on the man in seconds. Julius made the mistake of giving into his instinct and turning on his heel.

It was easy to say stand still in the face of a charging lion, but the reality of the situation was different. Even knowing he was inside the cage, he ran as fast as he could toward the truck, but the lion leaped and sank its claws into his back, bringing him down hard to the sandy floor like any other of its prey.

Lea turned away, unable to watch the slaughter. Ryan gritted his teeth and curled his hands into two tight fists as Julius desperately tried to fight the two hundred kilo beast. It was slapping him around with its paws, but not going for the kill. Not yet.

"They're not like tigers," Kruger said casually. "Your tiger is much more aggressive. Your average tiger is a heavier animal and goes straight for the kill, straight for the throat." He dragged his fingernails over the soft flesh of his throat to underline the point. "Rip it straight it open, but not these beauties." He looked at the lion with admiration and respect. "The lion has a whole pride of other animals surrounding it so when it decides to kill it can afford to play games with its prey for a while, like now."

The King of the Jungle was now batting Julius about from side to side, but keeping him alive. Lea cringed at the sound of the man's terrified screams, but Ryan felt nothing but rage.

"The tiger is a lone hunter so doesn't mess about with games," Kruger said. "Evidence from ancient Rome shows when tigers fought lions the tiger usually won."

Blankov's lips twisted into a smile. "This is true. I watched many of these fights at the Coliseum, but the tigers didn't *always* win."

His words made everyone but the lion freeze in disbelief. Kruger looked especially nervous. Something told Lea he was distinctly uncomfortable around his immortal masters.

Kruger winced when he saw Julius slapping at the animal's muzzle. "I wouldn't do that if I were you, Professor Cronje."

The lion's jaw muscles flexed as it opened its mouth and moved in for the kill, easily taking most of Julius's head into its mouth. The jaw closed, its claws plunging into the man's shoulder and torso. Hot blood spilled out of the gouge marks and ran over the animal's fur. The sun flashed on the beast's teeth as they sank deeper into the man's neck.

Julius's screaming was drowned out by the lion roaring loud and deep and then the thunderous sound of cheering as Kruger and his men celebrated the savagery. Thanks to the demands and perils of life in the ECHO team, Lea and Ryan had seen a lot, but never before had either witnessed this level of barbarity. They felt like they'd just witnessed a new low on the bar of human evil.

Blood pumped from his jugular and splashed up onto the lion's gums. Its hot breath blasted over its prey's face. They all heard a grinding, crunching noise as the beast ripped his throat open and hit some bone. Julius was slowing now, delirious with fear and losing blood pressure. Instinct and adrenaline drove him to fight back, but his slaps were weak and pathetic, mistimed and almost comical.

Kruger laughed, but Venter took a step back and found something else to look at.

Blankov offered no reaction at all as the beast jerked its head back and tore a chunk from Julius's throat. Bloody sinew hung from the lion's mouth and Julius finally collapsed dead, sinking back into the hot sandy dirt. With no more resistance, the lion relaxed as it started its work of tearing, ripping and shredding. Ryan heard a tinny shattering sound as more bones were broken but finally turned away when the animal started licking the horrible mess with a wet, bloody tongue.

Lea wretched. "I'm going to be sick."

"Not as sick as that fucker," Ryan said, gesturing at Kruger.

"You!" Ryan realized Kruger was pointing his finger at him. "You're next."

"This can't be happening!" Lea said.

"Hurry up," he snapped. "Mr Blankov here hasn't got all fucking day."

CHAPTER TWENTY-ONE

"You can't do this, Kruger!" Lea yelled. "You've already killed two innocent men today, isn't that enough for you?"

"Nowhere near enough."

Lea and Ryan looked at one another, both understanding that there was nothing they could do while they were trapped here by Kruger's men. They had zero chance of getting away from their captors and for now they had little choice but to sit in the stifling heat and sweat with the stink of lions all around them.

Worse, they'd seen the Athanatoi man meet his maker in the most vile and inhumane way possible and now it looked like Ryan was the follow-up act. Kruger, after all, had a long score to settle with the young hacker and they all knew he wasn't the sort of villain to keep dead wood hanging around.

"There's really nothing you can do, Lea," Kruger said, almost like he cared, like he wasn't in control of this madness. "Besides, don't you want to see how much Khufu likes the latest flavor of Kit-E-Kat, Chicken and Dork?"

Lea tightened her jaw to stop from crying in front of Ryan. She had been in situations like this before and she knew from experience that you only survived if you fought dirtier and harder than your enemy. They were ruthless and wanted her dead. They would kill her without batting an eyelid. You had to think like them if you were to get through this and come out the other side.

"Get them in the bakkie!" Kruger yelled.

Lea was confused and for a moment hope flooded her heart. The bakkie meant the pick-up. Had Kruger changed his mind? “What’s going on?”

The arms dealer looked at her like she was a child. “Can’t do it here – this lion’s had its fill on that bastard Julius. We need to drive out a way until we find Khufu.”

“Khufu?”

“The pride male.”

“I thought…”

“That the animal you just saw kill Julius was the pride male?” Kruger let out a deep belly laugh. “That was Huruma. He’s not even a fully-grown adult yet. Just a pup. Name means compassion. If you thought that was something, wait till you see how Khufu does it.”

You sick son of a bitch.

“You men over there, grab the boy and bring him over to the bakkie right away! It’s not a long drive. I want to see him torn apart right in front of my eyes and *yours*.” He looked at Lea with narrowing eyes and a greasy smile.

Venter grabbed Ryan by his shoulders and bundled him out of the observation area and toward a Hilux pick-up. They paused while Kruger and Blankov exchanged a few words. “It’s just over there,” Kruger said, pointing out across the savannah. “He’s been resting somewhere under the shade of that mopane tree over there. Don’t worry, when we turn up he’ll soon stir back to life. He’s very hungry.”

Hands still bound behind their backs with cable-ties, Scarface pushed them toward the trucks, a submachine gun in his hand. “Give me any trouble and I’ll tear you in half with this thing before you’ve taken two steps toward me.”

“Fair enough,” Ryan said. “But your body odor precludes any normal human from getting that close anyway, so why waste the ammo?”

The guard's response was savage, pistol-whipping him with the stock of his weapon and breaking open the skin on his cheek and temple. Ryan plunged to the ground and collapsed in the dust.

"You'll pay for that," Lea said.

"Shut up and get moving," Venter said. "You too, Superman." He kicked Ryan hard in the ribs and sent him tumbling over in the dirt. "For the last time, get moving."

Ryan dragged himself to his feet and winked at Venter. "Thanks for that. Now I can kill you without bothering my conscience."

Venter laughed. "You? Kill someone? You couldn't kill a catfish if your life depended on it, you domkop. Now get moving! You have an appointment with a lion and he's very hungry."

Lea's mind was busy planning their escape as Venter and his guards force-marched them through the scrub toward the Hilux. Memories of Joe Hawke drifted into her mind, each one a reminder of how they had escaped with their lives from a hundred dead-ends. Rather than give her ideas they simply brought back how much she felt for him and how hard it had been since their bust-up in London.

Had she reconsidered her feelings for him during their break? Yes and no. She knew in her heart there was no way she wanted to live without him, but the way he had reacted when he saw her with Danny had surprised her.

"I said move!" She was brought back to reality by Venter. He pushed Scarface out of the way and did the job himself, bringing the stock of his MP5 down hard between her shoulder blades and knocking her to the ground.

It was a shocking display of raw, animal violence that she hadn't expected, not even from him. She cried out, her pain heard by everyone as she crawled in the dirt with an acute, electric stabbing sensation radiating across her back and up her neck.

For a moment, she thought she might pass out from the pain and she was dimly aware of Ryan struggling forward to help her. With his hands tied behind his back he was easy to push back and silence.

Venter dragged her back to her feet and shook her like a knitted doll. "Are you going to behave yourself now, bitch? Or do you want some real man stuff?"

Her head was still spinning with the pain, but she managed to glance at his groin and raise an eyebrow. "Not sure you're up to *real* man stuff, Venter. You couldn't catch a fish with what's in your pants."

Venter's face turned red with rage.

"You hear about that, Ry? Last time Venter here went into a fishing tackle shop they mistook his dick for a bait worm."

"You bitch!"

"I will *bet*," she said, leaning into his face, her Irish accent hardening, "that your dates need to bring an air pump with them."

Ryan laughed. "Certainly not enough down there to hang a hat on, that's for sure."

"I don't think *Barbie* could hang her hat on yours, do you, Venter?"

He finally snapped and belted her, knocking her off her feet again.

She crawled back up and he dared her to go another round, but this time she kept quiet. Her plan to delay them had only bought a few seconds and she was no use to Ryan if this bastard knocked her out.

They continued through the pitiless sunshine of the veld until they reached the bakkie's tailgate. Ryan was also searching for a way to escape, but Lea already knew a man like Kruger would leave them no escape route.

Flashing in the sun out on the perimeter was another ten-foot high electrified razor-wire fence running the length of the enclosure. The mopane tree was clearer now and so was Khufu.

Kruger smirked. "The only way out is if you kill your way out."

The first bullet hit Scarface. He had been standing next to Venter and now a high velocity round blew a fist-sized chunk of his shoulder into mush. Blood pumped out of the wound as he passed out and crashed to the floor.

Everyone hit the deck in a hurry and Kruger and his men pulled their weapons as they desperately started scanning for any sign of the shooter. Out on the veld, Khufu bolted and ran into the long grass behind the mopane tree.

"What the hell is this, Kruger?" Blankov yelled. "I thought you said this place was secure?"

More incoming fire forced them deeper into cover, away from the bakkie and back across the scrub into the doorway of the safari lodge's main building.

"Over there!" Venter said. "But I don't know how many."

Lea looked up and squinted in the sun.

Camacho.

"Thank God," she muttered.

Ryan gave her a look and winked. "Looks like the cavalry has arrived."

And about time too, she thought.

Kruger wanted to fight, but Blankov ordered a retreat back inside the complex. Venter dragged Lea to her feet and one of his men grabbed Ryan and hauled him along too. "We're going inside, hurry up!" he yelled.

More gunfire struck one of the Athanatoi and blew half his skull off. He died before he hit the dirt, but the effect was to send everyone running in different directions as they desperately tried to protect themselves.

The every-man-for-himself strategy had left Lea and Ryan without a guard and they peeled off back around behind the Hilux.

Camacho and Kim sprinted down from the bluff behind the complex and skidded to a halt beside them, a cloud of dust billowing up in their wake.

"You two okay?" Camacho said, hurriedly cutting the cable ties.

"Oh yeah," Lea said. "I'm loving my safari vacation just great, thanks."

"Hey," Kim said sharply. "We did our best but it took a long time to find who had taken you, never mind where! These guys weren't exactly advertising this place online, you know!"

"Sorry," Lea said. "You wouldn't believe what we've just seen, it just shook me up."

"It's going to be great when it opens to the public though," Ryan said with a wink.

"You can tell us later," Camacho said flatly. "We've got to get in there and take them out before they get away. They still have the sword, right?"

Lea nodded. "And they had its symbols translated as well."

The sprint from the bakkie to the entrance was a hair-raising hundred meters as the Athanatoi and some of Kruger's former commandos fired on them from an upper level of the complex. Bullets ripped into the sand at their feet as they sprinted over the distance as fast as they could.

They reached the entrance and immediately headed for a circular staircase that led up to the mezzanine level. This was where Kruger and his men had been firing on them moments earlier, but when they arrived it was empty.

"They already moved out!" Kim said.

"No, wait!" Camacho pointed to the far end of the mezzanine. "There's someone there!"

"They're firing!"

"Get down!"

They hit the deck as the bullets traced over them.

"There's more downstairs on the lower level too!" Kim yelled.

"We need to split up," Lea said. "Me and Ryan will go downstairs and you two stay up here."

"Got it."

*

Camacho and Kim gave some cover fire as Lea and Ryan ran down the circular staircase and disappeared beneath them. Kim was already moving forward, gun raised and firing in controlled bursts at Venter. For a second, the CIA man thought she'd gotten the guy but then another Athanatoi joined him and an intense firefight ensued.

Taking cover in a doorway, Kim quickly emptied her magazine.

"I need help, Jack!"

"I'm on my way!" Camacho shouted over at her and crouch-walked along the mezzanine, carefully avoiding the spent cartridge casings. He reached the corner section and pulled his MP5 up over the wall, firing on the men below as he prepared to make the final dash to where Kim was holding her empty gun to her chest.

Venter then surprised him by making a break from his cover and running up the spiral staircase leading to where Kim was hiding out.

He knows she's out of ammo!

"Hurry up, Jack!"

"I'm almost there!" Behind him he heard Lea and Ryan engaging in what sounded like a heavy fire fight down by a waterfall in the lobby.

It was a race now, between him and Venter, to see who reached Kim first. They were both closing in on her at the same rate but Camacho had an advantage – all he needed to do was get close enough to throw a fresh magazine to his friend. When he reached that point, he pulled a new mag from his jacket pocket and threw it over to her. "Kim!"

She saw what he had done and leaped into the air to catch it. Instantly, Venter fired on her. In a hail of flying lead she grabbed the magazine and crashed back down onto the riveted floor of the deck. She smacked the mag into the grip of the SIG and sighed heavily with relief. Another five seconds and Venter would have peppered her with bullets and killed her right here.

Camacho had taken up a new position much closer to her now and joined her in firing on Venter. Kruger yelled at his man and Venter heard the warning and backed off. Kim watched him as he retreated back down the spiral staircase and then she crawled along the deck until she was beside Camacho. "You saved my life."

"You've saved mine enough times," he said with a smile. "Thought it was about time I repaid the favor."

The moment was cut short by a volley of automatic fire ripping into the wall behind the deck. From such a low angle, Kruger and his men were unable to hit them direct and had decided to keep them pinned down while they made another assault on them. Chunks of plaster burst and split and rained down on them. They covered their eyes with their forearms and waited it out.

"Shit! This is getting real, Jack!"

The stream of automatic rounds raked into the wall at their backs and snaked up the spiral staircase, spitting sparks and ricocheting bullets all over the place. One traced past Camacho's face and buried itself in the rubber plant at his side. "I'll say it is," he said, peering over the top of the wall. "Uh-oh…"

"What?"

"GPMG."

"Oh, fuck!"

"Looks like a Vektor," he said, starting to look worried. "We can expect a lot of fifty mil bottlenecked rounds heading our way in three, two, one…"

CHAPTER TWENTY-TWO

The large-calibre rounds tore holes in the bottom of the mezzanine's stainless-steel deck as if it were made of aluminum foil. A speechless Camacho and Kim watched the holes rapidly approaching where they were taking cover. "We're outta here!"

They leaped to their feet and sprinted away from the carnage created by the Vektor, taking pot shots at the gunner behind the GPMG as they went. "Keep going!" Camacho yelled and leaned over the top of the wall to get a better shot at the gunner. He fired and hit him, ripping part of his skull away and spraying brain matter and blood all over the man feeding the ammo belt into the gun.

"Get on that weapon, man!" Venter yelled.

The man now covered in blood slipped behind the Vektor and immediately pulled the muzzle around until it was pointing directly at Jack Camacho. With a fury the American had rarely seen before, he started firing the powerful GPMG at him.

The bullets traced and whistled all around him as he and Kim sprinted for cover like the devil was on their tails. One of the rounds blew through the wooden handrail and blasted a cloud of splinters into his path. He felt several embed themselves in his face as he threw himself into a dive and rolled down into the other corner dropping down beside his old friend.

Kim looked at his face. "Cut yourself shaving?"

"Funny."

"Seriously, you okay?"

He nodded. "Just a graze, but it was close."

Peering through the gap between the wall and the handrail, they saw another man feeding a fresh ammo belt into the Vektor and the blood-soaked goon operating it looked angrier than ever. Another volley of automatic fire came from the far end of the deck. "Looks like they're trying a pincer movement," Kim said.

Camacho felt his jaw tighten with rage and fear. He'd been in a few scrapes in his time, both in the CIA and with ECHO, but things around here were hotting up much more than usual. They'd been fighting for nearly ten minutes now and they'd only advanced the length of the mezzanine. He had no idea if Lea and Ryan were still alive and no way of contacting them to find out. Venter was fighting as brutally as he had ever seen anyone fight before. He guessed that was what twenty years in the 4 Special Forces Regiment did to a man.

"Down the stairs!" he yelled. "I see Lea and Ryan!"

They sprinted down the spiral staircase and met up with their friends in the lobby. "Way too hot back there," Kim said. "What about you guys?"

"See for yourself," Lea said.

Tucked down behind the wall at the base of the artificial waterfall, Ryan grinned and opened his bag.

"Holy shit!" Kim said. "The Sword of Fire!"

Lea smiled. "We found it in Kruger's study after a ten minute fire fight. We got the translation too."

"Guess they're not too happy about us having it, right?" Camacho said.

"See for yourself," Lea said.

Men carrying MP5s and Milkor BXPs burst into the giant lobby and immediately took up position behind the rocks at the base of the waterfall. Lea and Ryan moved toward them while Camacho and Kim provided cover.

Lea ran toward their position and fired on them with her weapon.

The closest of them turned and aimed his gun, a look of terror on his young face. He moved to fire but Lea struck first, landing two in his chest and one in his forehead. "Maybe you can hunt defenseless animals, laddo, but I'm a different story."

"Woah." Ryan slammed down beside her. "You get out the wrong side of bed this morning or something?"

"Yes."

Camacho fired on a man at the top of the waterfall, striking him in the head. He tumbled down over the edge of the falls and crashed down into the lake at the base, disappearing in the swirling foam. Ryan was closest and ran over to the dead man, snatching a belt of grenades from him.

The four of them ran from the lobby, pausing only for Ryan to hurl one of the grenades into the base of the waterfall. The explosion filled the space with smoke and flames and blew out the containing wall around the raised lake at the base of the waterfall. Thousands of gallons of water burst out through the broken brick and started to flood the lobby.

"That way!" Lea said.

A fire door behind the reception desk led to a service corridor, at the end of which was a staff elevator. Kim opened the doors and they bundled inside with the sound of Kruger's men screaming and shouting back in the lobby. One of them reached the other end of the service corridor and lifted an automatic rifle into the aim.

"Doors!" Camacho shouted.

Kim hit the button while Ryan and Lea opened fire on the man through the ever-narrowing gap. He returned fire, his bullets pinging off the elevator's stainless-steel doors and some entering inside and raking up the inside wall.

When the doors slammed shut, Kim blew out a deep breath. "That was too close."

The doors opened at the subterranean level where the facility's vehicles were parked. Lea turned and fired on the control panel, disabling the elevator, then turned and saw a sprawling parking lot. Due to the park's extremely remote location, most of the staff and guests flew in and out but there was still a good handful of vehicles to choose from, mostly used for moving around the enormous compound or even the main park itself.

Camacho's eyes soon alighted on a white Mercedes AMG G63 with black stripes designed to resemble a zebra's markings. The luxury super-SUV would normally be filled with rich men in big hats being chauffeured out to hunt big game, but today the former CIA man had another use for it.

They ran closer. Printed on the side in a red rectangle were the words KRUGER WILDLIFE & GAME RESERVE. Camacho ran to the driver's door and punched the air when he saw the keys in the ignition.

"This is our baby."

"Everyone in!" Lea yelled. Her ploy to disable the elevator had worked, but Kruger's men had simply diverted to the service stairs beside the elevator shaft. They poured out of the double doors with guns blazing, shooting up anything that moved in the parking lot.

"John McClane wouldn't take any of this shit in Die Hard," Camacho said with a sigh.

"I love his Homefries," Ryan said.

Kim was confused. "What the fuck are you two talking about?"

Ryan said nothing, but blew out the rear window of the Merc SUV with his handgun before picking off two of Kruger's men. He saw Venter now, reaching the bottom of the concrete steps and emerging into the parking level's yellow strip lights.

Lea climbed into the back and slammed down into the seat beside Ryan. The luxury interior of the G63 included a chunky console between the two rear seats and she was able to raise one knee onto it to get a better view out of the shattered back window.

"Venter!" she said.

Ryan was aiming at him. "The one and only and he's mine."

She watched him gently squeeze the trigger but the bullet went high as they tumbled forward. Camacho had stamped on the accelerator and flung him off his balance. The Merc lurched forward in a cloud of burnt rubber smoke and spinning wheels that filled the entire garage with an ear-piercing squealing noise.

"Dammit, Jack!" Lea said. "Ry nearly had Venter."

"Company employees are welcome to use the suggestion box," he shouted from the front, ducking quickly to the right as a bullet punctured his window and traced past his head. It blew another perfect hole in the opposite window beside Kim Taylor who screamed loudly before spinning around and scanning for the gunman.

"They're everywhere!"

Ryan flicked a panicked glance over his shoulder. "And they're never going to stop until they have the sword back!"

Camacho reversed at high-speed in the underground car park, smoke spewing from the wheel arches as the rubber tires spun on the polished concrete. Spinning the steering wheel hard to the right, he flung the vehicle around in a tight arc, changed into drive and stamped on the gas.

The underground parking lot filled with the sound of tires squealing as Camacho weaved the SUV in between the support pillars and hit the exit ramp. Bullets chased them all the way outside and when they emerged from the subterranean parking area it was into a soft African twilight. The intense heat and glare of earlier in the day had dissipated now and night was rapidly approaching.

Camacho pushed the Merc as hard as it would go as he steered it around to the left and followed the signs for the helipad, praying there was a chopper there. They got there seconds later and found their prayers had been answered. A nice, new helicopter was sitting beside Blankov's private jet. The jet offered a much faster way out of the nightmare but none of them knew how to fly it.

The former CIA man skidded the SUV to a halt a few meters from the chopper. "We'll have to destroy the jet when we're airborne. Everyone out!"

With the sword in the bag under Ryan's arm, they clambered out of the SUV and jumped into the chopper. Camacho made some instant pre-flight checks and then fired up the engine. As the rotors started to whir, a team of Athanatoi and some of Kruger's commandos appeared at the top of the car park ramp and opened fire on them.

Camacho lifted the chopper into the Transvaal dusk and rotated it to the side to allow Ryan and Kim to return fire on the enemy. They took cover behind a low concrete wall which marked the perimeter between the complex and the car park, giving Lea time to fire on the jet with the MP5.

With the chopper's rotors noisily whirring overhead, she leaned out into the downdraft and swept the powerful machine pistol up and down the wings, puncturing the aluminum as if it were foil. The jet fuel sparked and ignited and blew the private plane into a terrifying ball of fire.

"Get us outta here, Jack!"

Camacho spun the chopper and increased speed, swooping low over the complex as he steered around to the south. "Goodbye, assholes."

Lea twisted in her seat to see Blankov running out of the complex and staring at his aircraft, now no more than a black burning skeleton. The cloud of thick, choking smoke was the thickest she had ever seen. She high-fived Kim and Camacho set a course for home.

*

With the day long-gone, the exhausted four-strong team sat on the veranda running around the front of a large villa north of Pretoria. Set in the middle of a wildlife sanctuary owned by old friends of Danny Devlin from his South Africa days, they all agreed it was the safest place any of them could be right now.

The brother and sister owners of the property, Isaac and Lily Elsey, were away in France on business, but they had answered Danny's call for help in a heartbeat and now the place was theirs for as long as they wanted it.

But that wouldn't be long. Now, they cracked some beers, dressed their wounds and breathed a collective sigh of relief. Lea rubbed her temples and tried to force the stress away, but it wasn't going anywhere.

In the notes containing Julius's translation they had found references to an ancient shield that was made to match the sword. The Athanatoi scholar's deciphering of the symbols on the sword described the shield in intimate detail and both Julius and Ryan had instantly recognized the item in question as being the Shield of Pridwen.

It was a relic from Camelot, much like they believed the Sword of Fire to be and both men knew where it was last seen: in the National Museum of Archaeology in Athens. Ryan was especially pleased.

He'd had time with the sword before when they found it in Wales, but not enough time to make a proper study of the symbols etched into it. This plus Julius's hard work had yielded a fantastic result and they all felt like they were making real progress. It was a relief to all that the shield was in a museum and not at the end of a week-long treasure hunt.

But not all was great. They might have the information they needed about Athens, but so did Dirk Kruger and his psycho boss Ivan Blankov. It was true they had a good head-start on them, but there was still no sign of their puppet master, the Oracle. Lea felt the ominous signs of a migraine headache creeping around the sides of her skull.

Kim cut the call she was making and slipped her phone in her pocket. "I got some great news, guys – they got Lexi back!"

The relief was massive and they all shared a whoop of joy and a few high-fives on the veranda in the twilight. Lexi Zhang was not the closest member of the team, always keeping her emotional distance, but she was fiercely loyal and had risked her life many times to save them. The thought of her being tortured by the Zodiac assassins had given everyone a few sleepless nights and now it was over.

"Thank God," Lea said.

Kim frowned.

"What is it?"

"But Alex just told me she was pretty badly messed up."

"What do you mean?" Ryan asked.

"She didn't say, but I got the impression they screwed her up pretty bad before Joe and the others got to her."

Camacho punched the side of the wall. "Sons of bitches!"

"What about the Zodiacs?" Ryan asked.

"They got Rat in custody and Pig and Zhou died in a helicopter crash."

"Tiger and Monkey?" Lea asked.

"She said Lexi took Monkey out, but Tiger got away."

"So four down, one to go, in other words," Camacho said.

"Right," said Kim. "Tiger is still out there."

"And how do you go about catching a man like that?"

Camacho mulled it over. "You catch more flies with molasses than you do with vinegar, right?"

Ryan sank a beer and watched a crane heave itself up into the air over the dust-dry landscape. "You tell him about the Shield of Pridwen and Athens?"

She nodded. "They're flying there right away."

"Great," Ryan said. "We're closer than we've ever been guys."

They toasted their success in retrieving the sword, but in her heart, Lea knew the fight hadn't even started yet.

CHAPTER TWENTY-THREE

Hawke strolled along a side street in the center of Athens. The sun was setting over the Theater of Dionysus and couples walked together, hands clasped as they stole kisses in the twilight. It was a city he loved and after a long trip involving US Navy aircraft carriers and RAF transport planes he was glad to be here.

He thought back to his first mission with ECHO, before he even knew what that meant. They had come to the city in pursuit of a man named Demetriou. His ultimate betrayal of Hawke's trust didn't come close to spoiling this charming place for him.

Returning to his hotel, he crossed the lobby and spoke with the woman on the reception desk. Yes, the rest of his team had arrived from Pretoria around an hour ago and were waiting for him in their suite. He thanked them and made his way to the elevators, scanning all around him to check for anything out of place.

Old habits die hard.

And so did his pride, but tonight, die it would.

He owed Lea Donovan the mother of all apologies and now there was no getting out of it. She was upstairs with everyone else and his strategy of avoidance had worked about as well as he thought it might.

So get on with it and stop being such a bell-end...

Thanks, Cairo.

He opened the hotel door and there she was, right in front of him. She was on the bed, leaning up against the headboard and watching the TV with a bottle of water in her hand. She looked beautiful, as usual, if a little tired. He swallowed his pride and stepped over to the bed.

"Fancy meeting you here," he said, feeling like a fool. "All right?"

"I might be."

"You *might* be?"

"Sure," she shrugged. "Depends on how sorry you are."

Hawke realized every pair of eyes in the house was fixed firmly on him and he felt himself redden. Pulling his collar loose, he made a crack about it being hot in here and then asked Lea to step outside onto the balcony with him. When she agreed, a groan of disappointment filled the room. "Please no," Scarlet said. "I've been waiting for ages to watch this."

"Bugger off, Cairo," Lea said.

Hawke closed the sliding door behind them and surreptitiously flashed Scarlet his middle finger as he did so.

Out here, on the balcony with Athens crumbling away beneath them, all lit amber and red in the setting sun, Hawke was stunned all over again by how beautiful she was. A gentle breeze lifted the ends of her long hair and trapped the sun in it, creating a halo effect. Her eyes, which ignored him and looked out over the bustling city, sparkled in the dying light. He waited for her lips to move, to signal that she was about to say something but they stayed still and silent and offered no hope of redemption for his sins.

The sun dipped below the skyline. He contemplated a gag. Humor was a device he had used to great effect many times in the past to get himself out of trouble. It was a defense mechanism that had saved his bacon on more occasions than he could count but the stony expression on her face told him it was a poor strategy, so he bit the bullet.

"I'm sorry, Lea."

He heard the words as if someone else had said them and she was still ignoring him. Her eyes were tracing the path of a jet as it flew over the mountains to the west of them. While the rest of the ancient city was now fading into darkness, the plane's high altitude meant it was still catching the sunlight and it shone like a pink diamond on a dark blue canvas.

"I said I…"

"I heard what you said."

She turned now and faced him. He had missed this face. After London he had gone to ground. Enraged and humiliated, he had spent time dossing down with old SBS friends on England's south coast before being recalled by Eden for the Beijing mission. By the time he'd got to the ECHO leader's London HQ, Lea and the other team had already been dispatched to South Africa to retrieve the Sword of Fire. He hadn't seen her since the bust-up and now she was just a few inches away from him. He reached out with his hands and held her shoulders. "I mean it. I was a total idiot."

"Yes, you were. An arse, in fact."

"Yes, I was an arse."

"Was?"

"I *am* a total arse."

She turned her face back to the city and smiled at a million strangers. "Better."

He saw a glimpse of the old Lea and moved in for the kill. "Am I forgiven?"

"You're around five percent there, Josiah," she said with a sly smile. "Keep working on it."

Before he could reply, she kissed him on the cheek and slid open the suite's heavy glass doors. Stepping back inside the room, a sea of expectant faces turned to her. She glanced back at Hawke. "Oh, get inside, ya stupid eejit."

*

Back to business, the mission could be going better. The rescue of Lexi Zhang from the heart of the Chinese military-industrial complex had rapidly turned from covert ingress into farce and back out the other side into the realms of serious diplomatic scandal. The British and American ambassadors in Beijing had both been summoned to the Ministry of Foreign Affairs to explain themselves and rumors of sanctions were swirling in the loftier circles of international government.

South Africa had gone better. They had retrieved the Sword of Fire and had the pleasure of annihilating one of Dirk Kruger's major business ventures but it wasn't all champagne and strawberries. The man himself, along with his business partner Mr Blankov and a small number of his men including Venter were still alive and knew about the Shield of Pridwen. Now they had to watch not only for the surviving member of the Zodiacs, Tiger and the Athanatoi, but a band of former South African commandos.

One of Eden's diplomatic contacts in Westminster, Simon Underhill, could probably see off the Chinese and being on first-names terms with the sitting President of the United States would also help grease the wheels as well, but things were still dangerous.

On the other hand, they knew from the deciphered sword symbols that they were looking for its matching shield and only then would they have all the information they needed to locate the King's Tomb.

"Early start everyone," Hawke said.

Reaper stubbed out his cigarette. "Oui, and I must call my family in France."

"And I must go and find some more ceegarettes," Scarlet said in a French accent.

They split up and returned to their rooms, all except Hawke and Lea. She looked at him with a wicked sparkle in her eyes. "So, what number's your room then?"

"Well, I…"

"You what?"

"I was hoping to stay in here tonight, with you."

"That *is* hopeful, what with considering …

They embraced and kissed and as they fell onto the bed, Hawke reached out and killed the lights.

CHAPTER TWENTY-FOUR

The next day, Athens was like a dream. Blazing sun, blue sky and the streets were busy and hot. Cars and mopeds sped through the arteries of the city like blood keeping the entire place thriving and energized. On the sidewalks outside cafés people argued and shared jokes and laughed and haggled. Tourists sauntered around snapping pictures on their phones and cameras. Hawke envied them, wishing he could kick back with a coffee and enjoy the city instead of fighting through whatever the day had in store for him and the rest of his team.

The Plaka district was heaving with activity and the air was thick with fumes from the heavy traffic. It mingled with the hot sunshine and exotic aromas drifting out of the restaurants, reminding Hawke that life went on and one day they might be able to have one of their own, to join the human race again and enjoy the simple pleasures on offer in a place like this.

Despite the pressures, the team seemed to be on good form. Kim and Camacho were talking about old times, Scarlet and Lexi were teasing Ryan about his latest tattoo and Lea and Devlin were sharing a joke. He had learned his lesson in that department and believed Lea when she had told him she loved him. He glanced at his watch, looked up at the café and sighed. "What the hell is he doing?"

Talk of the Devil, Hawke thought. Reaper stepped out of the nearby café with a Greek coffee and a lit rolled-up cigarette hanging off his lower lip. He winced when he sipped at the strong, black brew and then took a long drag on the cigarette. "I'm not alive until I do this," he said, blinking hard in the daylight.

The team crossed the busy road at the lights and continued on their way to the National Archaeological Museum. Like the ancient city all around it, the impressive neoclassical building was an important part of ECHO's world.

Inside, they fanned out and systematically searched through the ancient artefacts and relics until they found what they were looking for. Except, they never did. Hawke expanded the search to include objects from other cultures much further afield than what seemed likely, but still they came up with nothing.

He took a moment out, watching the team as they checked and double-checked for the shield. The idea that they had come this far only to fail in this way was totally unacceptable. Ryan had assured him that the shield described by Julius before his death was in this museum and he knew better than to doubt the young hacker. His mind was like a labyrinth of esoteria and facts and that combined with his eidetic memory made arguing with him a mistake.

Usually.

But what if this time he had screwed up? There was no sign of a shield matching the description given by Julius in the NAM website, after all. They had travelled all the way here from Pretoria purely on Ryan's hunch, a faded memory he claimed he had about seeing the shield here.

Flying here from South Africa had cost them a lot of time and resources. Keeping a Gulfstream in the air for that many hours wasn't cheap, either. To think the whole thing had been a mistake wasn't a thought he wanted to dwell on. But if Ryan had cocked up, it would give Scarlet at least another year's worth of material to mock him with.

There was always that.

Ryan walked over to him, hands in pockets and a frown on his face. "I'm *sure* it was here. I know I saw it in a guidebook once."

"Heads up," Lea said. "Curator's on the deck."

The curator was a small man with diffused, thinning hair stretched over a tanned scalp in an impressive combover. He was wearing a neat, pale brown suit and polished shoes and fidgeted when he moved. Under his nose was a thick, black waxed moustache which curled up at the end and instantly reminded Hawke of Poirot. Looking across at Lea, he saw she had made the same observation. She stifled a chuckle and had to turn away from him to stop laughing.

After introducing himself as Panos Theodorakis, he said, "Can I help you, please?"

"I hope so," Ryan said, describing the shield. "Do you have that here?"

"I'm impressed you are even aware of such an artefact," he said. "The Shield of Pridwen has not been on display since 1941 and has never been included on our website. Its image was included in some of the earlier museum guidebooks printed before the war, but these were not very high-quality images and as far as I know there are very few of these publications left in print and they were only ever printed in Greek. Do you have one of these guides?"

Ryan shook his head.

"Then you must have an exceptional memory."

"He does," Lea said. "It's actually quite terrifying, especially when you get into an argument with him. It's like arguing with a computer database of uncomfortable facts."

"You said that the shield hasn't been on display since 1941," Hawke said.

"That's correct. As you may know, when the front finally fell and the Nazis invaded my country, we moved as many of our most precious artefacts to hiding places around Greece to stop the invaders getting their hands on them."

"We did the same," Ryan said. "Much of the contents of British museums and art galleries were hidden in Welsh mines and caves."

"Exactly, so," Theodorakis said. "We did what we had to do to stop those monsters plundering the riches of our lands. You used what you had – the mines and caves of Wales – and we used what we had. We moved many of our priceless relics to places such as the ancient tombs at Delphi on the north coast of the Gulf of Corinth. Other sites included the caves beneath the Acropolis or right here."

"Right here?"

"Yes, in the museum. Beneath our feet is a maze of hidden underground chambers interconnected by ancient tunnels. When the Nazis broke through the front and advanced on Athens many of the treasures you see around you were transported to this secret underground system. Very few people know this history and even fewer are aware of the secret underground sections here in our museum."

Theodorakis's phone buzzed. He checked the tiny screen and a look of confusion grew on his face. "Please, excuse me."

He put the phone to his ear and lowered his voice. A hurried, panicked conversation followed and then he turned to Hawke, visibly growing paler. "It seems we might have a major incident here in the city."

"A major incident?" Scarlet asked.

The curator looked terrified. "A terror attack on the Parthenon. We have to get everyone to safety!"

"The Parthenon is sitting on top of the Acropolis, right?" Kim said.

"Of course," said Theodorakis.

"You said there were caves under the Acropolis and an underground system beneath the museum right here, right?"

He gave a brief nod and looked like he was going to throw up. "This is unbelievable."

"Professor," Scarlet said, snapping her fingers in front of his face to get his attention. "Are the caves under the Parthenon and your underground facilities here at the museum linked together by tunnels?"

His eyes widened as he realized what she was driving at. "Yes, they are."

"We need to get down there mate, and fast," Hawke said.

CHAPTER TWENTY-FIVE

Lea took the steps down to the basement level two at a time. What had destroyed Theodorakis's day had made hers – someone was making a move to steal the shield and that someone had to be Dirk Kruger, only he was trying to access the museum's vaults via the tunnels under the Acropolis. This was their chance to nail him once and for all and take the final part of the puzzle for themselves.

"Ready for a fight?"

She turned to see Devlin at her side. He had already drawn his gun and looked like he was champing at the bit for a good old-fashioned showdown.

"I'm ready to bring Kruger to justice, Danny. He needs to serve time for all the damage and destruction he's brought to this world."

"He needs to die," Ryan said from behind them.

"We're not a travelling courtroom, Ry," Lea said. "If he gets killed in the crossfire then so be it, but our job is to secure the shield and let the authorities deal with Kruger."

Ryan said nothing more, but she knew what was making his heart tick at the moment. The grudge he held against the South African was as hard as they came and with good reason. It wasn't ECHO's policy to murder their enemies, but sometimes there was no avoiding it. Feelings ran high in a team like this, but they still had to follow the rules or they were no better than the people they were fighting.

Ryan would have to be watched.

She drew her gun as they crossed the basement and then followed the curator to a series of doors on the far wall. “Most of these are storage units, but this one is the access point to the underground system.” He fumbled with a heavy ring of old brass keys before finding the correct one and pushing it in the lock. “It’s so rarely used I can’t remember the last time anyone came down here, but there are other curators so perhaps more recently than I thought.”

“Let’s just get the door open, shall we professor?” Scarlet said.

Theodorakis paused and gave her an icy stare. “I’m doing my best! These keys are very old!”

Hawke got up in his face. “Just do as she says, professor. Whoever’s shooting up the Parthenon right now is on their way here. Don’t forget that.”

With trembling hands, he opened the door and they found themselves at the top of a long stone staircase. Bending around to the right, it was lit by a weak electric lightbulb hanging on a wire above them.

“Cosy,” Lea said.

“You go on,” Theodorakis said, handing Lea the keys. “If this is a terror attack on our city I must make sure my family are safe!”

They watched the curator shuffle back up the steps and then turned to make their way inside the vaults. They soon reached the bottom of the stairs and walked along a short corridor. Lea went through the keys and opened a second, unlocked door which opened onto another much longer and wider corridor.

High stacks of wooden crates towered either side of them, pushed up against the walls of the tunnel and closing them in. Most of the lids were nailed down, but some had been broken up at some point and straw used for packing poked out of the gaps. Hawke peeked inside one of the open boxes and saw an old vase with a depiction of Poseidon painted on the side. "Hello old friend," he said.

"What was that?" Kim said.

"Nothing. Keep looking for the shield."

"Oh my God," Kim said. "I think I found it."

Devlin peered into the box she was searching. "Well bugger me with a pair of long-handled hedge shears! She has, as well!"

Scarlet gave him a passing look of disgust as she joined them at the box.

Kim pulled the shield from its thick straw bedding and held it up to the others.

"Ryan?" Hawke asked.

"That's it," he said. "No doubt."

Lea felt a wave of relief. "Get on those symbols, Ry!"

They formed a defensive position around the young hacker as he scoured over the carvings on the front of the shield. "I think I've got it," he said at last.

"Well stay away from me then," Scarlet said. "Because if *you've* got it, I don't want to catch it."

He smirked at her. "That gag is older than you are and that's saying something."

"Don't be so damned cheeky," she said. "You mean that gag just has more experience than I do."

"Where's the location of the tomb, Ry?"

"Amphipolis, near Thessaloniki."

"We're outta here, guys," the Irishwoman said.

"Wait," said Reaper, indicating the other end of the corridor with a nudge of his square, unshaven chin. "Our old friends."

Kruger's men rounded the bend in the tunnel and saw the ECHO team huddling around the row of large crates. The electric light above their heads was flickering in the damp, stone tunnel but Dirk Kruger was instantly recognizable. So was Blankov, Venter and a number of other men.

Lea felt her heart skip a beat and gasped as she reached for her gun. Devlin was a step ahead of her and aimed his gun directly at the trafficker's face. "Drop your guns, fellas," the Irishman called out. "It's game over."

Ryan lifted his gun and pointed it at Kruger. "Goodnight, Dirk."

Lea heard scuffling behind her and turned to see Reaper pulling Ryan back and forcing his gun hand down. "Not now," he said. "You cannot kill him in cold blood, mon ami."

"Watch me!"

"Non!"

"No," Hawke said. "Reaper's right. We're not executioners. Not like this."

Kruger curled his lip and looked at Ryan with contempt. "Someone change that boy's diaper. It stinks in here."

Venter and the men laughed, but Blankov was looking decidedly serious about the situation unfolding in the tunnel. He smiled when a unit of Athanatoi streamed into the other end of the corridor behind the ECHO team. They were trapped between the two forces.

"You look like a bunch of sewer rats," Kruger said, chuckling at his observation. "A bunch of rats about to die down in this filthy hole."

"I don't think so, Krugs," Ryan yelled. "You're the only one who's going to die today."

Another cackle of delight. "The boy's making death threats now! Drop your weapons and hand the shield over."

Ryan gave a sigh of defeat and passed the shield to his nemesis. Kruger snatched it from his hands and curled his lip. "I hope this piece of crap is worth all the trouble it's given me, Blankov."

The Athanatoi chief took it from his hands and looked at him with contempt. "It is, now bring the prisoners with us to the chopper."

"Can't we just kill them here?"

"The Oracle has decided he wants to kill them personally."

Kruger and his men marched them along the tunnel toward the Parthenon, but just before they reached the entrance and with the top of the Parthenon visible in the distance, Hawke saw his chance. One of the cultists had gotten too close and now he body-slammed him into the tunnel wall and disarmed him. Firing the weapon at the Athanatoi he killed three of them before turning on Kruger.

"Drop dead, Kruger," Hawke said.

"No, that's your job," the South African screamed back. "All of you men, kill them now!"

CHAPTER TWENTY-SIX

As Kruger and his men opened fire on them and fled the tunnel, Devlin hit the floor and landed on a sea of empty shell cases. Bullets traced over his head and splintered through the rock in the tunnel wall. Kruger had surprised all of them with the speed and ruthlessness of his attack. The Parthenon was in view now and so was the chunky AugustaWestland AW101 powering up behind it. Kruger and his men were on the brink of escaping with the shield.

He snatched his weapon from his holster and scrambled to his feet. Up ahead, Hawke and Reaper had sprinted over to the cover of the east side of the Temple of Venus while Lexi and Ryan were providing cover fire from the south side of the Temple of Rome. Over by the gateway to the Acropolis on the outcrop's western edge, the chopper's four massive rotors were powering up and starting to whir faster with every second.

Images of his life flashed in his mind like a badly edited movie. His childhood in South Africa, his life in the Irish Army, his relationship with Lea and now his adventures with ECHO. He reached the top of the steps and found himself entirely without cover. He scanned the rocky escarpment and saw Scarlet. She was closest to him, having taken up an offensive position in what had once been the Altar of Athena.

She saw him and rolled her eyes. "Get your arse over here, you fool! You're standing out like a dick on a wedding cake!"

Devlin sprinted across to her, chased all the way by a line of automatic fire from Venter's MP5. The lethal rounds bit into the dust and dirt at his feet as he charged toward the cover of the ruins, skidding into safety with seconds to spare. Venter's bullets slammed into the altar's stonework and ricocheted into the dusk.

"You want to get killed or something?" Scarlet said.

"I don't know what happened," he said. "I was thinking about my life… I totally lost it, Cairo."

"You lost it a long time ago, Danny. Just stop whining and start shooting."

Devlin managed to give her a grin and nod in response. "Thanks, I needed that."

"I'm not your therapist, Danny. Just shoot!"

Behind them, Camacho and Lea were dragging an unconscious Kim up the stone steps out of the tunnel's mouth.

"What happened?" Scarlet called over.

"Hit her head diving for cover," Lea said.

Kim was still unconscious as Camacho hauled her up onto his shoulders in a fireman's lift and pounded through the dust and gunfire to the cover of the Temple of Rome. They were all out of the tunnel complex now, but with Kim still knocked out they were a man down and now Kruger was climbing into the chopper. Blankov was already buckling up in his seat. Venter walked backwards as he fired his MP5 from the hip.

The former South African commando leaped inside the chopper and the mighty machine powered up and lifted off the ground. It hovered for a few moments while the pilot slowly turned to port and then they all saw it at once.

Venter was sitting behind a M134 Gatling gun mounted in the side door.

"Fuck, fuck, fuck!" Scarlet cried out.

Venter laughed as he opened fire on the team who were struggling to maintain their cover in the ruins. The pilot casually flew the helicopter higher into the air and off the southern edge of the rocky outcrop. Spinning in the air like a bird of prey, he swooped down over the top of them as Venter let rip with the Gatling gun again.

Devlin and Scarlet clambered over the top of the ruins and sprinted for the more substantial cover of the Erectheion on the northern edge of the Acropolis. The ancient temple had once contained the most holy relics in the city, but today it was a skeleton of broken rocks and crumbling pillars. Whatever. Those pillars provided the cover they needed while they reloaded. They had to draw fire from Venter in the chopper to give Hawke and Reaper a chance to escape from the Temple of Venus and get to the Parthenon.

Above them, Venter was a new god of death, raining down fire and brimstone on them from the sky. The rounds blasted into the pillars and blew chunks of the ancient, priceless ruins into the sky.

Chank chank chank!

Devlin cursed. “I don’t think they like us very much, Cairo!”

“I don’t think they like the Acropolis very much either!”

The six-barrel rotary machine gun in Venter’s hands continued to fire on them at six thousand rounds per minute. The muzzle flashed white and orange in the dying light and one of the commando’s men was helping to feed the ammo belt into the weapon. Both men lurched to the side as the chopper tipped to the side and headed over to the other side of the Acropolis.

Devlin followed its path. “They’re after Hawke!”

Hawke and Reaper were halfway along the open ground between the Temple of Venus and the Parthenon. The AW101 speeded above them and spun around to starboard on a dime, Venter firing all the time. The powerful rotary breech raining 50 mil rounds down on them wherever they tried to go to escape the savage fusillade.

Devlin and Scarlet fired on the chopper from the Erectheion but their handguns were almost useless. Lexi and Ryan provided a second front, firing on them from the north side of the Temple of Rome, but the pilot responded by gaining some altitude and turning the machine in the air to expose the door on the other side. Kruger's face appeared from the shadows inside the helicopter's interior.

"Holy shit!" Devlin cried out. "RPG!"

Kruger squinted as he shouldered the RPG-7 and looked down the optical sight. He fired and the rocket-propelled grenade burst out of the front of the weapon. Smoke fired out the back of the launcher and dissipated out of the other door where Venter was still firing the Gatling gun. The missile streaked forward with a trail of smoke twisting behind it.

"Take cover!" Scarlet yelled.

Lexi and Ryan ran for their lives as the speeding warhead struck the north side of the Temple of Rome and detonated, blowing half of it into the sky in a cloud of smoke and flames. Lexi reached the cover of some olive trees and Ryan skidded down into a pile of rubble between the temple and the Acropolis's eastern perimeter wall, cursing loudly as he came to stop in the dust and dirt.

Camacho had used the attack on Lexi and Ryan to pound across the open ground with Kim on his shoulders. Lea was at his side, firing up at Venter, but now the chopper was heading their way. He saw Hawke and Reaper ahead, also providing cover fire as they peppered the chopper's front windows with lead in the hope of taking out the pilots.

"You can do it, Jack!" Reaper said.

Devlin watched with his heart in his mouth as the chopper swooped down behind them until it was almost ground level and spun around to give Kruger the shot he so badly craved. If he got lucky now he could take out Hawke, Lea, Reaper, Camacho and Kim and a good chunk of the Parthenon into the bargain.

"This is chaos!" he shouted.

The sound of fighter jets.

Devlin looked into the sky, shielding his eyes from the sun. In the sky to the north, flying through the dazzling blue sky were two F-16 Fighting Falcons.

Ryan and Lexi had regrouped and were running around the length of the perimeter wall until they slammed into the cover of the Erectheion beside Scarlet and Devlin.

"You see the planes?" Devlin said.

"It's the Hellenic Air Force!" said Ryan.

"Stupid bastard could have gotten away," Lexi said. "But his obsession with killing us has cost him this time."

Hawke and Reaper were still firing on the chopper, but then Kruger fired the RPG again. The grenade ripped away from the launcher and sliced through the air on its way toward Camacho, Lea and Kim.

"Incoming!" Reaper yelled.

They made the Parthenon's eastern side and scrambled up the stone steps. Hawke and Reaper continued firing as Camacho and Lea ran into the interior of the ancient temple. The CIA man slipped Kim from his shoulders as the grenade piled into the outer layer of pillars and detonated.

They watched in disbelief as the Parthenon's entire eastern section exploded in a giant fireball and filled the sky with a terrifying mushroom cloud of flames and black smoke. One of the F-16s screeched overhead as the pilot made a recce of the situation and counted the guns.

Chunks of two and a half thousand-year-old masonry smashed down all around them, crumbling on impact and rolling away down the steps back to ground level. Camacho shielded the unconscious Kim with his body as the rocks and debris rained down from the fiery sky above their heads.

Kruger's chopper gained some more elevation and swooped away from the carnage, partially obscured now by the enormous mushroom cloud rising from the ashes of the Parthenon.

The F-16 was long-gone now, flying back into an attack formation with the other jet out on the horizon. Below, Devlin was suddenly aware for the first time of the screams of citizens and tourists panicking in the streets. Sirens filled the air and the red and blue lights of the emergency services flashed on the buildings far below as they raced toward the Acropolis.

"This situation is getting distinctly out of control," Ryan said.

Scarlet raised an eyebrow. "Not going to let it get the better of you, are you boy?"

"Me? Never!"

"We need to get to the Parthenon," Devlin said. "Better cover."

They used the smoke for cover and made their way across to Hawke and the others who had tucked themselves down behind the northern side of the ancient temple. The carnage was even worse close up and they were forced to climb over the fallen pillars and blasted stonework of what had once been the world-famous Parthenon in order to reach the rest of the team.

"Kruger's not screwing around anymore," Camacho said. He was cradling Kim's head in his arms and she was slowly coming back to life. "He's going to pay for this."

"He already is," Lexi said. "Look!"

She pointed at the southern horizon where the AW101 was hovering above the city. One of the F-16s fired a surface-to-air missile which tore through the sky toward the chopper. The pilot spun around in a defensive manoeuvre which silently impressed the ECHO team and the missile blew past the side of it with a few feet to spare.

Two things happened at once. The missile slammed into the southern side of the Acropolis's escarpment and blew a substantial quantity of sandstone and marl out of the side of the famous outcrop. It disappeared up into a cloud of filthy dust before coming back down to earth all over the streets of Plaka.

Then Kruger used the chopper's new position sideways to the F-16 and fired the RPG-7 at it. The grenade scorched its way toward the fighter, its three hundred meters per second muzzle velocity making the short distance of one K in just three seconds flat and plowing into the bird's starboard wing.

The explosion was savage, igniting the jet's JP8 kerosene and blasting the fighter into a thousand pieces over the streets below. Kruger fired again and hit the second jet. It blew up into a fireball even bigger than the first. Both pilots had ejected with half a second to spare and were now drifting down to earth beneath the canopies of their escape chutes.

The merciless Kruger ordered the chopper to spin around and Venter filled the air force officers full of lead, killing them before they hit the ground. Then the chopper turned into the sun and disappeared into a mirage over the hills to the city's east.

CHAPTER TWENTY-SEVEN

Dozing on the rear seat of the Suburban, Hawke tipped his head back and closed his eyes but stayed tuned to the conversation going on around him. It felt good to have the team working together like this, but they still had problems. Elysium had to be restored if they were going to have a proper center of operations again, but while the Oracle was alive there was little point in spending time and money on something he could so easily destroy.

And then there was his private life. Lea had forgiven him, but their break up had made him rethink the marriage proposal. He was still carrying the engagement ring in his gear bag, but he was no longer sure it was the best for the two of them. Still haunted by the memories of his wife's murder and getting along so well with her without a ring on her finger, he started to think it was best to leave things as they were.

Lexi yawned. "How long till we get to Amphipolis?"

"One hour forty," Ryan said without hesitation. "Just checked it out on the satnav."

"Bummer the place doesn't have an airport," Scarlet sighed.

"Yes," Ryan replied. "How ignorant the ancient Greeks were, not providing an airport for you to land your private jet in."

She raised her middle finger. "Spin on it, Jemima."

Hawke said, "Pull it together everyone. Thanks to Ryan deciphering the shield back in the tunnel we know where the tomb is located, but the Oracle knows too. We have the sword but he has the shield. All bets are off as to how this thing ends."

Lea tied her hair back and blew out a deep breath. "And this is the Oracle we're talking about. Remember that. This is a man who controls presidents and prime ministers. For all we know he's already tracking us or something. Probably has an army of Athanatoi cultists waiting for us at the tomb."

Kim gave a heavy sigh. "This is starting to feel like I don't have a life anymore," she said. "Before all this my life had structure. I had a career – the CIA and US Secret Service. I knew where I was from and where I was heading, but this is different. Maybe you Special Forces guys are used to all these crazy deployments and fights without rules, but I'm not sure I can handle it anymore and I miss my friends back in the States like crazy."

"I understand what you're saying," Lea smiled, but then concern and sympathy twisted her lips. "But it's not so great out there either." She nodded with her head toward the car window. "We're a family here and that's something most of us just don't have anywhere else in the world."

"I get that, but don't you ever get tired of this life?"

"Sure, but I can't stop until I know what happened to my father and I've punished those responsible for his death. Until that day comes, I'll never give up."

A long silence passed and then Hawke spoke up. "So where are we on this tomb, Ryan?"

"Since we got the location of the tomb off the shield, I've been looking into the area in a lot of detail. It's near a site called the Kasta Tomb. This was first discovered back in 2014 by archaeologists and it immediately raised eyebrows all over the world because of the hype surrounding the possibility of it being the location of Alexander the Great's tomb. Since its initial discovery much more evidence has been found suggesting strong links between the tomb site and Alexander."

"Such as?" Kim asked.

"Such as certain inscriptions which imply Hephaestion, one of Alexander's top generals and advisors is buried there, for one thing. Another is the grandness of the place. There are two enormous sphinxes made of marble guarding the tomb's main entrance and some archaeologists say there's a good chance the entire complex was designed by King Alexander's chief architect, a man named Dimocrates, sometimes known as Dinocrates of Rhodes. All of this means they *think* they might have found the tomb of Alexander the Great, but only *we* know it."

"Thanks to the sword and shield," Devlin said.

"Exactly," said Ryan. "Now we know that they're digging in roughly the right place, but not deep enough and slightly to the west of the actual site of his tomb. With the information we have now we should be able to locate the tomb precisely."

"These little quests just keep dragging us deeper and deeper down the rabbit hole," Lexi said quietly from the Chevy's second row near the front. "Idols, maps, treasure hunts, immortal men, cults, secrets and lies. We're so deep now we might never get out again." Her tortured hand was hidden inside a leather glove which she tried to keep out of sight as much as possible.

Hawke considered her words as he let Camacho's smooth driving whisk them around the northern shores of the Strymonian Gulf. Part of the Aegean Sea, it was a world of olive tree-covered peninsulas stretching into the sparkling turquoise water and cirrus cloud-streaked skies.

Deeper into the rabbit hole.

He nodded with the thought and found himself working his way through all the men and women he'd been forced to take out on this crazy journey. Hugo Zaugg and his depraved henchman, the one-eyed Baumann. Sheng Fang and his insane belief that he was the Thunder God. Maxim Vetrov and his crocodile pit. Klaus Kiefel's masterplan to wipe out the United States with an ancient bio weapon. Álvaro Sala and his crazy pursuit of the elixir of life to the very ends of the world. Morton Wade and his Mexican coffee plantation full of slaves… It almost seemed like a dream now, unreal and impossible.

And yet it was real.

And so were Dirk Kruger and the sick and twisted man who pulled his strings, the Oracle. Thousands of years old, was he a man or a god? A demigod? This creature who had been tormenting them for so long could be either and it drove him mad just to think about it. He glanced forward to the next row where Lea was sleeping.

If it felt like he was losing his mind in all this, then he couldn't imagine what it was doing to her. This man Wolff, the Oracle, had ordered the murder of her father and had him slaughtered right in front of her eyes. If anyone here deserved closure from this nightmare, then it was her and he was going to make damned sure she got it, no matter what it took.

He looked down at his watch and sighed when he saw the shattered face. He'd smashed it on the rocks back at the Parthenon and broken it. He took it off and slipped it into his bag down at the bottom near the engagement ring. It was a present his mother gave him on his pass out parade. A long time ago now, to be certain and he would get it repaired as soon as some degree of sanity returned to his turbulent life.

Beside him, Reaper pushed his window open and fired up a cigarette. Some of the smoke blew back into the

SUV, but no one complained. They were all smokers or ex-smokers of one thing or another and they let him enjoy the thing in peace. It settled the nerves, he said and Scarlet lit one up to join him.

"Just imagine," Devlin said quietly. "Finally finding the tomb of Alexander the Great after all this time..."

Ryan turned around in his seat and faced the back. "Tell me about it. Archaeologists and historians have been searching for the tomb of Alexander the Great for centuries, hoping to find not only artefacts and relics relating to his life and conquests but also the vast amount of treasure he's generally supposed to be have been buried with."

Lea opened her eyes and sighed. "We want the idols," she said bitterly. "Just the idols."

CHAPTER TWENTY-EIGHT

Jessica Clark padded around her kitchen as she talked. She was scrunching her neck up to hold the cell phone at her ear the way a violinist holds their instrument, waiting impatiently for someone to get back on the line. It was late and dark and the LED under-cabinet lighting gave a calm, arctic blue glow to the neat and ordered room.

"Garcetti?" she asked.

"Aaand I'm back."

"You get the details I need, or what?"

"Does the Pope shit in the woods?"

"Give me the details, please."

"You got a pen or something?"

She sighed and fought to control her temper. "You think people who do what I do write shit down? Why do you think I'm talking on a pre-paid cell phone?"

"Just asking… As I explained before, there's a new international terrorist group on the scene."

"You already said that."

"Just listen up, Cougar. This is the official line and you need to know it. According to Pegasus, my contact in the CIA, they're called the ECHO team. That's Echo, Charlie, Hotel, Oscar and it stands for the Eden Covert History Organization."

"Doesn't sound like a bunch of terrorists to me." She woke her laptop up and accessed the FBI's Most Wanted Terrorists website.

"If Pegasus says they're terrorists, they're terrorists."

"They're not on the Most Wanted Terrorists list." She slid a box of full metal jacket nine mil pistol cartridges off the kitchen table and started to push the primer-end of the bullets into the back of the fifteen-round magazine. As the tension on the spring increased she slotted her speed-loader onto the top of the magazine and finished filling it up.

"And we both know that's the *public* Most Wanted list, Cougar. The list on my desk right now is the list of the real problem children."

"What are my orders?" Pushing a box of Cheerios away to give her more room on the table, she put the full magazine into her bag alongside her Glocks and started to fill another one. The second one was much older with a weaker, used spring so she set the speed-loader down in the bag and filled it up manually.

"It's the full package."

The words made her stop in mid-flow. "The full package?"

"Uh-huh. ECHO's members and everyone they know. All family and close friends are to be wiped."

"You know how big a job like that is?"

"I don't give a damn. You asked what your orders were. Now you know."

"Names."

Garcetti tried not to sound bored as he rattled off the names of everyone she was to terminate. There weren't many. Just ECHO for now. She would work her way out to their friends and family as she went along.

"Where are they now?"

"They just arrived in Greece."

"What, are they on vacation?"

"No, they're not on vacation. They're on a mission to obtain some relics they have no business trying to obtain."

"You want me to fly to Greece to do it?"

"No, I want you to pour yourself a bath with some Shizumi luxury salts and let the stresses of the day melt away. Of course I want you to fly to Greece, but you're only tracking them. You don't take anyone out until I give the final execution order, but it will be soon, so be ready."

Be ready. What an asshole. She was ready every minute of the day or night. That was how she stayed alive. "You're the boss."

"You got that right."

She heard him again now. He was along the short corridor in his little bedroom, coughing in his bed. She put down her bag and walked toward him. "Wait a minute, Garcetti."

"I beg your pardon?"

"You heard me."

"Don't you put the phone down, Cougar!"

She put the cell phone down on the hall table and opened the bedroom door. The ghostly glow from the kitchen lights shone onto the bed and lit up her son. Ten now, his young life had been spent fighting severe asthma.

"You okay, buddy?"

A thin, pale face emerged from the bedsheets and gave a solemn nod. "I guess."

She hated seeing him like this. The attacks came and went, but they were getting worse. Sometimes when she heard him coughing and wheezing for breath she broke down and cried before going to comfort him.

"You're going to be fine."

Fine. Sure, but it was relative term. She had no insurance. Wasn't even in the system. She was like a wraith, moving through the world the way a ghost drifts through a cemetery. No birth certificate, no ITIN number for tax, no *nothing* and yet look here – a young boy of ten who spent his life fighting to breathe.

There was a new operation they said could help. It had something to do with radio waves. She didn't understand all that stuff, but she knew how much it cost. A chunky five figures and she couldn't reach that high. That was why she was coming out of retirement, just one last time.

This goddam stinking pile-of-shit world wasn't going to get any more kicks torturing Matthew Clark and that was for damned sure. She knew what she had to do to stop his pain.

He peered over the sheets and saw the time. "You're going away again?"

"I have to, Matty. I'm so sorry, baby."

He started to cry and she felt her heart breaking for the thousandth time. She reached out to him but he pulled away. "I hate it when you go away."

"It's all right, baby. It's just a few days, that's all."

"You always say that."

She ran a motherly hand over his forehead and swept his hair back. "I know and I hate it, but it's what I have to do. I can't buy you the help you need unless I get paid, you know? This is all I can do, baby."

And it was. No one gave regular jobs to a ghost. All previous attempts had winded up working alongside illegal immigrant labor or plain old-fashioned stealing. This was all she could do, but most jobs paid only enough to cover the rent and pay for food and Matty's medicine. This job sounded different. It might just be the one to end their nightmare and start living a real life.

She walked back out to the hall and snatched up her phone. Garcetti might be her handler, but there was a healthy respect people like him had for people like her. After all, she could live with breaking into his apartment and taking him out, but he couldn't say the same about her. "How much?"

"Kind of you to join me again."

"I asked how much."

"One million."

She gave a weary sigh and raised her eyes to heaven. Money well-spent, she guessed, but it would be more than enough for Matty's operation plus plenty left over to get out of this apartment and start a new life down in Mexico. "Fine."

"You will be paid on completion of the mission. Got it?"

She looked along the corridor at the shape of her son in his bed. Watching his thin body shaking as he coughed and wheezed, she knew there wasn't a damned thing she wouldn't do for him.

"Got it."

CHAPTER TWENTY-NINE

Shouldering their weapons and gear without complaint, the ECHO team left the Suburban and set out for the top of the mountain. The day was already hot and the sun beat down on them as they made their way to the coordinates. Their destination was well away from any of the paths used by hikers and tourists in the area.

Over the last hour or so the terrain had become dry, dusty and rocky with scree. One misplaced foot could mean a fatal fall, especially considering how loaded up they all were with equipment, guns and ammo. Highlighting their isolation from the world, a black kite screeched in the blue sky high above them.

Hawke glanced up and saw several others join the bird of prey, circling on thermals and wheeling patiently in the sky as they waited for one of them to tumble in a ravine and die. He pulled his hood up over his head to protect it from the glare of sun. "No way those bastards are having me for dinner."

He turned his gaze back to Lea, Scarlet, Reaper and Devlin who were now several hundred meters ahead of them up the slope. Looking at Lexi, he said, "When they reach that break on the ridge they should be able to see the rift further to the north. We've got some serious pounding ahead of us before we get to the coordinates though."

"I love it when you talk dirty, Joe."

He gave the Chinese assassin a lingering look, studying her eyes and lips for a fleeting moment. They had once been lovers, but Zambia was a long time ago –

and yet… sometimes the way she looked at him made him wonder. He said nothing but laughed and pushed on up the slope. Behind them, Ryan and Camacho were straggling at the back and arguing over the best poker hand.

Time marched on, each minute full of thoughts of Kruger and where he and his army were. There was no sign of them yet – the air was still and silent and no one could hear any helicopters or Jeeps, but they all knew he was out there somewhere and would never give up until he was dead.

Hawke puffed out a sigh and paused to take another drink of water from his canteen. The dry, scrubby grassland had given way to trees and thick coniferous woodland now dominated the landscape. Pine-covered mountains stretched to every horizon as far as they could see in any direction. Here, among the trunks and undergrowth of the Pangaion Hills, they joined together again and took a short break.

Kim pulled open her backpack and started dishing out supplies. "I got cookies, I got nuts, I got chocolate…"

"Gimme everything," Devlin said. "I'm so hungry I could eat the fleas off a dead dog's arse."

"Mmm, yummy!" Scarlet said. "Thanks for that image, Danny."

"You're welcome."

They tucked in, drinking plenty of water and replenishing their energy reserves before the final push. There would be no time to reenergize and rehydrate if they stumbled on the enemy in a place like this.

One more punishing hour and they found themselves approaching the coordinates Ryan had extrapolated from the shield. Hawke felt the sweat trickling down his back and took in the sky once again. Clouds had blown in from the east and now the pure, blazing blue was mottled with gray and the humidity was increasing.

"Holy crap," Kim said as she reached the rise and scanned the slope. "We made it!"

With a stormy-looking sky stretching to every horizon, they worked as a team to clear the scrub and scree away from the entrance until they were left with a single boulder blocking their way.

Hawke looked at it with satisfaction. "What time is, everyone?"

They called back in unison. "C4 time!"

CHAPTER THIRTY

When the dust had settled and the earth had stopped shaking, they picked up their equipment bags and headed inside the tunnel. Somewhere ahead of them was the tomb of King Alexander the Great, one of the most hunted archaeological sites on the planet and they were on the verge of its discovery.

"I hate to break it to you, guys," Camacho said. "But it looks like we have company."

They all turned and watched as the CIA man pointed through the trees to a gentle rise in the south. "If I'm not very much mistaken that's Dirk Kruger, with Blankov and Venter walking a little way behind him."

"We knew it was just a matter of time," Kim said.

"Sure, but this is cutting it rather too close," said Devlin.

Scarlet watched the small army of Athanatoi marching behind their leader. "They've regrouped as well. That's at least a thirty-strong force."

"We can't fight a force like that," Hawke said as they walked into the tunnel. "That means we have to work fast."

They entered the gloomy tunnel and switched on their flashlights as the daylight slipped away. It looked like it had originally been a natural passage in the rock that Alexander the Great's men had widened at significant time and expense. The chisel marks were still visible in the rock as they walked down the incline toward the end of the tunnel.

Here, deep inside the mountain they soon found what they were looking for – a cavern not much higher than the height of a man. Elaborate carvings decorated the walls and an impressive mural of the night sky stretched over the ceiling. They had never seen a mausoleum of such exquisite beauty before, but it wasn't the star of the show.

An intricately carved marble sarcophagus dominated the center of the space and now they slowly wandered over to it, none of them really believing they had found the final resting place of King Alexander the Great.

"Bloody hell," Hawke said as he tried to take it all in. "We actually did it."

On top of the sarcophagus were two tiny sphinxes carved in smooth marble, facing each other as they had done for thousands of years in the darkness of the mausoleum.

Ryan instantly knew this meant they had been successful. "I'm speechless." His voice was a whisper in the dark.

Scarlet looked at him sincerely. "It finally happened."

"But don't you understand the significance?" he asked.

"Sure, you've finally stopped speaking. That's a miracle."

He gave her a sarcastic look. "I mean this tomb."

"She knows what you mean," Lea said. "And yes, we all get the significance."

They started their search of the tomb but found only bags of treasure – coins, statues, gems. Leaning against the base of the sarcophagus were three bronze discuses sporting inscriptions which Ryan told everyone were votive offerings to the gods, but what they were seeking was much more ancient and valuable than any of this.

"It's time to go into the sarcophagus," Lea said. "That's the only place left."

They tried to prise the lid off the sarcophagus, but it wouldn't budge an inch. "I don't understand," Hawke said. "We've opened heavier lids than this."

"Wait!" Ryan said. "The sword – the carvings on the sword say that it has the power to open the tomb!"

"Do your He-Man thing, Joe," Lea said.

A muted ripple of laughter went around the tomb as Ryan handed Hawke the Sword of Fire. He held it in his hands and weighed it, got the feel of it. "Now what?"

"Well, it seems to be glowing blue already," Ryan said.

"Fuck!" Devlin said. "Orcs!"

Scarlet rolled her eyes. "God, I really want to slap you sometimes."

Hawke raised the sword in both hands and a deep, rumble filled the tomb and shook the ground beneath their feet. They all felt a wave of crackling static electricity swirl in the small mausoleum and leap onto the sword's blade. The steel glowed brighter and then when enough energy had been converted from the static into a live current, a bolt of blue lightning flashed out the tip of the sword and wrapped around the sarcophagus.

The bright blue sparks and bolts leaped and flickered all over the ancient marble and they all felt the heat the electricity produced as it worked its magic on the final resting place of Alexander the Great. Deep down in their souls, they all knew they were witnessing an ancient technology. Something far deeper and more complex than any of them really understood.

And then they heard a loud cracking noise and the blue electrical bolts sucked back down into the top of the sword and instantly stopped.

The room fell dark. Hawke swore and dropped the sword. "Bugger me, that's *hot!*"

"Looks like it worked though," Lea said, approaching the sarcophagus.

The marble lid was cracked in two, with a deep fissure running down the length of it. The rest of them joined her and now they prised the lid off the ancient coffin. There, in the dark of the sarcophagus, they found the king, resting in peace exactly as his family had left him thousands of years earlier. Each of them stood in respectful silence for a few moments, almost unable to comprehend what they had achieved.

"Oh, crap," Ryan said. "It's another idol!"

He reached into the sarcophagus and pulled out a small golden idol, similar to the ones they had seen in Valhalla and Mexico. "It's Chronos, without a doubt."

"It's the guy your aftershave was named after!" Scarlet said.

Hawke lifted an eyebrow. "I think someone already made that joke."

Ryan handed the idol to Lea who held it with a mix of achievement and fear.

"But there are supposed to be more," Lea said anxiously.

"I see something else," Ryan said at last. "There's a ring on his finger."

He reached inside and gently took the ring, handing it to Lea. She gasped. "I've never seen anything like it before."

"And there's more," Ryan said. He lifted a dust-covered tome from the skeletal arms of Alexander the Great with trembling hands and turned to the rest of the team. Turning its fragile pages with care, he turned to face them with a goofy smile on his face. "It's all the research his priests and historians put together. It's really quite astonishing. It seems he spent most of his life obsessed with searching for eight rings and eight idols."

"I like what I'm hearing so far, mate," Hawke said. "What else is there?"

Ryan was running his finger along the lines of faded ancient Greek script. "Tons. If my ancient Greek is good enough and it is, then he was searching for the same idols we've been finding on some of our missions."

"What's their purpose, Ry?" Lea felt her heart quicken.

Ryan's face visibly paled as he lifted his eyes from the yellowed manuscript. As he turned to face his friends, his breathing grew faster and shallower. "He says there are eight idols in total… that he found only one – this one." He read on. "According to this, Alexander the Great dedicated his life to finding them but only found Chronos. It says he has no idea where four of them are, but the other three are in a temple in Pavlopetri, the famous sunken city! He died before he could get to them and took their location to his grave!"

"Well, we've got two of them now," Hawke said. "What else is there?"

Ryan's hands started to tremble again. "It says these idols are the key to the gateway."

"A gateway?" Scarlet said.

"No, *the* gateway."

Lea felt goosebumps flash over her body. "*The* gateway? The gateway to what?"

"Yes, to what?" Kim said.

"Even I'm starting to give a shit now, Ryan," Camacho said. "Spit it out."

Reaper laughed and shared a high-five with Camacho.

"The gateway to somewhere called the Citadel."

Hawke stepped closer to Ryan and the codex and looked the young man in the eyes. "I presume you can get more out of this book than *the Citadel*, right?"

"Oh my God!" Lea said. "Remember what Blankov said to us back in South Africa about his little gateway and the Citadel? This is what he was talking about."

"But what does it mean?" Scarlet asked.

Ryan said, "According to this, the Citadel is what Alexander called the capital city of an ancient civilization based in what we call Sumer."

"A Sumerian city?" Reaper asked.

"No, not at all." Ryan said, words trailing off into the darkness of the tomb. "It says this civilization they're talking about predated Sumer by thousands of generations. He calls it the Land of the Gods."

"Impossible," Devlin said. "Sumer is the oldest civilization in the world."

Everyone turned to stare at him with the obvious question on their faces.

"So I watch the Discovery Channel from time to time? Sue me!"

"But he's right, isn't he?" Kim said.

"Not anymore," said Ryan. "I think we just made the greatest discovery in world history. If Alexander and his priests were right, human civilization started hundreds of thousands of years before anyone alive today thinks is possible."

"Wow," Lexi said. "That's about as heavy as it gets!"

Ryan looked at her, a smile spreading on his unshaven face. "You'd think, yes…"

"What does that mean?" Hawke asked, starting to feel anxious. He took the ring from Lea and started to study it.

"It means that the antediluvian civilization described in this codex was an advanced culture with knowledge, technology and weapons superior even to those we have today."

Even Reaper looked impressed. "C'est pas possible!"

"So we thought until a few minutes ago," Hawke said.

"He's even sketched some sort of a map here – looks a mural of a bull, maybe. It could be some sort of identifying feature. This is gold dust! We need to protect this." With trembling fingers he carefully ripped out the page with the reference to the sunken temple in Pavlopetri. "We can't let them know where it is." He folded it carefully and slipped it in his back pocket.

"Good idea, mate." Hawke took the ring and looked for somewhere to hide it, then saw Lea's hand. "Put this on your finger," he said. "No one will ever know."

"You're so romantic, Josiah."

Ryan sighed. "I'm going to need some time to translate this. The chances of me making a correct translation under pressure are slim to zero."

"Especially when you're dead!"

They spun around, shaken from their awed state by a familiar South African accent. Kruger was in the tomb now and behind him they saw the first few faces of what they knew was a small army of Athanatoi.

"You just won't go away, will you?" Lea said.

"This is our property, not yours." Blankov pushed past Kruger. "The things in this tomb belong to the Athanatoi."

"Hand it over," Kruger said. "Like the man just said, it doesn't belong to you."

"Nor you, you son of a bitch!" Lea said.

"It doesn't matter what you think you know, Donovan. You can never know what the Oracle knows. You can never understand the gravity of what you found here today." He turned to Ryan. "Now, I'm getting tired of saying this you little squirt, but hand over the goods."

Ryan's heart was torn in two. To hand the manuscript over to Kruger meant they might lose the mission, but to refuse meant instant death. Not wanting to give the South

African any satisfaction, and reassured by the map page in his pocket, he controlled a sigh of frustration and walked it over to him.

"There's a good boy, now fuck off back to mum and dad over there."

Ryan returned to the other side of the tomb and Kruger handed the codex to Blankov. The Athanatoi general never even looked at it, but held it like it was no more than a briefcase. He casually turned to Kruger. "We have what we need. You can kill them now."

"But I thought the Oracle wanted to kill them?"

"He has changed his mind. You are to terminate all of them immediately."

Blankov left without a glance at them, followed by his contingent of Athanatoi bodyguards.

In the new silence, a fiendish grin spread on Kruger's face. "By the time I've finished with you this time, you'll be a nothing more than a pile of bleached bones strewn out in the sun."

"Oh la vache!" Reaper said. "That's not nice, Dirk."

"You're nothing more than their lapdog, Kruger," Lea said.

Hawke stepped forward, but was instantly forced back by Venter's submachine gun. "A dog with no teeth."

"Stick and stones may break my bones," he said with a curled lip. "But names will never hurt me."

"I'll fucking hurt you," Ryan said. "Just give me half a chance and stop hiding behind your goons."

"I'll have you know these are fine fighting men, not like your little ragtag bunch of amateur misfits. We caught you, after all."

Ryan stuffed his hands in his pockets, a frown on his face. He looked more beaten than angry. It had been a tough few hours since the initial raid on Kruger's Pretoria mansion and he was tired of running and fighting. Maybe Kruger really did have the edge. Maybe he really would beat them in the end.

"You won't get away with this, Kruger!" Hawke yelled.

His response was laughter. "You're making threats against me? You're in no place to do that. I'm going to execute you now, here. Say your goodbyes!"

CHAPTER THIRTY-ONE

Kruger ordered Venter and his men to step forward. Without a further command they slid the bolts on their weapons and aimed them at the ECHO team. If they fired in here it would be a bloodbath beyond description and no one would ever find their bodies.

Kruger took one last look around the mausoleum and that was the only chance Hawke needed. Grabbing one of the bronze discuses, he threw it at full speed like a Frisbee. It raced across the tomb and struck Kruger in the center of his face. He cursed and kicked and swore and when he looked back up his nose looked badly broken by the force of the discus smashing into it.

Hawke knew what came next, so before the arms dealer gave the execution order, he threw another of the Frisbees at Venter, causing him to duck to avoid the same fate. The discus smashed into the carved wall behind him and the ECHO team needed no order from Hawke to tell them what to do.

They charged Venter and the other men in the gloomy light of the mausoleum, piling into them and forcing their guns up to the ceiling. A few of the weapons fired off, blasting holes in the night-sky mural, but now they had a chance.

Reaper's opponent went down first. The Frenchman easily disarmed him and kicked his gun away. He punched him in the face but the man drew a combat knife from his belt. The former Legionnaire fought like a bull, strong and agile and cunning. Twisting the knife out of his hand, he drove the serrated blade up into the soft flesh beneath the man's ribcage and silenced his screams with his hand until he was dead. The man's corpse slipped to the floor of the cave and Reaper turned to help Ryan who was fighting with Kruger.

Hawke and another soldier were rolling in the dust over by the sarcophagus. The South African mercenary knew some moves but he was no match for the former commando. Hawke got the better of him and was soon pinning him down and pounding him in the face.

Camacho and Venter were taking swipes at one another nearer the door and Lea, Scarlet and Lexi were deconstructing a merc's ego on the other side of the sarcophagus, taking it in turns to hit him and then push him over to the next in the group for a go.

"That's enough!"

A gun went off in the semi-darkness and everyone froze where they were.

Hawke twisted around and saw Kruger with a gun at Ryan's head. The South African had captured him and was holding him hostage. "I said that is enough! Release my men!"

"Men? I thought I was fighting fairies," Scarlet said.

"Shut up, bitch!" He cursed. "Get me the sword Venter."

Venter picked up the Sword of Fire and walked it back over to Kruger.

Hawke climbed off the badly beaten soldier who joined Venter and the others with Kruger at the entrance to the tomb. "Just when I was having fun, too."

Kruger grinned. "Is it fun you want, boy?"

Hawke bristled at the insult, but kept his emotions under tight control. "Nothing could be more fun that watching you die, Dirk. How are you going to beat that?"

"You'll find out. Venter! Get your men out of here and use up the rest of our C4 on the entrance tunnel." He turned to Hawke. "That sound like fun to you – trapped in here under a hundred tons of granite?"

"You bastard, Kruger," Lea said.

"Not even the mighty Joe Hawke can dig his way through a fucking mountain, I'll bet. I bid you farewell, my friends and I thank God we'll never meet again."

Kruger pushed Ryan away and stepped back into the tunnel, the shadows of the tomb slowly obscuring his grinning face and then he was gone.

Seconds later they heard a tremendous explosion that made the entire mountain shake under their feet. Pieces of the carved walls fell to the floor and one of the bags of gold coins tipped over and spilled its precious cargo all over the dust of the mausoleum's floor.

"That's torn it," Lea said.

"I don't think so," said Ryan. "Start searching for the other entrance."

"What other entrance, mate?" Hawke said.

"The sarcophagus is marble, right?"

Hawke looked at him, unable to resist grinning at how his friend's mind worked. "If you say so, then yes."

"Well, it is. Does it look like this mountain is made of marble?"

"To be honest," Scarlet said. "I wouldn't know."

"Let me help then," Ryan said. "It isn't. As our good friend Dirk Kruger just said, it's made mostly of granite. That's because this part of Greece is in the Attico-Cycladic Massive region, obviously."

"Obviously," Lea said with a smile and a shake of her head.

"Still not getting why this means we're not suffocating to death tonight," Lexi said.

Ryan huffed and pointed at the sarcophagus. "How big is that thing, Lex?"

"Huh?"

"I'll give you a clue, the side panels alone are wider than the tunnel we walked through to get down here."

"Ah…"

"I get it, Ry,' Lea said. "The sarcophagus is too big to have been brought down the entrance tunnel and it wasn't carved down here because it's made from the wrong stone."

"Give that girl a cigar," Ryan said, resuming the search. "And there's another thing, too – where's the antechamber? A tomb for a man like Alexander the Great would have had an antechamber. In other words, we came in through the back door."

Hawke felt a wave of relief. "The lad's a genius."

"And that is so, *so* annoying," said Scarlet.

"C'est ici, je pense," Reaper said, heaving a small, square block of chiselled granite out of the wall. "On the north wall."

Kim crawled down and looked through the gap. "There's a tunnel."

"That'll be the connecting corridor to the antechamber," Ryan said. "Built after the sarcophagus was placed in here."

They crawled through the corridor until they were in the antechamber and found themselves staring at a much wider entrance on the far wall. Ryan pointed at it. "And *that* is where the sodding sarcophagus was brought in."

Hawke turned to Ryan and gave him a heavy slap on the back. "You saved our arses again, mate."

"I believe in the modern vernacular, that's because I'm a *boss*, is that right?"

Scarlet rolled her eyes. "Don't push it, neckbeard."

"Hey!"

"All right, let's move out." Hawke led the way into the tunnel.

They followed it up an incline but then it turned sharply back down again and they felt like they were walking to the center of the planet. Intrigued as to where it was going to break the surface, they soon found out when they heard running water.

Turning a corner in the wide tunnel they found a pool.

"My bet is we swim our way out through there," Kim said.

Scarlet looked at Ryan with a look of smug satisfaction on her face. "And how did they get the bloody sarcophagus through that pool, Poindexter?"

"My best guess is that when we come to the surface we'll find we're in a river and that they diverted the river to fill this pool after they delivered the sarcophagus." He returned the smug look with a raised middle finger. "How d'ya like *them* apples, Cairo?"

She twisted her lips. "I'll let you off, *boy*, but only if when we get to the other side we find ourselves in a fast-moving river!"

"Wanna bet on it?"

"I'm not afraid of wager."

"A hundred quid."

Camacho was impressed. "That's a hundred and fifty bucks – he must be pretty damned sure."

Scarlet thrust out her hand. "Done. Let's get on with it."

"No one's going anywhere until I've checked it out for safety," Hawke said.

Specially trained for deep dives and long periods underwater by his SBS years, the Englishman slipped down into the water.

They waited in the silence of the cavern for a few moments and then the Londoner broke the surface of the pool with a grin on his face. "Hope you've got some cash on you, Cairo. You own Ryan here one hundred smackers."

CHAPTER THIRTY-TWO

The ancient city of Pavlopetri is one of the world's oldest submerged cities and a popular site for divers to hunt for ancient treasures and relics. Laying off the golden shores of the Laconian coast of southern Greece, its name means Paul's Stone, a reference to the Christian saint. The settlement contains archaeological evidence dating back to Minoan culture, almost five thousand years old and today is a UNESCO site under the Protection of the Underwater Cultural Heritage.

As their boat speeded away from the coast, Hawke looked out across the sparkling turquoise water with a strange mix of excitement and anxiety. Frozen in time, the streets below the water were just as they were all those thousands of years ago when the ocean swallowed the city.

For a team like ECHO the opportunity to visit such a site and explore for relics and treasure was a once in a lifetime event, but they all knew Kruger must already be here, at least an hour ahead of them. Ryan was certain a close reading of the codex would have revealed Pavlopetri to the South African, but at least they knew the exact location was theirs alone.

He turned and looked at his team as they prepared for the battle ahead. They were tired. Bags under their eyes and sluggish movements. Adrenaline would get them over that, but he wondered for how much longer he could push these people. Now, sailing over the Mediterranean Sea, Hawke sensed for the first time that he might be nearing the end of this mission. Staring out over the vast expanse of water, he wondered what turmoil would be lurking beneath its calm surface.

Beside him, Camacho and Scarlet were sharing a kiss. Devlin rolled his eyes and took the moment to check his equipment. Reaper and Kim were talking quietly at the end of the cabin. Lea was sitting separately from the rest, eyes closed but still awake and for some reason Lexi was tweaking Ryan's ear and forcing him to apologize for something he had said. In other words, the team was acting as normal and all looked totally unfazed about the battle to come. That, at least, was something.

But his mind was far from satisfied. When Eden had called about hiring the boat, he'd had nothing new to report on the location of Otmar Wolff. Hawke had hoped the team might have found him down with Kruger in Pretoria, but it was a hope too far. The immortal monster known as the Oracle had been evading them for so long now it felt like they were never going to hunt him down.

Was it all worth it? A life on the road wasn't a good life. Never having anywhere to call home, never being able to relax without wondering if someone was going to attack in the night. It felt like life had been like this forever, but there had been somewhere he could call home for a short time.

He thought back to the first day he had seen the island. It seemed like Elysium was a totally different era now. The pristine white sandy beaches, the pure, clean warm ocean waters and the coconut palms. In the middle of it all nestling between two tropical extinct volcanoes was their former HQ, a sprawling complex of airconditioned glass and steel that had everything a team like ECHO could ever desire. And it was still in ruins after the Oracle's brutal attack.

Hawke guessed it would take millions of dollars and several months to bring it back together again, but there was no point doing it until the Oracle had been killed because otherwise there was nothing stopping him destroying their home all over again. Until then, they were nomads, wandering from hotel to military facility to friends' apartments. It was a turbulent, exhausting life he thought he'd left behind when he quit the SBS.

The captain's voice crackled through the boat's internal comms. A large ocean-going yacht had been spotted a kilometer or so away to the west. Hawke furrowed his brow and walked up to the bridge. He clamped a hand on the captain's shoulder and he turned and gave a thumbs up in response.

Peering through the windshield, the captain went on to describe the yacht as being over one hundred and sixty meters long with three decks and a helipad. Kruger was rich, but not in this league and that meant only one thing.

The Oracle was in town.

By the time he had made his way back from the wheelhouse, the ECHO team were already standing by on the aft in their diving gear, spearguns locked and loaded and ready for a fight. Lea was tying her hair back and the ocean breeze was blowing across the deck and whipping it around her face making her curse as she finished the job.

"What gives?" she said, her teeth glinting in the sunlight.

"The captain just got a call from a fishing boat on the other side of the peninsula about a very large yacht. No one recognizes it as coming from around here. Apparently, it's over a hundred and sixty meters in length."

"Holy crap," said Kim. "That's a big boat."

Camacho agreed. "That ain't Dirk's."

"No," Hawke said flatly. "I think it's safe to assume his boss has turned up to claim the grand prize."

"The Oracle?" Lea said, her face dropping.

"The very same, only thanks to Ryan's quick thinking back in the King's Tomb, he doesn't have the specific location of the temple Alexander was searching for."

"Maybe we should just go home," Devlin said, deadpan. "I mean, these guys are good. Better than us."

Now Scarlet was tying her hair back. "Hey, Danny?"

"What?"

"Fuck all the way off."

"Ouch," Devlin clutched at his heart. "She got me again, boys! There goes any chance of a date."

"There was never any chance of that, Ranger."

"You love me really, right?"

Scarlet couldn't resist a devilish smile of her own. "You made Hawke flounce off like a girl, so you can't be all bad."

Hawke opened his mouth to reply but Lea put her finger across his lips to stop him talking and then she kissed him. "I love that you flounced off like a girl."

"Not sure what to make of that," Lexi said.

"Anyway," Hawke said, changing the subject. "The captain of the fishing boat said there's a davit crane at the stern."

Ryan furrowed his brow. "Eh?"

"It's a device used for lowering heavy equipment off the back of boats, in this case my best guess is an underwater vehicle of some kind."

Lea's shoulders sloped. "So the Oracle's got a goddam minisub here?"

"Great," Lexi said. "We don't stand a chance."

Devlin put an arm around their shoulders. "Stick with me and you'll be all right."

They both gave him the same look and he removed his arms. "Just trying to be reassuring."

Hawke said, "All right everyone, listen up. This is our chance. We have to get down there and back up again before the Oracle works his way around the peninsula. I'm presuming he's got the best sonar equipment available on board and it won't take him long, so we have to work fast."

"What's the plan?" Kim asked.

"We do what we always do," Hawke said. "Make it up as we go along."

"Oh *crap*," she said. "Can't you at least say something like we'll improvise."

"Fine," Hawke said, deadpan. "We'll improvise."

Reaper flicked his cigarette off the deck. "Who's going down?"

Lea spoke without hesitation. "We're all going down, right?"

Hawke nodded. "We don't know how much muscle we're going to need down there and if our friends turn up we'll need all the fight we can muster. The priority is securing the idols and then getting back up here as fast as we can."

In full diving gear, Reaper was first to sit on the side of the boat and push back off the edge. He crashed into the water backwards and was soon under the waves. Camacho was next. He winked as he fitted his diving mask and gave a two fingered salute before slipping out of view. Then Scarlet went, followed by Kim and then Ryan. Lexi and Devlin went over the edge next and then Hawke was last out.

They dived to a safe depth to keep out of sight and then swam down to the famous sunken city. It was easy to see through the crystal-clear turquoise waters of the Med and they soon found themselves approaching what they all prayed would be the location of the last idols.

CHAPTER THIRTY-THREE

Hawke always felt at home under the waves and today was no exception. Even with the speargun he moved easily and quickly in the wetsuit as he dived down to the famous ruins on the ocean floor. He turned once and saw the rest of the diving team swimming behind him, each armed and prepared for battle.

"These ruins are incredible!" Ryan said through the comms device. The small transceiver was attached to the retaining straps of his face mask and used bone conduction to transfer vibrations to a small microphone.

"Just like old times!" said Lexi. It felt like she was gliding over the streets of a foreign city.

"It's very silty over to the west," Lea said. "Evidence of Kruger?"

"I can't smell anything too foul," Scarlet said.

"Good one."

Hawke flipped around and stared over in the direction Lea had pointed out. He saw a bank of thick silt drifting in the water on the western edge of Pavlopetri, but no sign of any human activity. "Maybe, but that's not where the map says the temple is." He brought himself about and continued on his original trajectory. "I think I see the entrance up ahead. Some of the silt is drifting over it now, but it's still visible. Anyone else seeing it?"

"Got it," Reaper said, his voice calm despite the growing excitement they all felt.

They swam down further and approached the city on the ocean floor. Eerie didn't begin to describe the sight of temples, homes, streets and alleys submerged in this watery grave just as they had been the day they slipped into the sea so many thousands of years ago.

Hawke imagined what it must have looked like back on land, soaked in the Greek sun and bustling with people going about their business, trading, living, loving. One day, he wondered, will our cities look like this?

They reached the coordinates on the map and touched down gently on the street beside the small temple. As their diving fins landed on the cobblestones they kicked up wispy clouds of sediment into the water around them and partially obscured the clarity of the temple for a few moments before clearing again.

“Who wants to be first?” Scarlet asked.

“I’m going first,” Hawke said in reply. “There could be boobytraps.”

“I can’t argue with that,” said Ryan, drifting back out of Hawke’s way.

He swam up the steps and made his way inside the temple, leaving the sun-dappled underwater world behind him and emerging into a newer, darker place. He flicked on his light and scanned the place for any sign of traps. “I think we’re good to go, guys.”

One by one, the team members headed for the temple, swimming up the steps and joining him inside. Jumbles of rocks and boulders lay on the floor alongside fallen marble support pillars and a few slabs of granite from the roof. A school of parrot fish flashed past them and burst out of the door and a large octopus drifted up from behind one of the granite slabs and pushed its way up out of a hole in the roof.

“Plenty of sea life,” Lea said.

“Yeah,” said Scarlet, “but where’s the pond life?”

“Just what I was thinking,” Ryan said. “The Oracle’s yacht is somewhere on the surface, but where the hell are they all?”

"Maybe they already got inside," Devlin said. "But used another entrance."

"I think they're still too far away," said Hawke.

Ryan swam over to a fallen pillar and gently swept aside a thick layer of silt and sediment. "Check out these carvings!"

"What have you found?" Kim swam over to him and passed her flashlight over the broken pillar.

Hawke turned in the water and joined them. He recognized what Ryan had found immediately – the carvings were almost identical to those they had seen all over the world, from the Aztec temple in Mexico to the ice caves of the Arctic to the strange jumble of ruins in Atlantis, not to mention the ones on the mysterious idols.

"We can add Pavlopetri to the list as well," Hawke said.

Ryan gave him a thumbs up. "Whoever created these symbols had a worldwide presence. It links up with what Blankov was saying about a global capital city."

"But they're so ancient," Kim said. "It doesn't make any sense."

"Wait, I think I see something," Lea said. "Over there where the octopus was."

Lexi spun around in the water and pushed herself across the temple. "I see it too!"

"It's a bull's horn!" Lea dived down to the floor and started to rub silt off the floor with her hands. "This is the mosaic in Alexander's map!" She cleared it off until the entire bull's head was visible, but one of the horns was obscured by a giant slab of granite that had fallen from the roof.

"It's the entrance, guys." Lea hovered above the slab with Lexi at her side and both women were shining their lights down into a narrow hole in the floor. "But it's partially blocked by this slab."

Hawke and the others swam over. "Damned thing probably came off the roof during an earthquake."

"Time for more Big Bang Theory?" Ryan said.

Hawke raised his hand and gave him the thumbs up sign. "I'll set the charge at the end of this gap between the slab and the mosaic. Should be enough to make a hole big enough for us to dive down."

He pulled the explosives from his bag and started to fix them into place.

"Wait," Lexi said through the comms. "Is that little fucker NG?"

"Of course."

"What's the problem?" Ryan asked.

Hawke replied as he worked. "NG, or nitroglycerine is best for this job. The other option is an ammonium nitrate explosive, but that needs a contact primer." He set up a NONEL, non-electric detonator and made some final checks. "Nitro is less stable but cheaper. We're on a budget after all."

"We have a private jet," Scarlet said.

"What are you?" Hawke finished setting the underwater explosives and looked up at her. "My accountant?"

"You couldn't afford me, darling."

He looked at her eyes hidden behind the gloom of her mask. "Shall we detonate?"

"You always know how to turn me on."

They shared a look and then swam back outside the temple with the others in their wake. Safely tucked down behind the wall of a house opposite the temple, Hawke pushed his thumb down on the trigger and activated the explosives. The explosion was muted by the water pressure, but the shockwaves were still powerful enough to blow them back away from the house and onto the street.

Hawke was first to his feet and saw the cloud of sediment forming around the temple as dead fish floated up to the surface. "I'd say that was a job well done."

"Fish killer," Lea said, yanking on his arm.

They swam inside the temple again and soon found the bull mural. The explosives had done the job and cleared an enormous hole in the floor. They dived inside and swam along a wide, natural tunnel which ended when they surfaced in an underwater lake.

Hawke scanned the area and then pulled his mask off. The others joined him and after swimming to the shore they crawled out of the water. Standing in the cavern, they took off their fins, tanks and diving masks and checked their weapons. When they fired up some glow sticks they soon realized they were standing in not just a cave but another manmade temple.

Kim gasped. "What now?"

"We follow this tunnel, I guess," Lea said.

They walked down into the tunnel and as her eyes adjusted to the darkness, Lea saw a marble column plinth supporting an impressive statue. "Wow."

"Minoan snake goddess," Ryan said casually.

Ahead of them a stone ramp descended into a lower level. Statues of unknown gods lined the sides of the tunnel, each one a little more obscured by the darkness of the caves. On the far wall was an enormous arch carved into the stone. At the bottom of it, on an elaborately carved stone table, was a beautiful shrine supporting three life-size statues. Just to the left of the shrine was a deep chasm filled with black water. Hawke shone a light down at the surface and winced.

"They're gods," Ryan said without hesitation. "Brahma, Pangu and Ra."

"Brahma, who and Ra?" Hawke said.

When Ryan looked at him, he shrugged. "Well, I've heard of two of them!"

"Thank heaven for small mercies," Ryan muttered. "Brahma was the Hindu creator god, their head deity. The same distinction applies to Pangu who was the creator deity in Chinese mythology and Ra for ancient Egypt."

"And their statues are in a sunken city off the coast of Greece… why?" Reaper asked.

"It's all connected to my parent culture hypothesis," Ryan said. "And if King Alexander was right there should be…"

"Too late," Lea said with a wink. "I saw them first… the idols!" She stepped closer to get a better look.

"And not just any idols," a voice in the darkness said. "But the *final* idols."

Lea felt her skin crawl as she turned slowly in the gloom and took in the Oracle's withered, ashen face.

"And your final destination," he said, lifting a speargun and aiming it directly at Lea.

With a depraved smile on his face he squeezed his thumb on the trigger and fired the weapon. The spear burst from the gun and darted across the small space before anyone could react.

"No!" Hawke yelled and dived in front of her, pushing her roughly to the floor and out of the way, but the triple-pronged spear head buried itself into his leg. He screamed out in pain and staggered back over the edge of the chasm.

CHAPTER THIRTY-FOUR

He tumbled down into the void with the harpoon buried deep in his leg. Crashing through the surface of the black water, he started to sink deeper. The pain was electric, radiating out from the wound over his entire body. He screamed in the darkness and lashed out with his hands, desperately fumbling for something to hang onto and stop his descent.

The slit of light created above him by the lamps in the temple was rapidly growing smaller as he sank faster in the underwater chasm. He checked his depth gauge and realized he was speedily approaching his maximum limit.

An experienced diver from his former life with the Special Boat Service, he knew the extreme dangers of diving too deep. As the inert gases built up in his tissues he could expect disorientation, tremors, exhaustion... Now, the icy water started to cause a serious cramp in his legs. If he didn't act fast it would be too late and he would die down here.

Glancing down he saw no end to the chasm. It was entirely possible that this hole was hundreds more meters deep. Waiting to hit the bottom was suicidal. He grabbed the harpoon in his leg and wrenched it out with all his strength. Only he heard his screams as the steel endblade ripped out of his thigh muscle and finally came free. A cloud of blood burst into the water behind the endblade's exit and twisted up above him in scarlet tendrils.

He grabbed the harpoon with both hands and held it above his head. As he brought it level it jammed up against the two sides of the narrow chasm's walls and acted like a bar fixed into place in the tunnel. He jerked to a sudden stop and found himself hanging like a marionette from the harpoon's main shaft. His plan had worked, but now he had to swim to the surface with a badly wounded leg.

His head started to swim around in the darkness. Disorientation, just as he had expected. He glanced at the depth gauge on his forearm but the glass face was smashed and it was broken. He must have belted it against one of the chasm walls as he plunged down through the depths. He cursed and craned his neck up. The slit of light was still visible – just, but was almost razor thin. He guessed he had fallen several hundred feet before he was able to extract the spear.

He was running out of air as well. Another curse. He pulled himself up over the spear and started swimming back up to the chasm's black surface. Lea was still up there, with the rest of his team – and all at the mercy of the Oracle. He hadn't come this far to let him win now. He had to get back to the others and stop that bastard getting his hands on the idols. Praying his friends were still alive, he forced his arms through the black water and powered himself to the surface.

The gaping wound in his leg slowed down his usual lightning pace and when he reached the top and broke through the surface he was surprised to find the chamber totally empty. He was less surprised to see the idols were all gone, too. Gripping the ground around the top of the chasm, he dragged himself up out of the water, screaming with pain when the wound on his leg scraped against the rocks around the edge.

"Dammit all!"

He blew out a breath as the blood pumped out of the deep cut and spilled out onto the sandy dirt on the chamber's floor. He was feeling a little light-headed as he tried to calculate how much blood he had lost. Pulling his torn wetsuit away from the wound, he immediately saw the three deep gouge marks made by the Oracle's triple-pronged spear head and the mess they had made when he had ripped them out of his leg. He thanked God the blades hadn't gone too deep and tore strips of rubber off his suit to use as a tourniquet.

Staggering to his feet, he walked carefully along the tunnel until he found the rest of his team. He saw a minisub on the surface of the lake they had entered the cave by, and realized from its size they could easily have used the hole they'd blown in the temple floor to navigate here.

He heard a scream and turned to see his team were fighting the Athanatoi divers. Lea knocked one of them out with the stock of her speargun and turned to see him limping along the tunnel.

"Oh shit!" she ran to him and looked at his leg.

"It's worse than it looks."

"Fuck that. Get over here out of sight." She grabbed her Scuba dry bag. Reaching inside for a bandage, she hurriedly cleaned and dressed the wound on his leg. "You absolute bloody eejit, Josiah."

"Eh?"

"You could have killed yourself, you damned fool!"

"Eeejit? Damned fool? I thought I saved your life?"

She finished securing the bandage and looked deep into his eyes. "I know."

"We have to get back to the fight," he said. "They need us."

"You can't be serious? With a leg wound like that?"

"I already told you it's not…."

The explosion knocked them both off their feet and sent then crashing backwards into the sand. When they sat back up, Hawke rubbed his head. "What the buggering hell was that?"

"Oh no!" Lea cried out. "They're firing grenade launchers at them!"

Before he could say anything, she ran forward to help her friends. He tried to follow, but collapsed down on one knee, screaming in pain at the bloody wound in his thigh.

A deep rumble boomed inside the underwater cavern as a section of one of the pillars broke away and crashed down on a frescoed wall. It smashed through the ancient tilework and almost crushed him. He dived out of the way and landed in a pile of rubble.

When he finally clambered to his feet he could barely believe what he was seeing. The Oracle and Blankov were climbing inside the top hatch of the submersible while the Athanatoi were firing on his team with grenade launchers. Kruger and Venter had taken Devlin and Lea hostage and were forcing them inside the minisub behind the Oracle.

"Lea!"

But she never heard and now he watched as the rest of the team sprinted for cover in every direction to avoid the grenades blowing up all over the chamber, blasting car-size chunks of roofing plaster and rock all over their heads.

"Bastards!" he yelled, struggling forward to help.

Scarlet fired on the sub while Lexi dragged a woozy Ryan away from more rubble and chaos, but they were submerged in seconds. Nothing was left except some bubbles on the surface.

Hawke ran over to them. "We can't let them get away! They've got Lea and Danny!"

They hurriedly got into their diving gear and grabbed the spearguns.

"This is it," Hawke said. "It's now or never!"

*

Venter grabbed the controls and increased power to the machine's propulsion system. The mighty combat submersible lurched forward, spewing a trail of bubbles in its wake as it widened the distance between them and the pursuing ECHO team.

They had turned just under the lake's surface and were now making good progress along the tunnel leading back to the temple. Lea and Devlin were gagged and bound and pushed up against the rear bulkhead wall, staring at the muzzle of Blankov's submachine gun.

Requiring two operators, one of Venter's men was sitting at the navigator panel while his boss steered the sub through the hole in the temple floor and out into the streets of Pavlopetri. "We're almost beneath the Anapos. We need to surface."

They heard a banging sound on the hull. *Clunk clunk clunk.*

The Oracle started wheezing and needed to grip the control consul to regain his balance. "Dammit! That's Hawke! Do something, Blankov!"

Blankov never hesitated, immediately ordering the sub to speed up and turn in an arc. "If they want to play games, then we'll play games."

"We have the idols!" Kruger yapped. "Why not forget about them? We're so close to getting what we want! We can afford to leave them behind and kill them later whenever we desire!"

"Kill them," the Oracle croaked. "Kill them all."

"Venter!" Blankov said. "Operate the claws."

Venter looked over at Kruger for his orders. The South African arms dealer immediately backed down and told him to sit at the claws' control panel. Venter followed his orders and seated himself in the small area at the front of the sub. Taking a joystick in each hand, the enormous metal claws at the front of the sub responded immediately, swivelling around and grabbing at the warm water.

"There's one of them!" Blankov yelled. "The Chinese woman!"

The Oracle smiled. "Crush her."

Almost on them now, Venter activated the grappling claws and extended them toward Lexi's legs. "We must get closer!" he snapped at Venter.

"I'm at full power."

The claws grabbed hold of Lexi's right fin. She was trapped, kicking out in the water. She turned and tried to take the fin off. Kruger laughed and Venter brought the other claw around and snapped at her head. Watching her struggling to save herself underwater raised a good laugh inside the sub.

Lea and Devlin watched in silent horror, their rage muted by the gags in their mouths.

"We're coming up to the Anapos."

"Radio the captain and have him destroy their boat."

"Yes, sir."

Lexi managed to free her foot from the fin and kick herself clear as the other claw scratched down her back and cut a groove in her suit. A plume of blood burst out in the water as she kicked herself away from the sub. Some of the others were in view now, Ryan, Reaper and Scarlet. The Oracle decided the clanging noise was Hawke trying to break in through the top hatch.

They watched the torpedo tube at the front of the yacht's starboard side open. "Good, they're firing."

The torpedo launched from the tube and raced at the head of a jet of bubbles toward the ECHO team's trawler. The impact of brand-new torpedo technology on a fifty-year-old trawler was predictable and the explosion lifted the forty-ton trawler partly out of the water before blasting its iron hull all over the bay in thousands of scorched, twisted pieces.

"Return to the Anapos," the Oracle ordered. "Their boat is destroyed and there's no way they can follow us, or rescue *you.*" He looked at the prisoners, wrapped in rope and duct tape and dumped on the floor behind the control consul. "We have what I want. We have the codex and seven of the eight idols. Something tells me getting the final idol from ECHO won't be too hard now we have something to barter."

CHAPTER THIRTY-FIVE

The exploding trawler had blasted the ECHO back through the water away from the sub and spiralling down toward the ocean floor. Hawke got it together first. Spinning around he gave the signal for everyone to get to the Anapos as fast as they could.

The sub was already at the stern, being hoisted out of the water by the davit crane and they all knew when the Oracle gave the order to move out they would be impossible to catch.

Reaper reached the yacht first, climbing up one of the many deck ladders and hauling himself on board. Scarlet and Lexi were next followed by Ryan. Camacho and Kim were next with Hawke and his wounded leg at the rear.

Hawke crawled on the deck, the pain coursing from his leg wound. Scarlet and Kim helped pull the wounded man up. "How are things up here?"

Scarlet said, "Apart from a handful of Athanatoi it's mostly a skeleton crew of not very well-trained oilers and wipers and a few stewards."

"Shouldn't take too long then," Hawke said. "And this time, can we *please* not let Kruger and the Oracle get away?"

Scarlet and Lexi ran up the steel steps and were soon heavily engaged in action on the promenade deck and Ryan was making progress on the portside of the same level. Camacho and Reaper had fought their way up the portside steps and were now pinned down on the navigation deck directly above Hawke's position.

He sprinted over the deck and shot his way up the starboard steps until he was also on the navigation deck but on the opposite side of the ship to Camacho and Reaper. His idea was to work with them to create two fronts pushing toward the bridge, but things changed fast when a grenade landed a few meters in front of him and instantly exploded, blasting him clean off the side of the yacht.

He flew through the air, struggling not to pass out. Realizing the awkward angle he was about hit the sea at, he tried to swivel around in mid-air but it was too late. The navigation deck wasn't high enough for him to make the manoeuvre and now he hit the ocean's surface hard and heavy. It felt like he'd landed on concrete as he sank down beneath the waves once again, desperately clinging onto his consciousness.

Deeper he sank, weighed down by the near-full ammo belt and his speargun. He managed to unclip the belt and watched the fresh rounds sink into the black under his feet as he kicked and strained to get back to the surface.

He burst through it and sucked in a deep breath to find Venter high on the sun deck firing at him with a compact machine pistol. The weapon chattered and spat fire as the gunman sprayed the sea around him with automatic rounds. Kruger was beside him, ordering him to kill Hawke at any cost as he fumbled with his own weapon.

Eyes wide with surprise and fear, Hawke heaved in a deep breath and flipped himself over to dive into the water. Swimming back down in the black and heading to the boat to use the hull for cover, he thought he'd made it when he felt a savage, searing pain in his arm. He spun around in the water, air bubbles exploding from his mouth as he screamed in pain.

He saw the wispy white line of an underwater bullet trail as the projectile ripped its way down into the depths. The trail was tinged red with blood. He turned and looked at the location of the burning pain and saw a neat, inch-deep gouge mark in his right shoulder. The bullet had punctured his upper arm and burst out of the other side leaving a deep channel of bloody, torn muscle in its wake.

He swam back up toward the relative safety of the hull's waterline with blood pumping from the fresh wound on his shoulder. He slipped under the boat's hull, swimming around the stern end of a chunky structural keel. He came to the surface, ready to surprise Venter. Closer now, the South African commando launched a renewed assault on him and pock-marked the sea's surface with more bullets.

Hawke fired back with the speargun. The projectile whistled through the air and wedged itself in Venter's stomach, spraying blood all over Kruger. He was so shocked he never even screamed. He reached down and held the metal rod sticking out of his stomach with a terror-stricken face and turned white in the face.

"Come on in," Hawke said. "The water's lovely."

Venter passed out from loss of blood and shock and tumbled off the side of the yacht. He hit the water with a tremendous splash and bobbed up and down in it face-down, allowing Hawke to use his body as a stepping stone as he reached for the stainless steel telescopic boat ladder.

With a sea of burning detritus from the trawler all around them, Hawke now watched with a crushing sense of defeat as a Kamov Ka-60 lifted off from the helipad on the sun deck, rotated in the air and swooped down low over the water. It headed back to the land and was quickly nothing more than a small black smudge on the horizon.

He climbed back up onto the top deck to find the rest of his team assembling around him. "Sorry, Joe," Scarlet said. "But they got Lea and Danny."

"And the codex," Ryan said.

Kim sighed. "And the idols."

Hawke tensed his jaw. "I'm calling Rich. We need to know where they're going and fast."

CHAPTER THIRTY-SIX

Dirk Kruger stepped out of the NH90's narrow cockpit door and walked through the helicopter's cabin until he reached the door to the Oracle's private suite. His shirt was still stained with Venter's blood and in his hand, he gripped an automatic pistol.

Outside, the warm blue waters of Biscayne Bay slowly melted into Card Sound. Tiny paradise islands were everywhere, little keys of palm trees and white sand dotted here and there like gems on a blue velvet cloth. They had boarded the chopper straight from the private jet in Miami and were now descending to land on the Oracle's private paradise island of Copperhead Key.

A small island in the Florida Keys, Otmar Wolff had bought it for the princely sum of $105 million dollars. He had used it for many things over the years – entertaining politicians and greasing the wheels of power, planning his archaeological ventures, even holding depraved parties for his fellow cultists. Its thirty acres offered total privacy and came with a small airfield and full service and dockage for up to fifty tons.

Kruger glanced out of the window just in time to see the clearing at the center of the island and the ominous outline of an airship sitting in the tropical dusk. A number of Athanatoi cultists were busy working in the airfield. Seeing it, the South African knew the plan the Oracle and Faulkner had been cooking up really was about to happen and there was no turning back now.

As he waited to be summoned inside, he turned to his left where Lea and Devlin sat. "All the trouble and misery you caused is coming back around again to you now. I literally cannot wait to watch you die."

Devlin winked and cocked his head, earning him a ferocious pistol-whipping with the gun's grip. The Irishman's head smacked back against the fuselage and then slumped forward. He was out like a light.

Kruger blew Lea a kiss and then the Oracle ordered him to enter.

He stepped inside the modest cabin at the rear of the chopper and found the Oracle screwing the cap up on a bottle of sparkling, glittering liquid.

The elixir.

"What do you want, Dirk?"

His eyes followed the golden liquid in the bottle. The Oracle slipped it inside his pocket and breathed a shallow sigh of relief. When was he going to get some of this stuff – this magical elixir that promised eternal life? He looked back up to the Oracle and gave his reply. "The pilot just told me we're landing on the island imminently."

"Good. Are all our preparations in order?"

"Yes, sir. What exactly is going to happen tonight?"

The Oracle smiled. "Tonight we destroy America."

*

When they landed, a number of Athanatoi cultists quickly whisked Lea and the unconscious Devlin away from the chopper and into what looked unnervingly like a dungeon. Like her, they removed his gag and untied his hands and then dumped his body down on the slimy stone floor before chaining him up beside her.

One of them kicked him in the ribs for good measure before they slammed and locked the floor. The foul chamber was plunged into almost total darkness, the only light shining through the bars in the tiny hole in the door.

She ran to him and lifted his head up from the cold stone. "Danny! Are you okay?"

With his head cradled in her arms, he started to stir. "Holy Mary Mother of Christ flying on the back of a flamingo, what the fuck was that?"

"He belted you because you winked at him, you idiot."

"You think it knocked any sense into me, girl?"

"Like buggery it did," she said, climbing to her feet. "What the hell were you thinking, winking at that son of a bitch like that? He could have killed you, Danny. You're lucky to be alive."

Groaning with pain, he crawled up to his elbows and rubbed the fresh wound on the side of his head. "On reflection, it wasn't the best idea I ever had."

"You're a fool, Danny Devlin, but a brave fool."

He looked into her eyes. The chains grated on the flagstone floor as he brought his hands up to brush against her face and then he leaned in to kiss her.

"Danny, no."

He stopped, lowered his head and sighed. "I'm sorry…"

"I love Joe."

His shoulders slumped down and he shook his head, but then she heard him laughing. "You're right, I'm such a fool."

"I didn't mean it like that."

"You won't tell Joe?"

"No."

"Thanks, because I think he's strictly a second chance only kind of guy."

She sucked in her lips but then returned his smile. "You're right on that one, Danny and we all love you being on the team."

"I read you loud and clear, Lea Donovan."

Her eyes had adjusted to the darkness now and she scanned the dungeon in search of anything they could use as a weapon, or even an escape route. It was a large, filthy space of cold, wet stone with water trickling down from unseen cracks and mould and fungus growing in damp, dark corners.

Metal chains hung from the walls and then she saw it – a skeleton in rags hanging by its wrists from a metal ring fixed into the far wall, its feet just touching the floor. She gasped and covered her mouth with her hand. "What the *hell* has been going on down on this island, Danny?"

He shook his head. "We have to get out of here, Lea, or that's us in a couple of years' time."

He was on his feet now, beside her. He pulled up the collars on his jacket, dusted himself down and swept his hair back. He turned to her, anxious but still in control. "I need to lose a few pounds but I don't think that particular diet plan is for me."

She twisted her head and pursed her lips. "Don't speak ill of the dead. Did you never hear that?"

He shrugged. "I'm just sayin', that's all."

"Eeijt."

They spent a quarter of an hour trying every crack and corner as far as their chains would let them move. They checked the door for any weaknesses but it was solid metal with only a small face-sized, barred window and there was no getting out of that. Then they heard the sound of a key in the door and took a step back as the Oracle and Kruger stepped into the cold dungeon.

"Still here?" Kruger snarled. "Must be losing your touch."

"Get lost, Dirk," Lea said.

"Unlock her," the Oracle wheezed. He looked like he was starting to fade.

Kruger walked over and unshackled her from the wall. "You're coming with us now, Donovan. We're going for a little flight."

The Oracle turned and walked back up the stairs.

Devlin stepped forward. "She's not going anywhere without me, Kruger."

The South African laughed heartily. "You're not going anywhere, but don't worry about being lonely. We've organized a new cell mate for you."

With his words still hanging in the air, an enormous shadow loomed on the wall of the circular staircase behind him. It looked like a monster was approaching and then he realized that was exactly what was happening.

Kruger stepped out of the enormous monster's way and laughed. "Meet Boboc."

Boboc now loomed into view. At least seven feet high, the Romanian bodybuilder was wearing a white vest which revealed an upper body totally covered in tattoos. Vampires and dragons fought for supremacy on his chest and arms, claws and tails and forked tongues twisted up his neck and throat, the ink twisting all over him in black and blue tendrils. In one hand he held a hatchet and the other gripped a flail mace.

Devlin took a step back as he took in the seven-foot monster with the medieval arsenal in his hands. "Holy Mother of God."

Kruger saw his fear and smiled. "Mr Boboc here has never been accused of being bad company. Apparently, the Oracle is going to increase his reward for every hour he can string out your death. Neat, huh?"

"You get away from him, you hear?" Lea cried out.

"He can't reply," Kruger said. "His tongue was torn out in a gangland dispute when he was a teenager, but don't worry. He's very good at expressing himself with his hands."

Boboc grinned and revealed a mouth of smashed, jagged stumps where his teeth had once been. He swung the flail mace around in a circle at his side and brought the spiked metal ball crashing down on the stone floor. It smashed through the surface and blasted splinters of granite into the air.

"Shit," Devlin said.

"And to think he wants to do that to your ugly little head!" Kruger said. "Goodbye, Mr Devlin. Forever."

Lea felt Kruger's hands squeeze her arm as he dragged her out of the dungeon and slammed the heavy door. "You can't let him die like that!"

Kruger chuckled. "If you think that's bad, wait until you see what the Oracle has in store for you."

CHAPTER THIRTY-SEVEN

Eden and Alex had liaised with the US authorities and quickly figured out the Oracle's flight plan to Miami, despite efforts to cover it up. Hawke and the rest of the team had landed in the city only minutes after the Athanatoi contingent.

A chopper was waiting for them on the apron and they were in the air before the engines on their private jet had stopped spinning. Tracking the Oracle's NH-90 south across Biscayne Bay had been meat and potatoes for Joe Hawke, but no one was prepared for the surface-to-air missile streaking toward them from one of the keys down on the twilight horizon.

"Brace for evasive action!" Hawke pulled on the controls and tipped the helicopter hard to port. Pitching the nose to the ground to raise the tail boom, he did all he could to stop the projectile hitting them.

"Holy shit!" Kim yelled.

The missile scorched through the sky at the head of a plume of white exhaust smoke twisting in the tropical breeze. The lethal weapon flashed past the chopper and screeched into the eastern sky behind them, before turning in an arc and heading back around to its target once again.

"Heat seeker?" Reaper asked.

Hawke gave a quick shrug. "Or remote control… hardly matters. Look out!"

He descended the chopper rapidly to avoid the incoming missile. Their ears popped as he piled the helicopter down toward the surface of the sea. The key was rising up now and approaching fast. A large swimming pool surrounded by loungers and palm trees was at the eastern end of the island and now Hawke saw a number of men in black setting up a grenade launcher at the side of the pool.

"Something tells me they don't want us to land!"

The grenade launcher crew fired on them and Hawke tipped the chopper aggressively to the left to avoid their rounds. He was too late. The grenade exploded and shredded the rotors, blasting them to pieces, instantly and fatally wounding the chopper.

He struggled with the helicopter's controls as the missile streaked past them and headed for the swimming pool area. The crew abandoned their grenade launchers and ran for their lives as the weapon smashed into the decking beside the pool and exploded in a massive fireball that lit up half the island.

The chopper burst though the cloud of smoke billowing up from the destruction below. Situated to the left of the pilot's seat like the handbrake on a car, the collective lever altered the pitch angle of the chopper's rotors. This normally changed the machine's lift and could even determine its rate of descent even if a helicopter's engine cut out. It was usually possible to glide the machine safely to earth using this collective lever in a process called autorotation.

This allows the pilot to constantly change the pitch to keep the rotors spinning even without the engine, but not if the rotors had been blasted to shreds by a fragmentation grenade. Fighting with the anti-torque pedals as he tried to keep the chopper straight and level, it didn't take an experienced helicopter pilot like Hawke long to know that this bird was going down, hard and fast.

He did all he could, desperately manipulating the pitch of what was left of the rotors in a bid to keep some kind of rotation going and slow the descent of the doomed aircraft. At the same time, he tried to edge the chopper toward the jungle running around the outside of the island. If they hit the hard ground at this speed, it was doubtful anyone was walking away, but if he could use the thick blanket of mangroves and palm trees around the island it might just arrest the fall enough to provide some sort of cushioning effect.

Hawke had flown many missions in helicopters, both as passenger and pilot and he'd had more than his fair share of close calls, but this was easily the most dangerous situation he'd ever had in one. Worse than that, the injuries on his arm and leg had been dressed on the plane from Greece but were still giving him a lot of pain.

The ground rushed toward him and the chopper now started to spin uncontrollably on its vertical axis. With time fast running out, he called over the comms to the rest of the team. "Brace for impact!"

"Not this again!" Ryan yelled.

The chopper plunged into the tropical canopy, its shredded rotors slicing the tops of the palms like two hot knives through butter and flinging the debris in all directions. Inside, the battered and terrified passengers held on for their lives as the machine smashed down through the trees and crashed hard into the sandy ground.

The landing skids instantly buckled and broke away from the main body. The spinning chopper's tail boom whacked into one of the tree trunks and tore clean away sending the tail rotor violently ricocheting off into the jungle. The horizontal stabilizer tails ripped off as it shredded its way through the undergrowth before coming to a dead stop in a wall of vines.

The main rotors jammed into yet more trunks like blunt axes, bending and stopping with a deep thud, halting the drive shaft and burning out the main motor before the forward-motion of the chopper's body ripped them off and sent them crashing to the ground.

The cabin of the helicopter, now without a tail boom or rotors, or skids, skidded along the jungle floor until they collided with a thick, low branch which punched a hole through the windshield. Nearly decapitating Reaper in the co-pilot's seat, it had the effect of spinning the chopper around one-eighty degrees and finally bringing them to a stop in the center of the thick jungle.

The aluminum on the main fuselage bent and crumpled, bursting open on the starboard side and sending fuel spilling out on the sandy ground. With the stench of jet fuel rising into the battered and dented cabin, Kim came to and tried to bring her eyes into focus. She was dazed, dizzy and nauseous. She realized she must have been knocked out at some point, probably after smashing her head into the window pillar on her left side.

She blew out a breath and tried to get her head together. She was shaking like a leaf and her heart was beating so hard and fast she thought it might just burst out of her chest. Then she smelled the fuel.

She could smell it strongly and hear it running out of the helicopter. She looked out of the window and saw a pool of it collecting around what was left of the chopper. It must be coming from a severed fuel line, she thought.

We have to get out of here.

She looked around the rear seats and saw Lexi Zhang trying to unbuckle Scarlet's belt and free her from her seat. The SAS captain was unconscious with blood trickling from a gash on her forehead. "Joe!" Kim called out in the darkness. "Joe, can you hear me? Are you all right?"

"I'm fine," he called back. "I think I hurt my shoulder, but the good news is my astonishing good looks are not compromised in any way."

"Good to hear your voice," she said, smiling at his joke but not responding to it. "What about Reaper?"

"Bad news I'm afraid."

She felt her heart leap. "What?"

"The crash hasn't made him any less ugly."

"Joe!"

"He's fine too, but he's out cold. How's everyone in the back?"

Ryan said, "Cairo's out too, but Lexi's fine."

"Nine lives," the Chinese assassin said as she kicked open the starboard door and started to haul Scarlet out of the chopper.

Kim unbuckled her belt now and started to climb. "We've got a fuel leak, Joe."

"I know, I can smell it – plus the Oracle will have sent an armed force out to finish us off. We need to get out of here right now."

Hawke grabbed his equipment bag, climbed out of the pilot's seat and ran around to the other side. He saw the pool of jet fuel getting larger by the second and knew one spark would send them all hurtling into the next world. He opened the door and unbuckled Reaper's belt. Pulling the heavy Frenchman from his seat, he dragged him out into the jungle to where Lexi had taken Scarlet. Kim and Camacho were there too, frightened and angry in equal measure, but unharmed.

"That right there," Lexi pursed her lips. "Was one fuck of a landing."

"My pleasure," Hawke said, crouching down to Scarlet and checking her pulse. "She's coming around."

"And Reaper too!" Kim said.

Scarlet groaned as she looked up at Hawke. "What the hell happened?"

"We had a slight hitch with the end of the flight," Ryan said.

"A slight hitch?"

Hawke shrugged and gave her a look of apology. "Kruger blew our rotors off with a grenade."

"Ah."

"You got knocked out, but you seem okay to me."

The Frenchman rubbed his head. "What happened?"

"You were knocked out, Reaper," Kim said.

"You hear that?" said Lexi. "Look, over there!" She pointed into the trees south of the crash site. "I see headlights."

Reaper was now also on his feet, brushing mud and dirt from his jacket and jeans. "Sounds like quads to me."

"Sounds more like trouble to me," Hawke said.

"There they are!" Kim said.

Hawke knew what to do. "Don't do anything until I give the order."

"But they'll be here in a minute or two," Camacho said. "We can get away."

Reaper started to trudge into the darkness of the jungle to the west. "Let's get out of here then!"

"No." Hawke stopped him. "Thanks to Kruger, we're at least a mile short of where we need to be to assault the villa. We need those quads!"

CHAPTER THIRTY-EIGHT

Danny Devlin had enjoyed better days. Chained to a wall in the dungeon of a freak like the Oracle while a meat mountain with medieval weaponry padded over to him was not his idea of the perfect evening.

Boboc grunted and swung the mace.

Devlin ducked and the spiky iron ball smashed into the wall behind his head and blasted a chunk of stone into the room.

"Are you not going to whisper sweet nothings into my year first?"

Another swing of the mace, closer this time. He actually felt the chain connecting the ball to the handle swipe past his face.

"OK," Devlin said. "So now I know how you really feel about me..."

He stepped fast to his right and flicked up the manacle on his right wrist, sending the chain whipping up like a skipping rope. It sailed through the air just as he thought it would and when it came back down he pulled it around Boboc's head and snapped it tight as hard as he could.

The chain-links cut into the flesh on the giant's neck and Devlin whipped it around a second time creating a kind of metal noose which he pulled on with all his strength. The man grunted in response and dropped the mace, bringing his fat hands up to try and prise the chain away from this throat.

Devlin sighed with disappointment. "So you can dish it out but you can't take it."

Boboc's mouth worked silently as he gasped for air. The powerful man spun around and threw Devlin back against the wall.

He started unravelling the chain from his neck, so the Irish Ranger knew he had to act fast. Reaching down he grabbed the mace and swung it hard at his enemy, catching him square between his shoulder blades with the heavy spiked ball. The bones in the man's back splintered like old pottery and he opened his mouth wide to scream hard and loud.

Devlin wrenched the mace ball from Boboc's back in a jet of blood and bone fragments and swung it again. It was a heavy, tough weapon to manipulate but Devlin was no slouch. He twisted his upper body to increase momentum and brought the spiked ball smashing into the back of the choking man's skull.

Boboc fell forward like a freshly-cut tree falling over, smashing his face into the stone floor with a toe-curling crunch as his nose and cheek bones shattered.

Devlin took the mace and then reached into the man's pocket and found the keys. Freeing himself he leaned forward and checked Boboc's breathing, but there was nothing. "Just staying on the safe side, you big ape."

Then he walked across the dungeon and slipped through the door, locking it behind him as he checked the corridor for any sign of the guards who might have overheard the festivities back in the cell. Nothing. "Good," he said. "Hold on, Lea. I'm on my way!"

*

Hawke waited until the men were almost at touching distance from the chopper and then fired at the pool of jet fuel at its base. The men saw the trap a millisecond before the fuel ignited. They turned to run but the explosion swallowed them whole and burned their fleeing bodies to a crisp before they could take two steps.

With fire consuming the chopper's twisted, gnarled wreckage in a fierce blaze, the other men backed up on their quads and turned away from the carnage. Spotting Hawke in the tree line, one of them alerted the rest of his team to his location and immediately headed for him.

Hawke darted back into the shadows of the jungle, allowing the men a long enough view of him to draw them in. As they approached, Lexi and Reaper opened fire on them and took another two of them out blasting them clean off their quads. The riderless machines spun out of control, one of them piling into the burning wreckage and the other smashing head-on into a tree trunk and spinning over on its side.

"There's another one!" Ryan yelled.

One of the quads turned sharply to the right and sprayed an arc of dirt and leaves into their faces. The man riding it lifted an MP5 and fired a long burst of rounds at them. The bullets slammed into the earth and ripped chunks off nearby trunks filling the air with splinters and misty clouds of palm sap.

"Take cover!" Hawke yelled.

He leaped into a trench and slid to a stop in a pile of rotten coconuts. Scrambling to the top of the trench, he returned fire, aiming squarely at the quad's fuel tank. He squeezed the trigger and emptied the magazine all over the man who had just tried to kill them.

The rounds snaked up the path behind the quad, blew out the two rear tires and then hit the target. The tank exploded in a ferocious storm of ignited gasoline and black smoke, blasting the quad into the air like a toy and propelling the rider into a palm trunk. He struck it with his back and slid down dead onto the jungle floor.

With the last of the men dead, they climbed on the quads ready to take off toward the villa in the center of the island when Scarlet's phone buzzed. She took the call and they all watched as her face dropped.

"That was Rich." She put her phone in her pocket. "He says the Five Eyes are meeting in a hotel in Miami Beach."

"Mon Dieu!" Reaper said. "Now there's a target worth hitting."

"What's Five Eyes?" Ryan asked.

Hawke fired up his quad and raised his voice. "It's an alliance of the intelligence agencies of the main English-speaking countries – America, Britain, Australia, Canada and New Zealand. It started after World War II when they created the ECHELON surveillance network."

"Right."

"They hold covert meetings every now and again to discuss stuff they don't want hacked or compromised. These meetings are so classified that only the very top tier of the governments know about it – presidents, VPs, prime ministers, you name it."

"Woah."

"Exactly," Scarlet said. "Usually it's just intel agency officials but this time the heads of state are involved."

"And the Oracle just happens to be in the vicinity!" Kim said.

Camacho swore loudly. "This is the mother of all assassinations!"

"Has Rich warned them?" Hawke asked.

"He's contacted a friend in MI5 who has briefed the British contingency, but they're not seeing it as a credible threat. They've swept the hotel and blocked all local airspace."

"So how can Wolff touch them?"

"That's what we have to find out and fast. They're not going to cancel a meeting of this level and importance and airlift everyone out until we can give them evidence of a solid terror attack."

"You told them there's an airship in the middle of this island, right?" Hawke said.

Scarlet nodded. "His MI5 contact has said that the Americans are very clear about defending the meeting. The second that airship crosses into prohibited airspace they'll blow it out of the sky. Their view is the president is safe and so are the other leaders and officials."

"I can see their point," Camacho said. "They get threats all the time and if they canned everything they were doing every time they got one they'd never get anything done. They've looked into it, done their checks and they're satisfied the president's not at risk. If all Wolff's got is an airship, I don't rate his chances up against a couple of F-16s."

"But this is Wolff we're talking about," Scarlet said. "He doesn't make mistakes like that. He's up to something and if they're not going to cancel the meeting and airlift the president to safety then it's up to us to stop it!"

"Plus the bastard's got our friends," Reaper said. "This cannot go unpunished."

"No," Hawke said coldly. "It's not going to. Everyone, with me."

*

Devlin stalked through the complex in search of Lea. He was sure the Oracle would be keeping her close to him, so he headed for what he guessed was the center of operations – the main villa in the center of the island.

He heard voices up ahead in an office and thought he recognized the sound of Wolff arguing with Kruger. Creeping along a corridor with the mace in his hand, he was approaching the door to the office when the game changed.

The serrated blade of a combat knife pushed into the soft flesh of his throat.

He stopped dead in his tracks. Could he swing the mace around and hit this guy before he drew the blade across his throat? No chance. "All right, you got me."

"You shouldn't give in so easily, Danny."

He breathed a sigh of relief.

Lexi's voice.

"What the hell, Lex?"

Scarlet stepped out of the shadows too. "You need to take five to change your pants, Danny?"

"Fuck off, Sloane."

Hawke said, "Good to see you, Danny – but where the hell's Lea?"

"You Know Who's got her. We were both in some kind of torture cell when he and his South African lapdog showed up and took her. They said they were going for a little flight, so I guess they've gone to the airfield. I haven't seen Blankov since we arrived."

A terrific explosion ripped through the pool house just outside the window, blasting the roof off and blowing out the windows. The shockwave expelled smoke and glass splinters away from the window at high-speed as a massive fireball bloomed up above the complex.

Then another explosion, and a third.

"What the hell's going on?" Camacho said.

Hawke punched the wall. "Scorched earth policy," he said. "He's pulling out and making damn sure he leaves nothing behind. I'd say every building on this island is rigged to blow, so we need to get the hell out of here!"

They sprinted from the office suite just as the room exploded. The power of the detonation lifted them from their feet and flung them into the swimming pool. They crashed through the burning wood and plastic from the pool house that was bobbing about in the surface of the water and sank to the bottom.

Hawke twisted around in the water and looked up to the surface. He saw black smoke, fire and pieces of roofing timber slowly falling back to earth. They splattered all over the surface of the water while pieces of metal shredded past them to the pool floor.

When the worst of the fallout was over he swam to the surface. The others followed his lead and they assembled on the surface of the pool, swimming to the edge through the wreckage.

Ryan saw it first and pointed it out to everyone else. "Up there! The airship!"

Hawke glanced and saw it. Smooth and silver and with the word Anshar painted on the side.

"Babylonian creator deity," Ryan said.

"Fuck it, he got away," Scarlet said.

Devlin cursed. "And he still has Lea!"

Hawke pulled himself out of the pool. "I don't bloody think so."

CHAPTER THIRTY-NINE

The sprint from the fountain in the center of the villa compound out to the swimming pool took seconds. The Athanatoi left behind as a rear-guard sniped at them from hidden positions but they ran like devils toward the jetty.

"Almost there!" Hawke yelled, ducking as a bullet traced over his head and buried itself in the side of one of the huts.

"I beat my personal best for fleeing psychos!" Kim said, glancing at her watch.

"I see the boats!" Ryan said.

They sprinted along the side of the main swimming pool until they reached the end of the island and found what they were looking for. A long, sun-bleached jetty stretched out into the ocean and moored at the far end were a number of airboats.

"Just what the doctor ordered, no?" Reaper said with a grin.

Hawke looked around. "We need some cover fire guys, or we'll get shot to pieces before we get fifty yards from the shore!"

The rest of the team moved into a defensive position and started firing on the Athanatoi as Hawke heaved the mooring line off the post and jumped down inside the boat. Ryan was looking at him expectantly.

"What?"

"I'm coming with you."

Hawke's hesitation said it all.

"Kruger's up there, Joe!"

Hawke climbed into the seat, flicked a small switch to his right and pushed the ignition button. The propellers burst to life behind the prop cage and the entire boat started to vibrate in the water. “Are you girls going to stand there all day or shall we get going?”

Devlin looked at Ryan and then back to Hawke, shrugging. “What the hell – I renewed my life insurance just last week!”

They leaped down into the boat as Hawke steered it away from the jetty and increased speed. Pushing the stick forward turned the boat to the right and pulling back on it turned them to the left. Speed was controlled by an accelerator pedal on the floor in front of his seat and now he opened the throttle fully and the airboat’s bow pitched up as they zoomed across the water.

Devlin and Ryan were standing either side of the prop cage, hanging on with one hand while the rest of the team fired on the guards back on the jetty. “Evasive manoeuvre!” Devlin yelled.

“Hang on!” Hawke said and steered hard to starboard, almost sending both his friends into the alligator-infested water.

Thanks to the cover fire provided by their ECHO teammates, the Athanatoi’s bullets blasted off course to the left, plowing into the sea and kicking up little foamy splashes in the airboat’s wake. Devlin and Ryan returned fire from the boat, blasting one of the men off the jetty and sending the others scrambling for the cover of the Oracle’s yacht.

Up ahead over the water the Anshar was still low enough for him to grab hold of the tether line, but it was gaining altitude all the time and if they didn’t reach it soon they would lose their final chance to get on board. Then the tether line started to retract.

*

The Anshar gathered speed as it lifted away from Copperhead Key. The Oracle stood front and center in the bridge, directly beside the captain. Blankov was on his other side and Kruger was behind him, gripping Lea in his arms. An ashen-faced Athanatoi hurried through the cockpit door and approached the men on the bridge. "We're being followed!"

"What do you mean, *being followed?*" said the Oracle.

"An airboat, sir."

"Hawke!" The Oracle scowled at him and walked over to the portside window. "But I don't see anything."

"He's almost directly behind us, Oracle, but he can be seen from the rear viewing deck."

The Oracle looked at the pilot. "Is there any way he can get on board?"

The pilot shook his head. "No. The tether lines are fully retracted, sir."

"Increase altitude at once!" he snapped. "This is Joe Hawke we're talking about, after all." He turned to Kruger and glared at him. "This is your fault, Kruger. Are you totally incompetent? I ordered you to kill that man!"

"Yes, sir."

The Oracle pulled a Walther PPQ from his jacket pocket and lifted it until the muzzle was pointing at the South African's right eye. He held it there for a second and watched the sweat break out on the arms dealer's creased face. Just one bullet, through the eye… the man would be dead.

He spun it around in his hand and held it at arm's reach. "Take this gun, Dirk and kill Joe Hawke. If he's alive by the time we reach Miami Beach, I will personally execute you and throw you to the sharks – understand?"

Kruger extended a shaking hand and took the pistol. "He's a dead man, sir. I swear it."

*

Hawke stamped on the throttle pedal so hard he thought he might just push it right through the bottom of the boat. They raced forward sending giant arcs of seawater into the air either side of them, all the time inching closer to the Anshar.

"It's gaining altitude!" Ryan yelled.

Devlin stared up into the sky. "We have to make a move now or it's too late, Hawke!"

He was right. "Take over the controls, Ryan! We're going up there."

The young man stood fast. "No way!"

Hawke knew this was coming. He opened his equipment bag and rummaged around, pushing aside his Kukri knife and a butcher's steel until he found what he was looking for – a compact rocket-propelled grappling hook. "We can't mess about, Ryan. We don't have time for an argument – I have to get the grappler prepared."

Devlin stepped up. "I'll take the controls while you two ladies decide what's going on!"

"Kruger's up there, Joe! This could be my last chance!"

Hawke made a split-second decision. His old friend was right about Kruger and the last chance, but did he have it in him to fight Kruger to the death? He recalled Ryan's failure to kill the South African when he had the chance back in Rio de Janeiro after the Lost City of the Incas mission.

Was this a chance to redeem himself, or was he risking the mission by replacing a seasoned soldier like Devlin with a dope-smoking hacker with a chequered background? When he looked into Ryan's eyes he knew what he had to do. "Fine, you go up after me and do as I say."

"Thanks Joe."

"Get us closer, Danny!" Hawke said, pulling the compressed air launcher from his bag. He turned to the young Londoner. How he had changed. The meek computer nerd was no more than a pale rasher of wind when he'd met him. He could have knocked him over with a feather, but he'd worked hard to prove himself. Tattoos on his toned arms, hair shaved down and a week's stubble on his jaw. He felt a bit like a father watching his son leave home. "Don't make me regret this, Ryan."

"I won't."

Hawke hoped so from the bottom of his heart as he prepared the grappling hook and aimed it at the bottom of the airship's gondola. Firing on a moving target was never easy, especially one that was not only moving to the side but also gaining elevation at the same time.

The range of the launcher was rapidly running out, but he stayed calm and aimed as Devlin kept the airboat smooth and steady. Taking the thing out of the sky would have been a simple matter of firing on the airship with their guns and blowing a few holes in the elevators and aft ballonet, but Lea was on board.

If an airship of that size crashed into water from this altitude she might survive, but she might not and that wasn't something any of the ECHO team, least of all him, wanted to live with. The only solution was to fire the grappling hook onto one of the struts holding the engine motors to the gondola and then climb up the hard way and do the job by hand.

He fired the hook and they watched it spiral through the humid Floridian twilight until it collided with the airship. For a second, he thought he'd missed, but then he saw its metal claws wrap around one of the support struts. Instantly, the massive coil of rope attached to it started to unravel on the airboat's tiny foredeck.

"It's now or never, Ryan!" Hawke said, grabbing the end of the rope. "Which is it?"

CHAPTER FORTY

Cougar had been tracking them since Pavlopetri, sitting up on a cliff with her binoculars watching them in a savage fight with some men on a yacht. Garcetti was vague about who the men in black suits were, but whoever they were, they sure could fight.

She had followed them back to the airport without a hitch and tracing their outbound flight to Florida hadn't exactly been tough with Garcetti's contacts. She was there at Miami airport's car hire before their plane's wheels hit the asphalt. Watched them pile into the SUV and then pulled out after them.

When the chopper nearly got blown out of the sky over Copperhead Key she thought her mission was over, but when she heard the gunfire on the island she knew they'd survived. Waiting for them to make their next move was easy.

Easy as cherry pie.

Now, sitting in the front of her truck, she looked at the picture of Matty that she kept on her dashboard. There he was, a rare smile on his young face. A moment without pain snapped by a forgiving iPhone camera.

Her phone rang.

"I miss you, Mom."

"I know. I'll be home soon. You go back to bed, you hear me?"

"I hear you, mom."

"I mean it, Matty. I don't want you getting tired. Did you find the soup I left in the refrigerator?"

"Already ate it."

She imagined him all alone in the apartment warming the chicken soup on the stove. Sitting at the kitchen table as he ate it by the spoonful. It broke her heart, but there was no other way. When you're going through hell, keep on going. She forgot who said that now, but it stiffened her resolve to get the job done.

"Listen, you make sure the place is locked up before you go to bed."

"I will."

"And if there's any problem you can speak with Mrs Kowalczyk across the hall, you got it?"

"I got it."

She hoped he did and she blew a kiss down the phone to him when she said goodbye. It was a tough conversation to have, but soon all this hell would be over. Justin had called earlier to tell her things were coming together south of the border. There was a neat little place just outside of Los Cabos he had his eye on for the three of them. All they were waiting for was this one last job and then they could be together forever.

And Matty could have his operation.

She opened the box of high velocity rounds and carefully selected exactly one bullet. She never needed more than one. More than one was useless. If the target survived the first round then he knew he was under sniper fire and took evasive action. The job always got done with the first round.

And this one had something etched into the side of it.

A name.

A marked round. Her specialty. The bullet with your name on it. It was why her name struck fear into the hearts of men and women all around the world.

Cougar.

Just one shot and it was over.

She glanced down inside the box at all the other rounds. Chunky, lethal .408 bottlenecked cartridges and each one carrying the name of the intended victim.

Taylor.

Camacho.

Devlin.

Reno.

Zhang.

Bale.

Each one of them a perfect killing tool. Solid bullets, not lead-core. Every one of the copper nickel alloy rounds delivering a violent and bloody end from over two kilometers away.

Lund.

Eden.

Sloane.

Each one of them nothing but death on speeding wings of lead.

Donovan.

Hawke.

She selected one of the named rounds and slid it inside the CheyTac M200 Intervention. The most lethal sniper rifle in the world, it could effortlessly power a .408 bottlenecked cartridge at over three thousand feet per second.

She set the weapon down in the footwell and leaned back in her seat with the monocular at her eye. It was dark now, but it was a high-quality night vision model and she was able to track the movements of the ECHO unit easily.

After a short time on Copperhead Key in what looked like some kind of firefight with a bunch of men dressed in black suits, Hawke, Devlin and Bale had climbed into an airboat and were in pursuit of an airship. Crossing back to the island, she saw the rest of the team fighting with more men in black. Looked like they were from that movie she liked when she was younger.

The Matrix, she guessed.

Crossing back to the airboat, they were still in pursuit of an airship which had risen from the center of the island and was now gaining altitude and heading out toward Biscayne Bay. She knew all of this must have something central to do with the kill order, but it wasn't her place to ask questions or second-guess. Her superiors didn't like that. They told her what to do and she did it. That was just about how it had always worked.

Government assassin, they called her. A ghost, others said. She didn't care what words they used, all she knew was, this was her last job. The dark reality of what she did for a living was no longer something she could live with. They got her when she was young, but now she knew better. She closed her eyes and thought about Matty and Justin. She thought about Los Cabos and the villa. She thought about going fishing in the Gulf of California. Watching her boy laugh and play in the bright turquoise water far away from the streets of LA. No more pain, no more suffering.

A life worth living and it was all hers for the taking.

All she had to do was execute Operation Crossbow and she was home free.

She opened her eyes and started to track the ECHO team once again through the monocular.

*

Ryan yelled back, "It's now, Joe!"

The rope was rapidly running out. Hawke threaded it forward until he was holding a section three or four meters from the end, giving Ryan the final section of the line to hang onto. "Keep us directly underneath, Danny!"

"No problem," the Irishman yelled back over the noise of the propeller.

"They're still ascending," Hawke cried out. "When the rope goes taught we're leaving this boat in a hurry, so hang on!"

Ryan nodded but said nothing. He swallowed hard and tried to look unfazed. Checked his gun was in his belt and gripped the rope with both hands. Now or never.

Now.

The rope tugged tight as the airship lurched upwards. Hawke was first off the deck and Ryan a second later. Their ascent was rapid and soon the Englishman was suspended in mid-air, fifty feet above the shark-infested water of Biscayne Bay. He looked down to check Ryan was all right and found him clinging to the rope for his life. His grip was good and he knew what to do, but getting up there was one thing – then they had to fight their way through an airship full of Athanatoi.

Craning his head up he saw the base of the gondola. He had around one hundred feet of rope to climb until he reached the engine's support strut. He prayed he could get that far without someone shooting at him and started to heave himself up the rope.

He'd spent half his life climbing up and down ropes, but he quickly found he was developing blisters on both hands. Maybe ECHO needed a long, hard training course to toughen themselves up for the hard stuff like this? Ten feet to go now and the portside door of the gondola swung open to reveal a man dressed in black.

Athanatoi.

He was holding a compact machine pistol he didn't recognize and now fired on him with a merciless fusillade of automatic rounds. Just as the airship had not been easy to hit with the grappling hook, neither were he and Ryan.

The rope was swinging wildly in the wind as the giant craft continued to gain elevation and the bullets went all over the place.

Hawke looked down and saw Devlin had used his common sense and was steering the airboat out of the gunman's line of fire. He coiled his left hand around the rope and moved his right hand across to his shoulder holster, ducking as another wave of bullets traced through the air inches from his head.

He pulled the pistol from the holster and aimed it at the young cultist. Immortality was no match for the lethal aim and shot of the former SBS sergeant and his first shot struck the man in the dead center of his forehead.

He tumbled out of the gondola and whistled past him and Ryan before crashing through the surface of the bay in a twisted, broken heap. Progress, Hawke considered, but these guys were like ants. Another would be along any second now.

A few feet from the strut, another Athanatoi appeared. This time Hawke was ready with his gun in his hand and his aim worked out in advance. When the face appeared in the door, Hawke fired and killed him instantly, this time blasting him back inside the gondola and hopefully causing an obstruction to stop others from leaning out of the door.

He dragged himself up over the support strut and made himself secure against the side of the gondola, firing inside intermittently to provide cover fire for Ryan as he climbed up behind him. When his friend was almost at the top, Hawke blasted his way inside the gondola and took out two more Athanatoi. The captain was standing at the bridge with his hands in the air. Beside him was a nervous-looking Blankov, but there was no sign of the Oracle, Kruger or, more worryingly, Lea.

"Where are they?"

"You can't stop this now, Hawke."

"Stop what?"

Blankov and the captain exchanged a nervous glance.

Hawke aimed his MP5 at Blankov's face. "Stop what?"

"The tsumami."

He and Ryan stared at each other for a moment. "A *tsunami*?"

"Yes, or a tsunami bomb to be more accurate. It's buried off the coast of Miami Beach. The Oracle is going to detonate it with a remote when we're in the right position to watch it flood the city."

"My God, you people really are insane. You'll kill thousands of innocent people!"

"We see the grand plan you are unable to see."

Blankov reached for a gun on the consul and Hawke released a burst of rounds from his MP5, mowing him down and killing him on the spot.

"You didn't see that part of the plan though, did you mate?"

Behind the terrified captain through the front window of the airship, Hawke saw a long golden line of sand and glittering tower blocks shining in the sunset. They were already approaching Miami Beach but taking care to avoid the no-fly zone. All the Oracle had to do was hit the remote and detonate the tsunami bomb and hundreds of thousands of innocent people would die, not to mention the Five Eyes officials, including President Brooke.

Hawke pulled back the hammer on his pistol. "I said, where are they?"

CHAPTER FORTY-ONE

With Ryan holding the captain at gunpoint, Hawke made his way through the door and started to walk down the length of the gondola. Around fifty feet long, a central corridor gave way to doors on either side and at the end of it at the stern was a large viewing deck. On the table was Kruger's backpack, complete with the codex and what looked like the base of one of the idols.

He had struck gold.

Now he saw the Oracle and a huddle of Athanatoi, then Kruger dragged Lea into view. There was a struggle and then the arms dealer slapped her hard across the face.

"Let her go, dickhead!"

Lea sighed with relief when she saw the Englishman.

Kruger shook his head. "Fuck me dead, Hawke. Can't you take a hint?"

The Oracle swivelled around, a bomb remote in his hand. "I told you to kill him! Kill him now and throw his dead body out of my airship!"

"Who do you think you are?" Hawke said. "Max Bloody Zorin?"

They fired on him with a vengeance, spraying the rear section of the deck with bullets and instantly blowing out the large observation window. Glass spewed out into the air and vanished in the twilight and a loud, howling noise filled the inside of the cabin.

Hawke dived to the floor and rolled behind the long wooden bar as Kruger dragged Lea across the viewing deck and toward some steps. He was trying to take her up into the space between the rigid structure of the airship and its helium bags.

Hawke raised his head above the edge of the bar as bullets drilled into it and forced tiny clouds of splintered wood and shattered glass into the air. He ducked back down just in time to avoid being shot in the face, slamming into the floor and cutting his hands on the shards of broken glass.

He cursed and looked down at the wounds but they were superficial. He'd just have to suck it up for now, he thought with a grim smile. An Athanatoi acolyte rounded the edge of the bar in pursuit of him. Finding him crouched in the detritus, he grinned and raised his gun.

Hawke grabbed the neck of a broken bottle of vodka and threw it at the cultist with all his might. It spun through the air like a dart and the jagged end buried itself into the middle of his face like a set of jaws.

He screamed in agony and dropped the gun as he reached up to pull the broken glass fragments from his bleeding face.

Hawke seized the moment and grabbed the dropped weapon. Still lying on his stomach, he held the gun with both hands and fired on the man, planting three rounds in his chest. With the glass fragments still wedged in his face, he stumbled back a few paces and then his legs collided with an upturned chair in front of the shattered observation window. Losing his balance, he tipped backwards and gave a heart-stopping scream as he fell out of the window and spun down toward the ocean hundreds of feet below.

"A new high-dive record, I think," Hawke said, peering outside the window. "Two tucks and a pike."

Someone else fired on him. The bullet slammed into the wall beside his head and he crashed down to the floor behind a long leather sofa. He cursed but at least he still had the gun. He checked the magazine and saw ten rounds remaining.

The man who had fired on him was reloading and Hawke used the moment to return fire under the sofa. The rounds strafed across the carpet, kicking up little puffs of rubber and polyester before tearing through the man's boots and burying themselves in his feet and ankles.

The cultist wailed and collapsed to the floor, howling in pain and desperately trying to drag himself into the cover of the central corridor.

Hawke fired on him and took him out before he'd made a yard.

Then he heard Lea screaming.

Scanning the room through the smoke he saw she was nowhere in sight. Kruger must have taken her into the top of the airship – but where the hell was the Oracle? He stuffed the gun into his belt and darted across the observation deck toward the steel staircase.

Taking a rail in each hand, he leaped up the steps two at a time until he found himself inside the space between the rigid structure and the helium balloons. It was cramped and smelled of oil but he had no time to assess the situation further. A gun fired in the darkness and he heard a bullet trace past his face and slam into one of the rigid structure support beams.

He dropped to his knees and pulled the gun from his belt. Looking ahead, he saw Kruger but still no sign of Lea. "Give up and I'll let you live, Kruger!"

"Get real, Englishman." Kruger fired again and Hawke buried his head in his crossed arms as the bullet blew past him and ricocheted off another of the steel girders. "We both know this is a fight to the death… Yours!" He fired on him again and the bullet struck a support strut and ricocheted down into Hawke's shoulder.

It felt like flesh wound, so Hawke fired back, but Kruger dropped away into the thin air like a phantom, leaving nothing behind but gun smoke.

"What the hell?"

Hawke ran to where Kruger had been standing and saw a maintenance hatch leading down to the bridge. There, on the floor, Kruger was fighting Ryan. He went to jump down when he heard Lea screaming. She was back with the Oracle and she needed his help.

Lea or Ryan?

Hawke knew Ryan needed to exorcise his demons when it came to Kruger, so he threw him his gun, turned on his heel and sprinted back down the inside of the structure.

*

Ryan saw the hatch burst open but had no time to respond. The man crashed through the hole and landed right on top of him, pushing him to the floor in the middle of the bridge with heavy work boots that almost knocked him out. When he staggered up to his knees and saw who had attacked him, he thought his heart had stopped.

Dirk Kruger.

"Fuck me," Kruger crowed. "I didn't know we had the Girl Guides on here."

Ryan saw the gun in the arms dealer's hand. His own had been knocked across the floor when Kruger crashed into him, but Hawke had thrown him another. It was out of reach. He started to panic, but knew he had to play for time. The captain took a few cautious steps back and steadied the airship's controls.

Then Kruger rushed him.

Ryan felt a surge of rage he had never known before. Before ECHO his life had been spent as a man on the run. When it came to fight or flight, he could write a PhD on running away. Mr Line-of-Least-Resistance, he always backed down, said sorry, walked away.

ECHO had changed all that. Hawke had changed it. Lea and the others had led him out of the darkness of timidity and into the light of courage and he needed to draw on that now, or he would die. He needed to use the intense, animal anger that Dirk Kruger was inducing in him if he was to survive.

The arms dealer's sweaty face was right over the top of him now, looking down with a grin as he tightened his fingers around his throat. Visions of Maria Kurikova flew through his mind like starlings. What heaven was she in now, he wondered… and would he soon be joining her?

The fingers squeezed tighter. He felt Kruger's fingernails burying themselves into the soft flesh of his neck, the fingertips pushing into his veins and blocking the circulation of blood, choking the windpipe. Maybe, he thought, it would be easier just to let go. I'd be back with her then. We'd be together in a better place and all this suffering would be over forever.

"You're fucking weak, Bale!"

Ryan strained for air.

"I should have killed you when I had the chance. This time I'm putting you down like a rabid dog."

The periphery of his vision started to fade out and he saw stars forming wherever he turned his bulging eyes.

"Men like me will always beat pathetic, weak bastards like you. As long as you're in this world you're just wasting my oxygen. Your Russian girlfriend must have been fucking insane to go with you, boy. Too bad she's dead, eh?"

Motivated by a depth of burning anger he'd never known before and never wanted to know again, Ryan heaved Dirk Kruger away from him and leaped to his feet. The South African did the same and reached for a knife on his belt.

Ryan lunged at him, snatching up the gun Hawke had thrown down and stuffed it into his stomach.

"You won't do it!" Kruger said. "You're a girl."

Ryan felt a kind of sick pleasure rush through him as he buried the muzzle of the Glock in Kruger's belly. It felt good. If only he had the strength to ram the barrel right through this bastard's stomach wall and out of the other side. As it was, he'd have to settle for using it the way God intended.

He fired point blank. The flesh of Kruger's stomach acted a little like a muffler and reduced the ferocious sound of the weapon. The man's eyes opened wide as the rest of his face froze. He knew what had happened. He was a dead man walking.

Ryan wondered what it felt like to have a nine-mil slug fired through your stomach at point blank range and then fired another one to see if it made things better. And a third and a fourth.

The captain rushed Ryan, but he spun and fired, hitting him in the head and killing him on the spot, then he emptied the rest of the mag into Kruger's stomach and pushed the dying man away. "You're not supposed to speak ill of the dead, Dirk, but in your case, I'll make an exception."

Kruger tried to talk but bubbles of blood formed in his mouth, popping like bubblegum as he took his last breaths. Behind him, air rushed in through the open gondola door and rippled through his hair. He reached out a trembling hand, a look of terror on his face. It was the face of a voiceless man begging for help, but he wasn't going to get, Not today. Not from this man.

Ryan hurled the empty gun to the floor and walked over to the kneeling Kruger. Raising his leg, he planted the sole of his boot squarely on the South African's chest and without saying a single word, he pushed his defeated enemy out of the gondola. There were no screams as he tumbled down to the tropical waters of Biscayne Bay.

An ugly splash formed in the water below. It wasn't the sort of splash you survived, but Kruger was one lucky bastard, after all. Ryan blew out a breath and for a moment he thought he saw the familiar outline of a great white shark swimming toward the splash. He looked closer and saw he was right.

Maybe Dirk Kruger's luck had run out after all.

CHAPTER FORTY-TWO

Hawke reached the observation deck and saw Lea struggling with the Oracle. He was forcing her toward the shattered window at the rear of the cabin and the tsunami bomb remote was lying in the splintered glass on the carpet beside an upturned barstool. The bag with the seven idols was on the floor and the codex was upside down on the carpet beside it.

Hawke leaped from the top of the steps and crashed down into Wolff's back, piling him face-first into the broken glass. The Athanatoi chief cried out as the glass splinters embedded in his face and he fought like a madman to get the Englishman off his back.

"How long can an immortal spend in jail?" Hawke pulled his arm in a half-nelson and made him squeal like a pig.

"You're dead a lot longer," he snarled and whipped a knife out with his other hand.

Hawke saw it coming. He'd been reaching for the very same arm to pin them both behind his back and tie them together, but his right hand was weakened by the bullet wound Kruger had planted in his shoulder.

The Oracle struck out wildly with the knife, but surprised Hawke by not attacking him. Instead, he threw the knife at Lea and it sliced through her thigh.

She screamed and kicked the knife away, but she had lost her balance and started to tumble back to the open window. She started to grow faint and her eyes rolled up into her head.

"Lea!" Hawke released the Oracle and sprinted to her, pulling her roughly back from the gaping void and resting her down on the sofa.

He turned. "You fucking bastard, Wolff."

The airship pitched forward and knocked them all off their feet. The idols rolled down to Hawke and Lea but the codex stayed up at the other end with the Oracle.

Hawke watched his eyes crawl over the idols. "If you want them, come and get them."

The old man's eyes leaped from the idols to the codex. Time was running out.

Lea came to and looked at the Oracle with disgust. "God, I wish you were *dead!*"

"Let me give you a goodbye kiss, instead." The Oracle reached into his pocket with a withered, bony hand and pulled out a grenade. Snatching up the codex, he put on a backpack and climbed over to the open window. He pulled the pin and tossed the grenade at them. Then he jumped into the void and fell away from the bottom of the gondola.

"The grenade!" Hawke yelled, rugby tackling Lea to the floor. "Get down!"

The grenade detonated and blasted the back of the observation cabin clear off the gondola and sent debris ripping across the fins and elevators. Fire wrapped up around the roof and snaked back down the walls toward where they were taking cover. When the smoke cleared, the Oracle had escaped and the airship was a dead bird, pitching down and speeding toward Miami Beach.

USAF F-16 fighter jets closed in on them as they approached the no-fly zone.

Lea watched with disbelieving eyes as a parachute canopy popped open from the backpack and unfurled in the gathering night.

The Oracle twisted down for around a hundred feet and then dropped down onto the deck of a submarine. He slammed the hatch down behind him and seconds later the enormous boat was under the waves.

"I don't believe it, Joe." She fought the tears back. "He's done it to us again!"

Hawke could offer no more than a heavy sigh and wrapped his arm around her shoulders. "It's not over. We have the idols now, remember. If he wants them, he has to come and get them and then we'll kill him."

"But he has the codex."

"And we have Alexander's ring."

Lea wiped a tear from her eye. "Am I imagining it or are we plummeting to the ground?"

"Eh?"

"Look… outside."

Hawke didn't have to look outside. As she spoke, the airship pitched down even more, sending all the broken furniture and glass sliding along the floor to the front of the cabin.

"This isn't good."

"It feels like we're on the sodding Titanic!" Lea said.

"Except we get to crash into the sea before we sink in it," Hawke said. "Brilliant."

They ran down the central corridor where Ryan was desperately fiddling with the controls at the front of the bridge.

"Er. We've got some major problems guys!"

"What's up?" Hawke asked.

"The Oracle's goodbye kiss wrecked everything. The primary control surfaces are out, including the elevators and rudder."

Hawke frowned. "Not what I wanted to hear, mate."

"I don't know what to do!"

“Let me have a look.” Hawke walked over and fiddled with the dials and levers on the consul, checking the response each time he operated one of the control surfaces.

“Well?”

“It’s going to be rough, but we’ve got enough elevator control to bring the pitch up and make a shallower descent. You get on the radio and tell those F-16s we’re friendly!”

He wrestled with the controls as the stricken airship plummeted to the beach. Buffeted by the wind which howled in through the smashed bridge window, Hawke fought hard to bring the nose up just as the bottom of the gondola smashed into the sea a little way off shore.

Lea screamed and Ryan swore loudly, neither able to look as the impact blasted tons of water up over the sides of the gondola. Hawke cursed as he pulled the controls back to keep the nose up. The last thing he wanted was for the force of the impact to plow the gondola under the surface of the sea and drown them all.

Successfully pitching the airship’s nose up again, the gondola skidded across the surface of the ocean for a few hundred meters before plowing up into the sand and screeching toward the large collection of emergency vehicles that had assembled on the beach as first responders.

“You two OK?” he yelled.

Two scared nods.

“In that case, please wait until the aircraft comes to a full and complete stop before unbuckling your seatbelts.”

Slowly, the friction of the sand against the gondola’s glass-fiber hull brought the wrecked airship to a stop less than ten meters from one of the fire trucks.

He saw the rest of the team he had left back on the island and now Camacho and Scarlet sprinted over from the fire trucks as Lea draped her arms over his shoulders and kissed him on the back of the neck.

It was over.

Almost.

*

It was full night when they crawled from the crumpled gondola. The lights of Miami Beach glittered all around them and the sounds of the city were playful and innocent. Music boomed from a Porsche convertible cruising along Miami Beach Boardwalk and laughter echoed from a nightclub's rooftop terrace.

Hawke was exhausted. He cricked his neck and strolled over to the rest of his team with his hands in his pockets. He wanted nothing more than a good night's sleep and then another good night's sleep straight after. When he glanced at his leg, he thought that maybe a trip to a local hospital might also be in order.

The entire team was together now except Devlin. He was piloting the airboat in from Biscayne Bay.

"There he is!" Kim said, pointing out into the darkness.

Devlin waved back as he navigated the airboat toward the beach.

"Why the long faces?" Hawke said. "And no horse jokes."

"He got away, Joe." Lea kicked he sand with her boot. "The bastard got away."

"But this was a successful mission!"

"Not if he got away it wasn't."

"What are you talking about? We now have all eight of the idols and that weird little ring… and we killed Kruger!"

Ryan coughed. "Who killed Kruger?"

Hawke patted him on the back. "We all know what you did, mate. Well done. That settles an account, right?"

Ryan reddened a little. "I guess so."

Reaper lit up a cigarette and blew the smoke into the night air. "That day you fired on him in Rio, do you remember?"

"I'll never forget it," Ryan said. "I let everyone down that day."

"That day was the day you started on your journey to becoming a real man, Ryan. Today you finished the journey and I am proud of you."

Lea started to well up.

Scarlet rolled her eyes. "Is there a fucking bar around here? I mean, it's Miami, right?"

Hawke huffed out a tired laugh. "When Danny gets here, I promise we'll find a bar. Somewhere nice and seedy where we can drink this nightmare away."

"Debriefing first," Lea said, pointing to a group of men in suits at the top of the beach. "The Five Eyes survived a serious terror attack tonight and those dudes are going to want every inch of it on paper."

"Dotted Is and Crossed Ts," Camacho said. "Gotta love the CIA."

Lea looked at Hawke's leg and shoulders. "And then hospital for you, mister."

As the others walked over to the authorities for a debriefing, Lea kept watching her old friend and lover as he drove the airboat to the beach. When she saw the tiny red dot on the surface of the water she knew at once what it meant. She felt her skin crawl as it slipped effortlessly onto the airboat's curved hull and then up over Devlin. It danced over his shirt and then settled on his left temple.

She cried out, "Danny!"

He couldn't hear her and then it was over. A high-velocity round drilled into Danny Devlin's head and blasted him off the airboat. He crashed down into the dark water and the airboat spun out of control, tipping up and cartwheeling over and over until it broke up and smashed into a hundred pieces.

No one in the team moved or spoke.

CHAPTER FORTY-THREE

Hawke leaned on the edge of the wall and looked out across Galway Bay. The sunset was lighting the sky in pinks and ambers and a new hush was descending over the world. A swallow dipped and dived and twisted in the twilight. It landed on a telephone wire above his head and chirped in the dying light.

He considered Danny Devlin and how he had died fighting alongside him for the good of the team. He wasn't quite sure what to feel when he thought about what had happened. He'd barely known Devlin but in the short time they had worked together he'd seen how brave he was and he felt a wave of guilt when he realized how badly he had misjudged the man when he'd hugged Lea in London.

Everyone in the ECHO team except Sir Richard Eden had attended the funeral in Dublin. Over a hundred friends and family had been there, including former colleagues from his army days and relatives from South Africa. No one could believe the great Danny Devlin was dead, but they raised many good glasses at the wake in his memory before the day was done.

That was a week ago and the rawness was starting to fade now. Scarlet and Camacho had travelled to visit her brother Spencer at Rytchley Manor in England and Ryan had returned to London to spend some time with a few friends from his hacking days.

Reaper had taken Lexi back to Provence where they planned to go to his summer home with his wife and twin boys. Her time at the hands of the Zodiacs had left her drained and she needed time to recover. Reaper's wife knew a good plastic surgeon who had promised to help mend her tortured hand.

As for Kim, she had returned to Washington DC and her job with the President. Hawke knew in his heart that was where she really longed to be and he guessed she wouldn't be coming on many more ECHO missions.

And there was Lea. After the funeral, when everyone had flown away and it was just the two of them, they had walked on the cliffs around Galway Bay and visited places she knew as a child. He'd watched her come back to life as she spoke in Irish to the older people in her family and realized just how damaging the lives they led really were.

Devlin's murder had been hard on her. They'd lost team members before and this time it was no less painful. Lea was visibly crushed when he was killed, but she had been too focused on the mission to think about it. He knew it would hit her later, like a ton of bricks. The former Irish Ranger was an old friend of hers and they had once been lovers. There was no way she could process his murder without going through a lot of pain and asking a lot of questions.

And if that weren't bad enough, she hadn't even begun to deal with the impact of her grandmother's letter. Or who she had thought was her grandmother, but turned out to be her sister. The stunning revelation of her father's discovery of the elixir of life had shaken her to her core but the events of the last few days had shielded her from its brutal truth and enabled her to hide from it. They both knew that soon she would have to face all of this and much more.

Some people cruised by on a boat below in the bay. They looked happy and peaceful and completely ignorant of what was really going on in the world. They carried none of the burdens he felt pressing down on his shoulders morning, noon and night and he envied them for it. They could laugh without fear and enjoy their lives. Relax with loved-ones and pursue their lifetime ambitions, when he was compelled to risk his life day in and day out to protect them from the likes of Mr Blankov and Dirk Kruger. And Otmar Wolff and the Athanatoi.

And what drove that compulsion?

He didn't know. He didn't want to know.

They had killed Kruger and Blankov and their goons, but something told him there would be more bloodshed and death before they finally took the Oracle down. He glanced over the ocean and felt a shudder when he considered which of the team would die next in the cause. It was too dark to contemplate and when Lea walked over to him he put the thought out of his mind. It was what they did and that was all there was to it.

"Hey," she said and peered over the cliff.

"Hey."

"Thinking about jumping?"

He gave her a sideways glance and smiled. "I'm sorry about Danny."

Her face straightened. "Me too, but he knew what he was getting into."

She was putting on a front which he knew would crack sooner or later and when it happened he wanted to be there for her.

"Why's your hand moving around in your pocket like that? Ireland's not *that* pretty."

She could still joke. A good sign.

He pulled out the box and she gasped. He didn't need to say anything. Before he had even opened it, she said yes and kissed him on the mouth. The swallow leaped from the wire and flew away into the sky. The sun finally slipped below the watery horizon and a chill wind whipped up from the water.

She wiped a tear from her eye and laughed and he put the ring on her finger. "And about bloody time, too."

They laughed and kissed again. She was right – it was about time and now as the stars came out over the bay he knew he'd made the right decision.

EPILOGUE

Magnus Lund watched Sir Richard Eden cross the floor of his study and pick up the report on his desk. Before the coma he was one of the strongest men he knew, but for the time being at least he was dependent on a cane. Eden shuffled back over to Lund and handed him the file.

"And you're certain about this?" Lund said as he flicked through the papers.

Eden collapsed down in a soft leather chair and sighed. "All the post-mortem notes are in there, Magnus. The bullet which killed Devlin was marked."

"Which page?"

"At the end."

Lund flicked through some more pages until he saw a series of high-definition macro shots of the fatal projectile. A single word was etched neatly into the lead: DEVLIN. Scratch marks from the calibrated barrel crossed through it diagonally, but it was still clear enough to read. As clear as day, just as the message it was intended to send.

"This is a bad development, Richard."

"You don't have to tell me that."

"Any ideas who the shooter was?"

"No. That bullet is probably the most forensically examined object in the history of the science. We know the exact round and the exact weapon that fired it, but it refuses to tell us who squeezed the trigger."

"I don't like it."

"You haven't turned the page yet."

Lund flipped over the page and gasped. He was looking at another series of photos of the other side of the bullet that killed Devlin. Etched into it were two more words: WHO'S NEXT?

"We're in trouble, Richard. This is a vendetta."

"It's a professional hit and whoever is behind it is clearly planning on taking out the entire ECHO team, probably including us."

Lund felt the blood drain from his head and he started to feel dizzy and a little sick. "This can't be happening."

"It's happening, Magnus and get a hold of yourself."

"I'm sorry, but it's different for you. You're a military man. The idea of being hunted by a sniper of this skill is... *terrifying* to me."

"I'm not exactly thrilled by it myself."

Lund stared down at the picture of the bullet.

Who's next?

He closed the file with trembling hands.

Who's next, indeed.

THE END

AUTHOR'S NOTE

I hope you enjoyed reading *The King's Tomb*, which is the tenth novel in the Joe Hawke series. The next installment, *Land of the Gods* is scheduled for release during the autumn of 2018 and will bring the current arc to a close, as well as killing off not one but two other valued members of the team. After this, the ECHO team are plunged into a brand new and extremely lethal adventure.

If you enjoy following the adventures of Hawke, or any of my other series, please leave a short review on Amazon. Independent writers request this of their readers all the time, but without your support the books lose their visibility and then their viability – and I massively appreciate your support!

JOE HAWKE WILL RETURN IN LAND OF THE GODS

Other Books by Rob Jones

The Joe Hawke Series

The Vault of Poseidon (Joe Hawke #1)
Thunder God (Joe Hawke #2)
The Tomb of Eternity (Joe Hawke #3)
The Curse of Medusa (Joe Hawke #4)
Valhalla Gold (Joe Hawke #5)
The Aztec Prophecy (Joe Hawke #6)
The Secret of Atlantis (Joe Hawke #7)
The Lost City (Joe Hawke #8)
The Sword of Fire (Joe Hawke #9)
The King's Tomb (Joe Hawke #10)

The Cairo Sloane Series

Plagues of the Seven Angels (Cairo Sloane #1)

The Raiders Series

The Raiders (The Raiders #1)

The Avalon Adventure Series

The Hunt for Shambhala (An Avalon Adventure #1)
Treasure of Babylon (An Avalon Adventure #2)

The Harry Bane Thriller Series

The Armageddon Protocol (A Harry Bane Thriller #1)

Website: www.robjonesnovels.com
Facebook: https://www.facebook.com/RobJonesNovels/
Twitter: @AuthorRobJones
Email: robjonesnovels@gmail.com

Made in the USA
Middletown, DE
22 April 2020